The Death Merch... agent, were 300 yards from the dome's pressurized pool entrance when they saw the first Soviet divers—four of them, 50 feet to the right and 25 feet above them.

It was the third Russian in line who spotted them. He did a half-loop in the water, tugged at the line securing him to the next comrade, and pointed at Camellion and Forran.

The Death Merchant knew that if one of the enemy divers managed to cry out an alarm to the surface ships above, or to the KGB security in the dome, he and Forran would have to fold their tent and run like hell for home.

"Kill them," he said calmly into the mike to Forran. He turned his spear gun toward the nearest Russian and pulled the trigger. There was a short *whooshing* sound, then another as Forran aimed and pressed the trigger. Two of the Russians, taking 3½-inch darts in the chest, jerked, went limp, and started to sink toward the bottom. The other two Russians, now being pulled down by their dead companions, reacted quickly. One kicked sideways and at the same time fired his spear gun at the Death Merchant, who fired again.

The third Soviet diver fired at Forran only a moment before Forran fired. Forran's dart caught him in the stomach and lodged against his backbone. The Death Merchant's little 3½-inch missile stabbed the last Russian high in the right arm and tore through the biceps muscle. He was trying to dive to the cover of sea ferns when Camellion's next dart buried itself in his chest, the tip touching his heart and switching off his life.

Slowly, silently, the four dead Russians sank to the bottom of the Caribbean. . . .

THE DEATH MERCHANT SERIES:

#37 in the incredible adventures of the

DEATH MERCHANT
THE BERMUDA TRIANGLE ACTION
by Joseph Rosenberger

PINNACLE BOOKS   LOS ANGELES

DEATH MERCHANT #37: THE BERMUDA TRIANGLE ACTION

Copyright © 1980 by Joseph Rosenberger

An original Pinnacle Books edition, published for the first time anywhere.

First printing, February 1980

ISBN: 0-523-40701-7

Cover illustration by Dean Cate

Printed in the United States of America

PINNACLE BOOKS, INC.
2029 Century Park East
Los Angeles, California 90067

"Now, my suspicion is that the universe is not only queerer than we suppose, but queerer than we *can* suppose. I suspect that there are more things in heaven and earth than are dreamed of in *any* philosophy. That is the reason why I have no philosophy myself, and must be my excuse for dreaming."

—*J.B.S. Haldane.*

Nothing is more amazing and fantastic than natural phenomena not yet recognized and classified by human intelligence. In this respect, there are neither miracles nor mysteries. There are only undiscovered laws—*and new realities man has yet to reach.*

—*R.J. Camellion.*

THE BERMUDA
TRIANGLE ACTION

Chapter One

As calm as a sheet of blue glass! Colonel Anatole Bersenko, swaying ever so slightly from the motion of the large work platform, stared across the wide expanse of water and thought of how pleasant it was to watch the Caribbean change color. A leaden overcast, an orange sunset, the passage of clouds across the face of the sun—all would change the color and mood of the sea.

"Colonel Bersenko, how is the work here progressing? The expedition has been here six weeks and Moscow wants a full report."

Bersenko didn't reply immediately. For a moment, he let his eyes sweep over the other men on the platform. At the north end of the rectangle, which was half the size of a football field, Russian technicians were at the controls of an A-frame winch, preparing to lower rounded sections of silvery gray titanium steel into the water. Watching the technicians were Haroldo Pinsario and Vincente Nobiles, the two Cubans who were high officials in the *Dirección General de Inteligencia,* Castro's intelligence service, which was dominated by the KGB. Next to the two DGI officers was Captain Petyr Stashynsky, Major Ivanov's right-hand man. Like the other men on the platform—except the technicians, who wore white coveralls—Stashynsky and the two Cubans were dressed casually, in sport shirts and slacks.

To the left of Colonel Bersenko was Dr. Paul Rostislav Trovtsev, the oceanographer from the Lomonosov Institute in Leningrad and the senior scientist of the Russian force. To Bersenko's right was the man who had just spoken—Major Yuri Ivanov, the head of the KGB in Cuba and the real boss of the Cuban DGI.

1

Bersenko looked at the patient Ivanov. "We're on schedule with the overall project," he said, then glanced at Dr. Trovtsev, a thin, wrinkled face man with a small beard and sharp bird-like features. "I think Comrade Trovtsev can supply the technical details better than I."

"The assembly of the tenth cell on the ocean floor will be completed today," the scientist said, his voice surprisingly deep. "As soon as the first three cells were completed, we began our sea-solar-power experiments in ocean thermal energy conversion, and we have been studying ocean currents ever since we arrived in the area, conducting them from the two ships." He nodded to the two vessels less than a tenth of a mile from the floating work platform, the enormous *Mikhail Tukhachevsky* and the smaller *Vitiaz*. "We have also set up a solar power station on one of the Pedro Cays group. As for the—"

"How far are we from those Cays?" interrupted Major Ivanov, adjusting his green-tinted sunglasses.

"We're only four miles south of the Pedro Cays," said Trovtsev. "If they weren't so low in the water, we would be able to see them clearly from here."

"What about the drilling project? Keep in mind, Dr. Trovtsev, that is the main reason for this expedition. The drilling takes precedence over all the other experiments. Remember that."

"My memory is excellent, Major," Trovtsev said icily. "I remind you to report to Moscow not to expect miracles. We began drilling a few days ago, but we must go down twenty-one thousand feet. Drilling through *sima* is difficult enough, but to do it at an angle, to reach a precise position in the fault, requires the greatest of technical expertise."

"This *sima*," inquired Ivanov. "What kind of rock is it?"

The scientist blinked rapidly and smiled. These KGB men were so stupid . . . country dolts, who loved the feeling of power and control their positions gave them.

"The continents of this planet are composed of granite rock called *sial*, while the ocean basins are underlaid by dark, heavy rock known as *sima*. To a reasonable approximation, the ocean basins are virtually exposures of the earth's interior mantle. Frankly, I think the entire plan is a masterpiece of foolishness. There isn't any hard evidence that six hydrogen bombs of seven hundred megatons each will cause a shifting of the entire fault and trigger tremendous earthquakes along the eastern and southern coasts of the United States. That is only Dr. Bubchikov's theory! And to widen such a hole to a diame-

2

ter of seven feet! Why even with lasers the task is almost beyond our technology."

Colonel Bersenko's cold brown eyes crinkled ever so slightly and the ruddy skin stretched a bit tighter across his wide cheekbones.

"That is quite enough, Doctor. Aleksandr Bubchikov is one of our most brilliant geophysicists. To demean his theory is to tarnish your own professional background."

"Besides, it is not our place to pass judgment," added Ivanov sharply. He stared sternly at Dr. Trovtsev. "Our job—and yours, Doctor—is to obey the orders of the Central Committee."

Colonel Bersenko cut in brusquely, "Apparently, Comrade Trovtsev, it has slipped your mind that the drilling of the shaft is only for possible use in the future, in case of war between the United States and the Soviet Union, or should the planners in Moscow feel that exploding the H-bombs would be to our benefit."

"Precisely," agreed Major Ivanov, pulling a handkerchief from his back pocket. "An explosion that deep underground will register on American seismographs, but they won't know whether it's an underwater volcano or us."

A tall, well-built individual, Ivanov took off his open-vent Panama straw hat and wiped the handkerchief across his forehead. "Let's get out of this heat," he suggested. "I suppose you have air conditioning in some of these buildings on the platform?"

"Only in operations," explained Bersenko, "and we can't talk in there without the engineers hearing us. Only nine of us know the real reason why the shaft is being bored. Come, we'll go under that canvas canopy by the side of the crane. At least we'll be out of the sun."

He turned and, with Ivanov and Dr. Trovtsev following, headed toward the single boom crane used to lower the long plastic boxes, containing pipe, to the drilling station 700 feet below.

"Naturally our quarters aboard the *Mikhail Tukhachevsky* are air conditioned," said Bersenko, "otherwise life in this temperature and humidity would be unbearable." Noticing that Captain Stashynsky and the two Cubans were standing underneath a canopy stretched from the left side of the Operations building, Bersenko added, "Why did you bring the Cubans along? Those idiots think we're experimenting with Extracting energy from ocean currents."

"I brought them along merely for show," Ivanov said with a

3

thin smile. "It's a matter of psychology, of making the Cuban fools feel that they still make decisions regarding their own destiny."

Colonel Bersenko chuckled. "Like fighting and dying in Africa."

"Ah, Comrade, those Cubans are only too anxious to volunteer." Major Ivanov, reaching the protective canopy with the two other men, fumbled in the pocket of his printed shirt for cigarettes and sat down on a long wooden crate. "There's a lot of dissatisfaction in Cuba," he finally said, "but there isn't anything those fools can do about it. We have the stinking island in the palm of our hand."

Colonel Bersenko took a deep breath and watched Ivanov light a cigarette. "Since I'm responsible for all the security out here, my only concern is the Americans. As you know, they arrived eight days ago. Their vessel is only ten miles west of us. As far as we can determine, all they've done is send down divers. No doubt the divers set up transponders for the submarine that accompanied the ship."

"Yes, I know." Ivanov looked thoughtfully out across the calm blue water and his voice sobered. "The ship is the *Atlantis II*. It's the biggest and the best oceanographic vessel the Americans have. Technically it's owned by the Woods Hole Oceanographic Institution."

"Do you have the name of the submarine?"

"*Nyet*. We think it's the *Kingfisher*. We can't be sure. But you can bet it's nuclear powered and of the Polaris class. We can also assume that the Americans know about our own submarine lying on the bottom."

Dr. Trovtsev said definitely, "The Americans have not made any attempts to investigate what we are doing below."

"They don't dare approach us," snapped Bersenko. "They don't want an international incident any more than we do. They realize we have our sub down there and that we have alarms around the entire area." He turned and looked at Major Ivanov, permitting himself an indulgent smile. "Frankly, I don't expect any trouble from the Americans. We are on the high seas. We haven't infringed on any international law. Neither have the Americans. They have a right to be where they are. But those ten miles might as well be ten thousand. Yet do I have to tell you what is troubling the Americans?"

Ivanov's answer was prompt. "Of course. They are wondering why we have chosen this precise position in the Caribbean—why we are here and what we are doing. That's the worry of American intelligence."

4

"Therein lies the real danger," Bersenko said quickly. "Should the Americans discover what we have learned about the overlapping faults, I think they would act against us. Understand, Major, that is only my personal opinion."

"The Center doesn't think so," Ivanov said, his tone business-like.

Colonel Bersenko frowned. "On what does the Center base its predictions?"

"On the past behavior of the American government. The American President is weak and an unrealist. He did absolutely nothing to prevent the disaster in Iran, and for the Americans, what happened in Iran was a major disaster. Turning over the Panama Canal is another example. Still another glaring example of stupidity is the situation in Rhodesia. To obtain the good will of American blacks, the American government is taking the side of Communist revolutionaries in Rhodesia. And what has the American government done about the Cubans in Africa, except talk?"

Bersenko was thoughtful for a short time. Finally he said, "I don't doubt what you say is true, but in a real emergency the American military would force the President to act. And those American agents in Kingston, the ones you spoke of earlier, we can't simply ignore them— on the assumption that they actually are agents of some branch of American intelligence."

"We observed Joshua Forran for almost six months," Ivanov said, putting his hands on his knees. "We didn't have any trouble doing it. We do pretty much as we please in Jamaica. Those black Caribs running the government are always open to bribes. This Forran is an American. He's been in Kingston for several years and supposedly makes his living taking tourists on deep-sea fishing excursions."

"Why do you think he's an agent of American intelligence?"

"Forran has had too many contacts with persons we suspect of being either British or American agents. Then there's William Coopbird, the Jamaican who works for Forran on his boat. We've tailed Coopbird, and once saw him meet and have a long conversation with a known agent of British SIS. This agent operates from the British Embassy in Georgetown, on Grand Cayman."

Colonel Bersenko nodded slowly. "On that basis, I'd say that Forran and Coopbird are both agents. What about this newcomer, Camellion?"

"Six days ago, a Mr. Richard Camellion arrived in Kingston, flying from Miami, Florida. Supposedly an American sportsman and big game hunter, this Camellion registered at

5

the Sheraton Kingston. The next day, he went down to the harbor, looked up Forran and stayed on board the *Baby Doll,* Forran's boat, for almost three hours. The following day, Camellion, Forran, and Coopbird went out in Forran's boat. Camellion actually did some fishing. Several of my men watched with binoculars from another boat."

Ivanov then tossed a quick glance at Bersenko, after which he turned and gave Dr. Paul Trovtsev an even quicker look. Unable to detect any particular emotion in either man, Ivanov felt uncomfortable over their lack of warmth and informality.

Da, it was true what they said about Anatole Bersenko. He was as cold and unfeeling as the middle of a Siberian winter. Well, most members of Department-V[1] were icebergs. They had to be, to kill the way they did. This was especially true of men like Bersenko who were members of two divisions. In Bersenko's case, he was not only an officer in Department-V., but was also a member of Directorate-T, the Scientific and Technical Directorate.

Never one to be caught off guard, Bersenko said evenly as he looked out across the placid water, "We are well aware of Forran's Boat, *Baby Doll.* It approached within six miles of our northern operations perimeter that first day, and came within three miles of our western edge several days later. Yesterday it was eight miles from our eastern fringe. It was yesterday that either Camellion or Forran caught a Marlin. I presume it was Camellion, since he's supposed to be the 'tourist.' The report I received was that he did a fine job reeling it in."

"Excellent work," responded Ivanov, secretly disappointed over Bersenko's efficiency.

"Standard procedure in security. It's not unusual for venturesome fools to try to approach us. It's sheer curiosity on their part. We let them get close enough to take down the name of each boat, then wave them off if they get too close. Most swerve off the instant they see our flag. We're not liked in this part of the Americas."

"Castro is the main reason," Ivanov said slowly. "All these years, he's acted like the complete ass that he is."

Concerned with only the present, Colonel Bersenko shook his head with professional distaste. "Camellion and Forran,

---

[1] Technically this is the Executive Action Department, the one the KGB most wishes to hide from the world. It is this department that is responsible for murder, kidnapping, and other forms of violence the world over—actions called "wet affairs", *mokrie dela,* in KGB parlance.

6

and the Jamaican. They are your responsibility. What action do you intend to take against them?"

A crafty look crept into Major Ivanov's eyes. "Those three will be captured and brought to the *Mikhail Tukhachevsky*. We'll find out what secrets they have."

"And the contact?"

"The moment my men have them, they'll contact Havana. I'll contact you with the special Y-code, using the scrambler."

While Bersenko nodded in satisfaction, Dr. Trovtsev tilted his egg-shaped head to one side and peered at Major Ivanov with calculating eyes. "There is one more matter we must discuss with you, Comrade Yuri Ivanov. The last reason why this expedition is here in this forsaken part of the world, our studies of Unidentified Aquatic Objects."

Ivanov's eyes twinkled and his voice sounded amused. "You are referring to that nonsense about the Bermuda Triangle?"

Colonel Bersenko bridled as much as Dr. Trovtsev.

"Moscow is convinced that the project is worthy of study," Bersenko said tersely. "More than a dozen times the Soviet navy has detected underwater craft that were more than ten thousand feet down and traveling at a fantastic 250 knots per hour. No nation on earth has a submersible that can move with such great speed underwater. Furthermore, many of those UAOs have been seen by the U.S. Navy in the Caribbean, a few even in this general region."

A grave expression dropped over Ivanov's well-tanned face. "As I understand the situation, the operation here is some miles from the southwest area of the so-called Bermuda Triangle."

"There is entirely too much EMI in the Bermuda Triangle," Dr. Trovtsev said, as if speaking to a child. "That's electromagnetic interference to you, Comrade Major. EMI would seriously interfere with our sensitive instruments. Even so, we had to choose this exact position because of the pattern of the two faults."

Colonel Bersenko cut in, "We scientists know that these objects are not natural underwater phenomena. We are convinced they are metal vehicles made by intelligences far greater than the race that dwells on the surface."

Toying with his pack of Camel Lights, Major Ivanov stared at Bersenko, who was short and chunky. A snout of a nose fronting a square head did not add to his looks.

"Intelligent life in the depths of the oceans. Very interesting." But Ivanov's voice lacked conviction, a lack of belief detected at once by Bersenko and Trovtsev.

7

"We are only beginning to understand the life process," Trovtsev said coldly. "It is very possible that organic life might undergo certain modifications. This process could lead to forms that, according to our present ideas of life, are impossible. Changes could be gradual. On that basis, it is quite possible that intelligent life might very well dwell in the depths of the ocean, even inside the earth itself."

Major Ivanov cleared his throat. "I can only report to the Center what you tell me, Comrade Doctor Trovtsev. "I presume your experiments in this direction, whatever they might be, are going well?"

"*Nyet,* they are not," replied Bersenko.

"There is no way to experiment with UAOs," said Dr. Trovtsev. "All we can do is send our searchers."

"We did that several days ago," explained Colonel Bersenko. "Three of our divers went on a scouting mission in one of our small deep-dive vehicles. Their intention was to monitor the area over the Cayman Trench, northwest of here. Our watch stations below picked up the craft on sonar as it was returning. Then, only four miles northwest of here, the submarine vanished. One instant it was there. The next moment— gone. We sent four more baby subs to investigate. They found no trace of the vessel. There was no evidence of a wreckage . . . nothing."

Major Ivanov brooded in silence for a long moment. At length he said, "Comrades, what is your evaluation of the strange disappearance?"

"A disappearance that cannot be explained by any conventional means," Bersenko said matter-of-factly. "That is all you can state in your report."

"*They* got the submarine and the men aboard," interposed Dr. Trovtsev, scratching the end of his long nose.

"They?" Bersenko tried to sound business-like.

"They—the *Other Intelligences.*"

Chapter Two

The several dozen photographs on the small table were as clear as air over the Antarctica. Richard Camellion, sitting on the edge of the extension berth in the stern cabin of *Baby Doll,* studied intently the 11 inch by 14 inch glossies, which he had taken with a camera equipped with a wide-angle telephoto lenses. The photos contained every detail of the work platform and the two Russian ships, every detail, from all angles. Not at all bad photography, he thought—considering that he had to snap each picture from below decks, from the first window on the starboard side, while wedged in the bow's tiny rope locker.

Barefooted and dressed only in white duck shorts, the Death Merchant hunched down over the table, his eyes searching for new details. There, on the platform, were the two cranes, the operations shed and three DDCs[1]. It was the storage area, where long boxes were stored before being lowered into the sea, that intrigued Camellion. Each box was handled with the utmost care, as if it contained delicate porcelain or fine China. Camellion knew why each box was handled with such tender loving care: the Ruskies didn't want the boxes dropped, or they might split open and reveal the contents to the ever-watching eyes of the Americans.

Lengths of pipe or drills? Camellion wondered. But the pig farmers couldn't conceal the rounded and curved sections of metal, and he had little trouble envisioning how the sections would appear when welded together: they would form a large, long, lopsided cylinder.

[1] Deck compression chambers attached to decompression chambers.

Camellion picked up the photographs, arranged them in order, and slipped them into an attaché case. There were three grim facts, the first being that the Soviet Union was engaged in vital underwater research, some kind of highly important project on the bottom of the sea. The second fact was that *Titan* had vanished—three months ago, before the Russians had arrived in the Caribbean. A nuclear submarine of the Polaris class, the *Titan*, had vanished in the Atlantic, in the vicinity southeast of Bermuda—the third nuclear submarine to be lost by the United States Navy.

The first had been *Thresher*. She had died off the coast of Maine, in April of 1963, when something went wrong during her deep dive. Parts of her were still scattered in 8,500 feet of water.

Scorpion went down south of the Azores, in May of 1968. She, too, was still a prisoner of the ocean bed, lying there nearly two miles down.

Both *Thresher* and *Scorpion* had been located by DRVs, Deep Sea Research Vehicles, but even *Jethro*, the U.S. Navy's latest DRV, which could descend to 3,200 fathoms, or 19,200 feet, had not been able to locate *Titan*. The Western Atlantic Basin was only 21,000 feet at its maximum depth. There were some undersea mountains, or seamounts, but none were very tall, certainly nothing resembling the tremendous seamounts of the Pacific. Using the most modern of microelectronic depth-sounding sonar and television-scanners with image intensifiers, *Jethro* should have been able to locate *Titan*.

Unless the sub wasn't there! reflected the Death Merchant. Only *Titan* was. At least, she had been. She had sent her last radio message at 21.00 hours, giving her position at 124 miles southeast of Bermuda. Cruising on the surface, *Titan* had not even had to send up her radio antenna on a float. The message had been a Mayday, the coded signals frantic! *"The sky and moon have vanished and we don't know our position. The compass is spinning in all directions. Ten minutes ago we were 124.11 miles south by east of Bermuda, but now we can't get any bearing. The water all around is is glowing with a bluish light and—my God! We're being pulled down! We—"*

That was all. End of message.

Titan had vanished so completely that it was as if she had never existed, as if the 320 men aboard had never existed. . . .

A look of concern crossed the Death Merchant's lean, hard face.

She vanished right smack in the middle of the Bermuda Triangle!

10

The third disturbing fact was that for any number of years the intelligence community of the U.S. had known that something very deadly was in the area, which was colloquially called "The Bermuda Triangle."

The first intense investigation had begun in 1946 after five TBM Avenger torpedo bombers vanished 225 miles northwest of Fort Lauderdale, Florida, on December 5, 1945, along with the Martin flying boat rescue mission that had flown out to search for the five missing aircraft.

The investigation scored zero. Subsequent investigations over the years, into other mysterious disappearances, had scored also come up with nothing.

More evidence that "something" was out there in the Bermuda Triangle came in 1976, from NOAA. The National Oceanographic and Atmosphere Administration reported that its polar orbiting satellites, moving from north to south at an altitude of 800 miles, would malfunction only while over the Bermuda Triangle. Taped signals would cease transmission, and telemetric and electronic impulses were also wiped out.

There wasn't anything anyone could do about it.

Then the Russian expedition arrived in the Caribbean.

Since the area involved was water, the United State Navy's Office of Naval Intelligence got into the act. Working with the CIA, NSA[2], and DIA[3], ONI decided to bring down two vultures with one big bang . . . solve two mysteries with one expedition. A private expedition, supposedly sponsored by the James Mellin Institute, would go into the Caribbean, supposedly to study gravitation, geomagnetism, continental drift, undersea oreogenesis (or mountain building), and various meteorological, hydrological, and seismological events. The real study would be to ascertain what the Soviet Union was doing on the floor of the Caribbean.

And also to study Gravity-XX, in relation to the strange disappearances forever going on in the Bermuda Triangle. Gravity-XX was the postulation that certain gravitational and "wave" effects on the surface of the earth—and especially on,

[2] *National Security Agency*, which concerns itself with electronic intelligence gathering . . . spy satellites, etc. NSA spends twice as much as the CIA and employs far more people than the CIA, which gets all the adverse publicity. Its base at Fort Meade, fifteen miles northeast of Washington, is almost twice the size of the CIA's complex in Langley, Virginia.

[3] *Defense Intelligence Agency*—a "spook" bureau assigned to the Joints Chiefs of Staff.

11

over, and in certain specific maritime areas—could be responsible for the strange "vanishings." The same theory also maintained that these effects could be detected by present scientific techniques.

The CIA wouldn't have it, pointing out that there simply wasn't time for such elaborate deception. Even if there had been ample time, the ruse wasn't likely to fool the Russians, in which case the "private" expedition would be in great danger. The KGB was not noted for either mildness or patience. The Company argued that it would be far wiser to send a force that would elicit respect from the Russians. Such an expedition would involve an oceanography research vessel that the Russians knew was connected with Uncle Sam, and a nuclear submarine.

The brass of ONI objected. The project was their baby, not the Company's. However, the Company was bigger, better, and more influential with the President's Foreign Intelligence Advisory Board. The CIA won.

The Company also stubbornly insisted that it have the final say and make all decisions regarding the Soviet force in the Caribbean. Again ONI objected vigorously. Again ONI lost, but only after having effected a small compromise. The CIA would not involve itself with the experiments regarding the Bermuda Triangle. The company agreed, but tacked on a rider to which ONI agreed: the Russian riddle would be top priority. The Bermuda Triangle would be No. 2-P. Agreed.

The research vessel chosen was *Atlantis II*. The submarine that would accompany the ship would be *Kingfisher*.

The man tapped by the CIA was Richard Joseph Camellion, the Death Merchant. . . .

Camellion was putting the attaché case in the locker below the table when Joshua Forran came in from the bow cabin, carrying an SD-10 portable depth sounder. The ONI agent swayed slightly as William Coopbird, at the helm on the flying bridge above the deck housing, turned *Baby Doll* slightly to port.

"I've said it before and I'll say it again," growled Forran as he sat down on the berth opposite Camellion. "Going in as close as two miles stinks. They know damn well I'm in the intelligence game. We're stretching our luck."

"You don't have any actual proof that it was Russian agents who searched your boat a year ago." Camellion crossed his legs, and began tearing the wrapper from a box of dried figs. His manner was deferential, but his icy blue eyes regarded

12

Forran with some concern. It wasn't that Forran was losing his nerve. It was just that he was not used to taking such enormous risks. *Maybe so,* Camellion thought. *But a turtle only moves ahead by sticking his neck out.* . . .

"On the other hand," continued Camellion, "ordinary thieves would have taken your high resolution cameras and the two auto-pistols. So I'd say maybe you're right, Josh. The ivans have got you made."

Forran went on, "We know that the sea floor below the Russians is seven hundred and eighty feet. And we don't need a crystal ball to know that their sub is damned close by, unless it's out scouting. I don't see any sense in triple-checking what we've already double-checked."

The Death Merchant removed a dried fig from the cardboard box.

"I want to be absolutely positive of the depth. Today ends our game of tag with the Russians. Tomorrow we'll establish ourselves on *Atlantis* and pick up the mission from there."

"Expect Commander Webber to give you a hard time," Forran said, his tone serious. "I met him several years ago. He hates the CIA and any 'civilian' connected with it. Don't worry though. He'll go by the book and follow orders. He'd attack the Russians with his bare hands if D.C. ordered him to."

The Death Merchant didn't comment. He was chewing a fig. He never spoke while chewing, and became annoyed with people who did. He didn't find Forran's comment about Webber unusual. The stiff-necked professionals always resented civilians intruding into their private world of shadows. At first, Camellion had even detected some resentment on the part of Forran, who was a career officer in ONI. But the man was a realist, and had quickly accepted the factuality of the situation. Camellion liked him, mainly because he was highly intelligent. And he enjoyed the company of William "Billy" Coopbird. The tall Jamaican was indeed a paradox. Not only was he educated, having majored in psychology at the University of Mexico, but his speech was totally free of Jamaican inflections and provincialisms, except when they suited his purpose. He always played the "friendly but dumb black" with tourists.

Camellion finished chewing. "I'm only thankful that the scientists on board *Atlantis* won't resent my intrusion," he mused. "My concern is the Russians. I couldn't care less than Friday about the Bermuda Triangle. That mystery will not be solved in our day, if ever."

Forran, a muscular man in his early forties, whose skin had

13

been burned the color of chocolate by the tropical sun, gave Camellion a peculiar look, his face clouding with curiosity.

"That's a rather dogmatic statement, although I'm inclined to agree with you. Like everyone else, scientists tend to have mental 'sets.' They tend to pick out whatever their minds are set for, and most experts in the physical sciences—the biological disciplines, too—are reluctant to even admit that there is something mysterious about the Triangle. I suppose you're aware that the Navy has pinged in on submarines as deep as 25,000 feet and going at speeds in excess of 200 miles per hour. I use the term 'submarines' only because the vehicles were underwater. Who knows what they really are."

Camellion looked thoughtful. "Among other things, it's those alien craft that worry scientists the world over. They don't like to contemplate living entities more intelligent than human beings, especially metallurgical experts, of humanoid form, living at the bottom of oceans we consider our own private preserves." He laughed bitterly. "I personally find it very amusing, not only because it bedevils the know-it-all experts, but because the whole business is just another crooked wormhole in man's reality, a reality that's ninety-nine percent egocentric, anthropocentric, and terracentric pride. We're crawling around on a speck of dust that's revolving around a middle of the road star in the boondocks of our galaxy; yet we still have the nerve to think we're 'special.' It's that kind of stupidity that forces scientists—most of them—to close their eyes to the true secret of the Bermuda Triangle."

"Your own theory could be incorrect," Forran said spontaneously.

"My own theory makes more sense than Gravity-XX," laughed Camellion. "Gravity can bend light waves, but it can't make them vanish. Gravity can't make people disappear either. My own hypothesis is that the Bermuda Triangle and other maritime areas are 'points of entry' into a different reality, probes controlled by aliens that employ techniques involving manipulation of space and time."

"Such as the Devil's Sea off the east coast of Japan—right?" commented Forran, who suddenly was puzzled. "But if these aliens are in a different dimension, what are their submarines doing in our reality? The Navy's sonar picked up solid objects. One even surfaced and was photographed. The damned thing was gray, didn't have any diving planes, no conning tower, nothing. No signs of a rivet or seams. Almost three hundred feet long. Or don't you feel that these vehicles are a part of the Triangle problem?"

14

The Death Merchant finished chewing a fig.

"Call it nonsense or call it intuition, but I know that the true underlying reality is one of pure vibration. It's a primal frequency realm, one that is beyond time and space. In a sense, it's analogous to the frequency patterns in a hologram. This world appears real to us because we can sense only one microscopic slice of this underlying reality at any particular time. This mode of reality would also explain the mechanism operating behind telepathy, precognition, clairvoyance and other paranormal activity."

"Well, maybe so, but how does all that tie in with the Triangle and alien submarines?" Forran asked, his manner impatient.

"Entities with a knowledge of the structure of this underlying reality could control matter. They could convert matter into energy, and energy back into matter. This ability would permit them to 'crossover' into our own space-time continuum. They could either enter as pure energy, then transform themselves and their machines into solids. Or they could project mental images—holographic images—of what they wanted any particular observer, or observers, to see. UFOs are a prime example. Some are solid. They're metal. They leave impressions on the ground when they land. Others, like balls of light that sometimes explode, are only images. And not infrequently, UFOs have been seen diving into the sea."

"Then you feel that *Titan* was sucked into one of the probes, the one in the Bermuda Triangle?"

Camellion nodded sagely. "I think so. But I haven't any hard evidence. The problem is that we don't have the right kind of instruments to detect these alien energy forms. I don't think they register as life forms, not in the sense that we know life. The scientists will fail because they'll be looking in the wrong direction. It's like using a thermometer to measure the distance from earth to Jupiter. What is needed is new constructs, totally new frames of reference."

Forran cleared his throat, took off the battered captain's caps and sighed. "The cosmologists do it all the time—form new frames of reference. There's the anthropic principle. By invoking the anthropic principle, cosmologists can explain the observable state of the universe. This principle states that if the universe were different in any significant way from the way it is, we wouldn't be around to wonder why it is the way it is. Put another way, humanity exists because the universe is the way it is, and the universe is the way it is because we are

15

here. It's a circular argument to me, but it satisfies the boys with the brains."

"But it doesn't help us with the pig farmers," Camellion said with a remote smile. "All it takes with those lying barnyard swine is firepower. Brute force is the only thing they understand."

The Death Merchant crumpled the empty fig box, turned on the bunk, and tossed it through the open window. Then he stood up and picked up the SD-10 depth sounder.

Slight surprise flicked over Forran's face as he stood up and tugged at the waist of his blue jeans, which were cut off at the thighs. Ordinarily, sounding the depth was his job.

"You're not going through with your fishing act today, huh?"

"Why bother? We're not fooling the Russians," Camellion replied with quiet finality. "I'll take a twenty-yard-length sounding when we're swinging around from the two-mile limit.

"Right. In that case I'll stay on the bridge with Billy." Forran glanced at his wristwatch. "We must be about forty miles from the platform. I'll ask him."

The Death Merchant, heading toward the aft door, paused and turned around. "Listen, Josh. Just in case, you'd better bring the Colts and the ammo bags. I'll see you on deck."

"Will do." As the Death Merchant went up the four steps to the door, Forran removed the mike from the wall and pressed the "talk" button. "Billy, what's our position?"

"About thirty-eight miles from the five-mile mark." Coopbird's cultured voice floated through the mike, the accent unmistakably British. "I trust we're not going to stop in their front yard?"

"We might as well," Forran said spiritedly. "Camellion insists on going as close as two miles from the platform. How does that grab your black balls?"

"Mon, I think we all crazy!" Coopbird cried with alarm, deliberately using the Jamaican dialect. "We make old Russian bear mad. Old Russian bear, he gobble us for supper."

"Not this day, Billy boy. I'll be topside in a few minutes."

"Sure, mon."

Forran hung up the mike, went back into the bow cabinet, opened a locker, and took out two Colt XM177E2 submachine guns and two canvas bags. Each bag contained nine magazines. In each magazine were twenty 7.62 millimeter cartridges. Forran closed the locker and headed for the deck.

The Death Merchant sat in the fisherman's chair, on the stern deck of the sleek Viking cruiser (which was advertised

16

as "The World's Best Superfast Fishing Machine), scanning the aft area. Regardless of what danger might be lurking, Camellion was enjoying himself. The average person was always looking for contentment in the future, as if happiness could be bought and boxed and tied with a red ribbon. Camellion knew better. He grabbed his peace of mind on a day-to-day basis. Besides, the sweet, powerful throbbing of *Baby Doll*'s twin Diesels was pure music to his ears. The crystal blue water was not an unfriendly plain, and the circle of sky stretched out into infinity, wide open, with only a line of mud-gray clouds on the western horizon. Several miles to the east were several fishing cruisers. Beyond them, a sailboat, a fairly stiff wind billowing out the canvas. Beyond the sailboat was a tramp steamer—no doubt having just departed from Kingston—moving slowly southeast, her hull dimly outlined against a hazy backdrop of sea and sky.

Camellion swung the chair around on its ring-mount, and started studying the quadrant to the west. Almost at once he spotted the British L-7 motor torpedo boat[4], its knife-like prow cutting the water masterfully. With the black, green, and yellow flag of Jamaica flying from the mast behind the bridge deck, the craft was headed at a full speed of 47 knots toward *Baby Doll*—a very obvious fact since the vessel was moving at an angle by which, within five miles, it would intercept *Baby Doll*.

The Death Merchant didn't like what he saw. Other than the dark-skinned men in uniforms on the bridge, the stern, and behind the 40mm automatic cannon on the forward deck, there were several Caucasians on the bridge. They might as well have had a hammer and sickle stamped on their foreheads.

Hearing Forran emerge from the aft cabin, Camellion said, "Josh, put the Colts on the deck and take a look."

He swung around toward Forran, who was placing the two submachine guns on the deck. When Josh straightened up, he handed him the binoculars, his mouth twisted in a sardonic leer. "They're sticking to us like a tick to a hound's ear. Have a look-see."

Forran had a long look-see, muttering, "Rape a ragged raccoon," while he studied the approaching B-L-7. At length, he

---

[4] Slightly larger than a PTF, a U.S. Navy fast patrol boat, the British L-7 has a length of 90 feet, a beam of 21.6 feet, a draft of 5.8 feet, and a complement of 17 men. The L-7 is armed with a 40mm antiaircraft gun and two 30-caliber Vickers machine guns.

handed the binoculars to Camellion, saying, "I don't like it. They're headed for us, but why? We're a long way beyond the limit. Those dumb bastards don't have any authority on the high seas. And the two white men on the bridge! It all stinks."

"Yeah, they smell like a barnyard," declared Camellion with feeling. "I can smell their commie stink even at this distance."

Anger, mingling with understanding, flashed over Josh Forran's face. "The goddamn boat's a KGB trap. Well, we can't outrun 'em, and we can't outshoot 'em. Our only chance is to outwit 'em with the element of surprise. Any ideas?"

"How much explosive do we have?"

"A pound of plastic stuff—C-4—and the timers to go with it. But they'd gun us down before we could toss it."

"How about Primacord?"[5]

"I think so. I'm not sure." Forran gave Camellion a questioning look. He would have argued with another man. But he had heard whispers about Richard Camellion, and knew that the lean Texan hadn't built his rep by merely saying what he could do.

"Get the C-4 and the other stuff," Camellion said, sliding from the fisherman's chair. "I'm going up to the bridge and clue in Billy."

"We're going to have to get the lead out; that boat's getting closer," Forran said, then turned and hurried to the aft cabin door.

Camellion picked up the two Colt submachine guns and the bags of magazines, and went up the steps to the flying bridge, which was surrounded on three sides by short steel walls and over which was stretched white canvas on a frame of aluminum tubing.

Billy Coopbird had already spotted the Jamaican gunboat. He said to Camellion in a serious voice, "I saw you two chaps discussing the problem. I presume we shall use an element of cunning to facilitate our escape, and that the submachine guns will assist us. I don't wish to appear obtuse, but what do you want me to do?"

On his knees below the top of the portside wall, the Death Merchant was checking the Colts, to make sure they were ready to be fired. "Right now, slow down to one-third," he

[5] Primacord consists of a PETN cord, protected by six layers of material. Detonating cord explodes throughout its entire length, with enough force to detonate any standard military charge to which it is properly attached.

18

said, and pushed the firing lever on one Colt to automatic. "When they're ten yards away, come to a full stop. Keep the engines on. When I say 'go'—after the fireworks—get us out and fast."

His tar-black face shiny with sweat, Coopbird cut speed. The power of the engines slackened and the Viking slowed, the prow tossing back less water against the sides and over the forward deck of the bow.

"The Ruskies have made one big mistake," Camellion said in a low voice. "The damn fools think we're going to respect the Jamaican flag. Those poor fools. They're less than ten minutes from eternity."

Billy grinned, revealing even white teeth. "I am not anxious to go with them, mon."

Camellion stood up and glanced at Forran who was coming up the steps with a block of C-4 in one hand and a Mertex electric timer in the other. Forran first glanced at the approaching Jamaican Coast Guard cutter, which was less than a mile and a half away, then looked at Camellion.

"No Primacord," he said. "The timer will do just as well."

Keeping his hands well below the top level of the short starboard wall, Josh handed the block of Composition C-4 and the timer to Camellion. The Death Merchant was also keeping a wary eye on the Jamaican cutter that was coming in fast from the northwest and, because *Baby Doll* had previously been cutting through the water at top speed, was now to the starboard bow of the fishing boat.

"Come to a full stop, Billy," said Camellion. "But keep the engines running."

Coopbird's hand went to the throttle and *Baby Doll* began to slow.

"Camellion, how do you want to do it?" Forran was all business, his voice dry ice. "All we can do is rake the whole damn boat, toss the boom-stuff, and get the hell out of here."

Camellion—checking the Mertex timer to make sure the contact pin had pierced the slick brown paper of the plastic C-4—agreed with a slight nod of his head.

"Dead right, if you'll pardon the pun," he said. "You take out the men on the bridge and the dummies behind the forty millimeter job. I'll give the long sleep to the boob behind the machine guns and the men on the stern."

"Good enough, but why not the other way around. Not that I care. I'm just curious."

"Because I'm a better shot than you."

Forran didn't comment. He knew that Camellion was not

boasting. From the tone of his voice, he had only stated what he knew to be fact, indicative that Camellion had been in similar situations, such as this, many times.

"They won't shoot unless they have to," Camellion said softly, "and that's what gives us the edge."

"They could have blown us out of the water long ago, with that forty mill job," commented Forran.

"They could have, but they didn't," declared the Death Merchant. "They haven't and they won't, because they want us alive. The KGB wants to ask us some questions."

"I'll see those commie bastards in hell first," Forran said grimly.

By now *Baby Doll* had stopped and was rocking slightly in the placid water. To the starboard bow, the Jamaican cutter had cut speed to three knots, the man at the helm preparing to bring the craft alongside *Baby Doll*.

"Call out to them, Josh," Camellion said, a slight edge of mockery in his low voice. "Let's see what kind of excuse they have."

He glanced down at the Colt submachine gun, which was leaning against the short wall and prevented from falling by his right leg. Next to him, Forran stood with his hands on the top edge of the bridge wall, his Colt braced against his leg. Already he had switched off the machine gun's safety lever.

Billy Coopbird, too, was watching the cutter edge in until its port side was only six feet from *Baby Doll*'s starboard. Coopbird had taken a fully loaded Ingram M10 submachine gun from the bridge locker. The Ingram lay at his feet, ready to be fired.

There were no white men on the bridge of the Jamaican cutter—*They're waiting below decks, waiting to get their pig farmer hands on me and Josh and Billy*. There was only a Jamaican in a white captain's uniform and four non-coms. Several sailors were behind the 40mm pom-pom on the bow deck, and perhaps a dozen more clustered on the stern.

The Death Merchant's only real concern was the tar baby in the square turret just behind the radio mast on the bridge deck. The sailor's hands were only inches from the deadly brace of 30-caliber Vickers, the barrels of which were pointed at *Baby Doll*.

Forran cupped his hands to his mouth. "What do you want? We're in international waters. Your authority does not extend to the open sea."

The man in the captain's uniform picked up an electric bullhorn. "Captain Forran, I am Captain Thomas Montroy."

The man's voice was friendly . . . too friendly. "We have word that smugglers of dangerous drugs are in the area. We are scarching all boats."

Forran pretended amazement and resentment. "Damn it, you know me. I've operated out of Kingston for over two years. I'm not a damned drug smuggler."

"I am sorry, suh. But my orders are to search all vessels," the Jamaican called back apologetically. "I suggest you cooperate and permit us to come aboard, or you will find your permit to operate from our nation suspended, and your visa will be canceled. Will you give your permission, Captain Forran?"

"Tell him yes," Camellion interposed, "then send him to his ancestors."

"Very well, Captain Montroy," Forran called in a loud voice. "I give my permission. Send your men aboard."

"*Go!*" hissed the Death Merchant. He stooped slightly and grabbed the Colt XM177, all the while mentally aiming at the sailor in the turret. In grabbing their weapons, Forran and Coopbird were only a thin slice of a second behind behind Camellion.

The Death Merchant fired. The Colt 177[6] roared, a stream of spitzer-shaped projectiles chopping into the Vikers machine guns and the sailor behind them. Chest ripped open by the impact, the dead man was slammed back against the rear wall. He slid to the floor, tiny pieces of bloody flesh sticking to the rims of the five burnt holes in his shot-apart shirt.

Forran and Coopbird were firing, their weapons chattering and shuddering in their hands. Forran's first long burst raked across the open bridge of the Jamaican cutter and the storm of high velocity slugs killing Captain Montroy and the three men with him. The only reason the fourth man escaped was that he was one of the men who was supposed to go aboard *Baby Doll*, so he had turned and started down the steps when the slugs struck.

The sailors on the bow and the stern also received the final surprise of their lives. Forran and Coopbird's slugs riddled the men behind the 40mm cannon, as well as the six sailors not far behind them, close to the front of the deck housing. They all fell like bricks and lay still, their blood making a mess of the deck.

[6] The Colt 177 was carried by special forces during the Vietnam war and has a wide variety of uses—for sniping, assault and even grenade launching.

21

Eight men were bowled over on the stern deck by the Death Merchant's sweep. *Like shooting bass in a bathtub!* he thought. Another sailor tried to dash up the steps to the machine gun turret—and he almost made it. But he screamed and stopped and tumbled back down the steps when two of Camellion's bullets tore off his left foot at the ankle. He was sinking into the gray fog of unconsciousness when the Death Merchant's next two slugs zipped through his right side and killed him on schedule.

"Get us out of here, Billy," yelled Camellion. He dropped the practically empty machine gun, bent down, picked up the C-4 pack from the floor, and turned the small black knob on the timer to 1-M, giving them one minute to clear out. For a second he measured the distance. Carefully then, he tossed the bomb to the forward deck of the enemy vessel, the deadly little package landing between two corpses.

Simultaneously, Coopbird shoved in the throttle, and Forran blew up three men who had come from below decks. Two jumped, jerked, did the two-step of death, and died. But the third man managed to get off a short burst from a Spanish Star machine gun before he crashed to the deck. Several projectiles zipped past Camellion's head. Another 9mm hollow-point narrowly missed Coopbird. Several more hissed by Forran's right shoulder. One hit one of the steel tubings supporting the starboard wall and richocheted.

Baby Doll leaped forward, her engines roaring, her twin screws churning the water. She was not quite a hundred feet from the doomed Jamaican vessel when the final second clicked off on the timer. The electric spark detonated the blasting cap, the force of the small explosion touching off the C-4. To the Death Merchant, who loved noise, the blast was a beautiful symphony of sound. To Forran and Coopbird, the explosion was a crashing sound of destruction.

A blink of flame, and the forward section of the cutter disintegrated into blazing, twisted junk, which flew upward and outward. The bridge, with its complement of dead bodies, shot fifty feet upward, the corpses turning over and over like rag dolls. The whole mess splashed into the sea, while what remained of the rapidly sinking gunboat blazed with crackling flames and belched oily black smoke.

"The poor bastards," intoned Forran. "Fifty years from now I just might feel sorry for them. Well, there goes the last of her."

The gunboat hung there, her stern upended, the hull perpendicular, propeller and rudder stark naked to sun and sky.

Slowly, then more quickly, the hull knifed downward and slipped beneath the water, leaving behind debris and ever-widening rings of water, which expanded into final nothingness.

Camellion glanced at the compass. The practical Coopbird had already turned west, knowing that now the only refuges were *Atlantis II* and the *U.S.S. Mohawk*, the amphibious LCC command ship of the American force ten miles west of the Russian expedition.

"Billy, head us straight for the Americans," Camellion said. We've worn out our welcome in Kingston, and there's no way of knowing if the Russians have a secondary plan."

"I doubt it," Forran said. He shoved a magazine into one of the Colt XM177s. "I don't think they expected us to fire on a Jamaican Coast Guard cutter. Well, we fooled them and soured the KGB's borscht in the process."

Camellion twisted his mouth. A tiny piece of fig had lodged between two left molars and was annoying him.

"We've only won a single skirmish," he reminded Josh. "The real war has yet to begin. Who's got a toothpick?"

Forran glanced at him in surprise. "Did you say toothpick?"

"Yeah. Be true to your teeth and they'll never be false to you. Do you have one or don't you?"

Coopbird turned and grinned. "Try the left side locker, mon."

Camellion opened the locker and, among several pints of rum, a P-38 Walther auto-pistol, a copy of *Without a Trace*, and several signal flares, found a half-full box of toothpicks. He took one out and began to attack the particle of fig.

Racing through the water, *Baby Doll* charged west, Coop bird's hands steady on the wheel. On either side of the tall Jamaican—he was six feet seven inches—the Death Merchant and Forran scanned the circular horizon through powerful binoculars.

Finally, far to the west, they saw their destination—the American force. There was *Atlantis II*, her white paint bright in the sun; and *Mohawk*, with her bow and stern double masts, and her midship tower loaded with radar and other electronic detection gear. Not far from the two vessels was the *South Dakota*, a DD class destroyer.

The Death Merchant lowered the binoculars. "Gentlemen, there's our new home for a while."

Forran and Coopbird didn't comment. People who live in

the Caribbean for any length of time develop a strange sense of intuition. Both men had a nagging presentiment about the undertaking, an eerie foreboding that Death was always a few steps behind them. It wasn't the Russians. They were flesh and blood; they could die.

It was the Bermuda Triangle. . . .

Chapter Three

"To begin with, I'd appreciate a complete rundown on the security," Camellion said to the gray-haired, stern-faced Commander Jason Webber, who was seated at the head of the long table.

Webber coughed deprecatingly. "We've taken all the standard procedures," he said, staring steadily at the Death Merchant, who was at the other end of the table. "We have our first warning line at a five-mile radius from Operations. We have a transponder at every one hundred feet. The second transponder circle is two miles from Operations. Other than the transponders, we have two four-man subs constantly circling the five-mile radius, one moving clockwise, the other moving counterclockwise. *Kingfisher* is six point three miles east of us, sitting on the seabed between us and the Russians. Her forward, aft, and side-scan sonar is going at all times—full range max. Finally, we have twenty-six wide-scan television monitors scattered around the five-mile radius. Can you suggest anything better, Mr. Camellion?"

The Death Merchant smiled and said what he honestly thought. "You've done an excellent job, Commander. I would say your security is first rate."

Lieutenant Commander Willard Norris added, "And four to ten of my men are constantly swimming about the two-mile perimeter. They carry pulse-spacing oscillators in order for the operators to ID them on the transponders. There isn't any way the Russians could infiltrate. They could try, but we'd know it. They know we'd know it."

Christopher Humbard, one of the ONI agents, looked impatiently from Commander Webber to Camellion, and said in a firm, demanding voice, "I'm not inclined to think the Russian force out there is going to attack us. The Russians don't want a confrontation any more than we do."

Humphrey Frimholtz cut in slyly, "I am positive that your orders are not to engage the Soviets in any kind of showdown, but to find out why they are at that particular position in the Caribbean, and what they are doing there. I should think the *why* will tell us the *what*."

The Death Merchant was silent for a moment . . . thinking. Besides himself and Forran—sitting at the first position to Camellion's left—there were six other men at the table in the planning room below the radar compartment in the *Mohawk*. Commander Webber sat directly opposite the Death Merchant. He was Navy all the way, and had seen a lot of action in the Korean War.

Next to Forran was Humphrey Frimholtz, the senior ONI agent of PINK INK, the code name of the American expedition. Sixty-five years old, and resembling a retired banker (minus the pot belly), Frimholtz was an old-timer in the intelligence and espionage game. His career went back to World War II, when he had been the sole American with the British XX-Committee, which specialized in manufacturing and delivering false intelligence through the Germans' own espionage network. The XX-Committee had even built a machine called Ultra, a complicated gadget that could and did emulate the cryptographic engines of any nation, the idea having originated with the clever Frimholtz. Strategic deception was still Frimholtz's trade.

Christopher Humbard had the chair next to Frimholtz. In his middle thirties, Humbard was a good-looking critter with wavy blond hair and medium mustache to match. He walked with a slight limp, the result of an airplane crash. His M7 File also listed him as a collector of, and an authority on, comic books.

To the Death Merchant's right was Lt. Commander Will Norris, the commanding officer of the 100 SEALs, a tough, square-jawed man with close-cropped red hair.

Next to Red Norris was Doctor Robert Tyler Mabroless, the chief of the seven oceanographers aboard *Atlantis II*. One of the world's leading authorities on the oceans' role in weather, the beefy-looking Mabroless, who resembled a bartender more than a scientist, had done research with the Scripps Institution of Oceanography at La Jolla, California and with the Woods Hole Oceanographic Institution at Cape Cod, Massachusetts.

26

The Death Merchant regarded Frimholtz with cold eyes, saying in formal tones, "I never do a job with hip boots when I can get the same results by running barefoot through the sand. But let's get something straight right off. I can't give you a guarantee that we won't lock horns with the Russians. And the home office knows it."

"But I presume we will try to avoid trouble," purred Commander Webber, tapping the polished table top with long fingers. He smiled indulgently. "I know you prefer to use intellect over muscle."

"Just as I prefer realists over fools," said Camellion, fully in control of the situation. "Only realists can deal with the Soviet Union, whose philosophy is that the end result justifies the means employed."

"If those Russian dirt diggers get out of hand, we'll settle their hash," Will Norris said dourly between sips of iced coffee. "We can't live in peace indefinitely with the Soviet Union—with any Communists for that matter."

Commander Webber made an angry face and sat up straighter.

"Fortunately, the decision to start World War Three is not yours to make, Norris. This is a situation that calls for scientific techniques. Brute force is to be avoided at all costs. If we—"

"Hold it, Webber!" the Death Merchant lashed out savagely. "Shift your damned gears, back up, and get on the right track."

Webber drew back in boundless astonishment. Josh Forran leaned back and smiled. The five other men, unused to such curtness, turned to Camellion in surprise.

"We're here to get a job done," Camellion said, looking directly at Webber, "And if it takes brute force to do it, then it's brute force we'll use. Forget that nonsense about 'at all costs.' You might as well say 'Better Red Than Dead.' Another thing: 'When I give an order, I want it obeyed without any excuses, or you can explain to D.C."

Not a pussycat, Webber snapped right back, "You haven't given an order yet, hotshot. When you do, we'll follow it. I have always felt that World War Three was inevitable and that it would be triggered accidentally—or by an idiot."

Camellion grinned and locked fingers on top of his head. "At least you don't have to worry about a second childhood, Commander. You've never left your first. You never will!"

"Gentlemen, I suggest we focus our attention on the Soviet

force," advised Dr. Mabroless as he continued to draw tiny circles on a yellow notepad. Ignoring the red-faced Webber, he suddenly turned to the Death Merchant. "It would be an illogical premise to conclude that the Russians have chosen that position at random."

"We've already eliminated why they are not there," Frimholtz said, no less confidently. He pushed back his chair slightly and crossed his legs. "Sea-farming is out. So is ocean-mining, oil, and studies in marine biology, geomagnetism, oreogenesis, volcanicity, seismology, and what-have-you. The Russians could have done all that back home. We concentrate on what is left, or rather on the improbable."

Forran commented with a touch of irony, "There are species of marine life here not found in and around the Soviet Union. But I hardly think the Russians would bring all that equipment and travel that far from home to study, say, triggerfish, snake eels, and green turtles."

"Highly unlikely," Will Norris said with a slight chuckle.

Camellion said, "Give me opinions on the long crates we saw the Russians unloading. My own conclusion is that the length, width, and depth of the boxes indicate sections of pipe."

"Long tanks are not an impossibility," offered Christopher Humbard, "tanks that could be used for some sort of assembly, some kind of complete unit."

Dr. Mabroless shook his head. "No. They wouldn't use that many tanks for oxygen regeneration or the desalting of water."

Announced Webber in a carefully controlled voice, "They wouldn't come all the way from the Soviet Union to carry out conventional experiments. I think Camellion's pipe theory makes good sense. Whatever the Russians are doing, I think it involves drilling into the ocean floor."

Humbard said, "We haven't discussed how Castro and his stooges figure in all this." He looked from face to face, last of all at the Death Merchant. "I submit that Castro and his people don't have a say in the project and, depending on the nature of the Russian project, might not even know the truth."

The others nodded, including Camellion. "I agree," he said. "The KGB wouldn't trust the Cubans to wash socks in rainwater. But let's not forget the firepower Castro can give the Reds."

"Which makes Castro a direct military threat to us," Norris said evenly. "Provided all his troops aren't being massacred in Africa."

Ignoring Norris's attempt at humor of the macabre, Camellion caught Dr. Mabroless' intense eyes. "We need a geologist, preferably one whose branch of the discipline is geognosy.[1] Do you have one on board. I'm certain you must have geodetic survey charts of this quadrant of the Caribbean."

"Dr. Wilderstein," Mabroless said. "He should have been at this meeting."

"I'll call him." Commander Webber pushed back his chair and stood up, then proved that, in spite of crossing swords with Camellion, he was a morally honest man. "Camellion, it's my fault that Dr. Wilderstein didn't come to the meeting. He had some work to do and asked to be excused. I didn't think he would be needed."

"Thanks, I should appreciate it," Camellion said pleasantly.

Commander Webber nodded, then walked over to a table on which rested a dozen telephones, each of a different color. He picked one up and began to dial.

Lt. Commander Norris didn't surprise anyone when he said, "We're never going to know what the Russians are doing until we get over there and see for ourselves—and I'll argue with you on that, Camellion!"

"We could," conceded Camellion, amused at the bulldog expression on Norris's face, "but we won't. We can't argue about something we agree on."

"I thought your view would be similar to mine," Norris said with relief. "Naturally there are technical problems."

It was Humphrey Frimholtz who put Camellion and Norris's thoughts into words. "How do you intend to get past the Soviet transponders, not to mention Russian frogmen and other protective devices?"

"Dr. Wilderstein is on his way," announced Webber, walking back to the conference table. "What was that about Russian transponders?"

Lt. Commander Norris told him. Immediately it was apparent that Webber was opposed to the idea of scouting the Russian base.

"The transponders would warn the Soviet security the instant you penetrated the barrier. You'd end up dead, or prisoners." His voice took on an almost mournful note. "What would either solve?"

"Bypassing the Russian transponders is the problem," Norris said simply.

[1] That branch of geology that studies the constituent parts of the earth, its envelope of air and water, its crust, and the condition of its interior.

Josh Forran, exhaling cigarette smoke, turned his head toward the Death Merchant. "You know, even if we used a scrambler and loused up the frequency of the transponders, the Ruskies would still investigate, to find out the cause of the trouble."

Forran and the others waited for an answer. But Camellion was deep in thought. When he did speak, he didn't say what they had expected to hear.

"Commander Webber, who's the captain of *Kingfisher*?"

"Damn it, he can't help us scout the Russians!" protested Norris dramatically. He stared increduously at Camellion. "He's not about to risk his boat. I don't blame him."

"Captain Claude McConachie," replied Webber, glancing in annoyance at the angry-faced Webber. "But Norris is right. McConachie will not use *Kingfisher* to scout the Russians. I know McConachie. He'd consider the scheme madness."

"I wasn't thinking of using the *Kingfisher*." Camellion was emphatic. "I have something else in mind. I'll dicuss it later in private with you, Webber . . . with you and Captain McConachie."

"And with us, with Mr. Humbard, and myself!" Frimholtz sounded more than a little aggrieved.

"Sure, if you have an L-Y-One." Camellion knew that the two ONI agents had top clearance, but he derived a kind of perverse pleasure in cutting them down to size.

"We have!" snapped Humbard, rubbing one of his long sideburns. "Or we wouldn't be here. I might add that it strikes us as most peculiar that you, a man who is not an employee of any U.S. Government agency, should have command. Having an unknown quality make vital decisions doesn't exactly inspire us with confidence."

The Death Merchant's expression did not change. If he's on a fishing expedition, he thought, he'll find I'm more mute than the sphinx.

"I find a lot of things peculiar in this world, Mr. Humbard," he said in an easy manner. "The naked singularity of a black hole perplexes me, but there isn't anything I can do about it. Cosmic censorship is too strong."

Humbard and Frimholtz, trained to conceal emotion, especially anger, only smiled slightly. They had been put down and knew it.

All eyes turned to the man who had just walked through the open bulkhead into the room. Dr. Morris Wilderstein was of medium height, paunchy, and had a strikingly bald dome. Carrying a gray attaché case, he hurried to the table. As he pulled out a chair, Commander Webber introduced him to Camellion and Forran, both of whom acknowledged with a nod.

"Doctor Wilderstein, we're interested in the sea bottom," Camellion said, watching the man sit down. "We feel it's possible that the Russian technicians are drilling through the sea floor, and not in search of oil. I ask you: is there anything unusual about the bottom in this part of the Caribbean?"

Wilderstein continued to polish his eyeglasses with a handkerchief. "I see. You want a description of the physiography and submarine morphology."

Speaking as though he were lecturing, Wilderstein explained that the Caribbean Sea is a suboceanic basin, approximately 2,640,000 square kilometers (1,020,000 square miles) in extent, lying between 9 to 22 N and 89 to 60 W, and that it's divided into five submarine basins, which are roughly elliptical in shape and separated from each other by submerged rises and ridges.

"It's best that I show you," said Wilderstein, and stood up. "I'll put a map on the wall, which will make it easier for me to explain."

He picked up his attaché case, placed it on the table, opened it, and removed a thick square of folded paper. He then walked over to a large corkboard on one side of the room, Camellion and the other men getting up from the table and following.

Dr. Mabroless helped Dr. Wilderstein in thumb-tacking a morphological map of the Caribbean to the corkboard, after which the geologist picked up a slim wooden pointer and proceeded to explain the various features of the sea floor.

He pointed out the Yucatán, Cayman, Columbian, Venezuelan, and Grenadan basins, explaining, "The Yucatán, the northern most of these, is separated from the Gulf of Mexico by the Yucatán Channel, which runs between Cuba and the Yucatán Peninsula. The sill depth of the Yucatan Basin is about fifty-five hundred feet at the deepest point."

"Doctor Wilderstein," interrupted Camellion. "Speaking of sill depth. I presume that's the same as the depth to bedrock, to the *sima*?"

"Ah, I see you know your basic geology. Very good, Mr. Camellion." Wilderstein smiled at the Death Merchant. "Yes, that's the depth to the *sima*. Now, as I was saying . . ."

Camellion and the others rapidly learned that the Cayman Basin, to the south, was partially separated from the Yucatan Basin by Cayman Ridge, an incomplete finger-like ridge that

31

extended from the southern part of Cuba toward Guatemala, rising above the surface at one point to form Cayman Island. Jamaica Ridge, a wide triangular ridge with a sill depth of 4,000 feet, extended from Honduras to Hispaniola, bearing the island of Jamaica and separating the Cayman Basin from the Columbian Basin. The Columbian Basin was partly separated from the Venezuelan Basin by the Beata Ridge. The two basins were connected by the submerged Aruba Gap at depths of over 13,000 feet. The Aves Ridge, incomplete at its southern extremity, separated the Venezuelan Basin from the small Grenadan Basin, which was bounded to the east by the Antillean arc of islands.

Annoyed with Dr. Wilderstein's academic manner, Norris and Forran exchanged bored looks. To make matters worse, Wilderstein talked as if he had to blow his nose. As irritated as Norris and Forran, the other men shifted on their feet impatiently. Finally the Death Merchant interposed, "Doctor, what you're saying is very interesting. However, I want specific information about the area in which the Russians are working. Would you please show us the area on the map."

"Certainly." Dr. Wilderstein tapped the map with the end of the pointer. "The Soviet expedition is at that position in the Columbian Basin. The depth there varies from five hundred to nine hundred feet. I mean at that local area. The minimum depth of the entire basin is about two hundred feet; thirteen thousand at maximum."

Josh Forran spoke up, "It's more likely five hundred where the Russians are. We know they've built an underwater base of some kind. Such a project is extremely difficult at five hundred feet, even with the most modern of technology. Deeper would require even more knowhow."

Humphrey Frimholtz adjusted his glasses. Standing, he was stooped and had to use a cane. "I take it then that there isn't anything spectacular about the Columbian Basin?"

"I didn't say that," replied Wilderstein stiffly. "There isn't anything unusual about the depth, that is, where the Russians are doing whatever they are doing."

The Death Merchant shifted his mind into high gear. "Tell me, Doctor, what is the nature of the *sima* where the Russians are located."

Wilderstein thought for several moments. "Granite, like any other *sima*. There is a lot of slippage in the area, all the way from Central America to the Mid-Atlantic Range. The is particularly severe in Central America and Mexico, which explains the earthquakes those nations have. Of course, these plates slip right on over to the Pacific Ocean, where they merge with the volcanic zone."

"Let's not wander off course, Doctor," Camellion urged gently. "Let's stick to the Caribbean."

"There's a lot tectonic activity and crustal slippage all over this region. If we could magically empty the Caribbean of water, we would see long grooves, many thousands of miles long. We call them *graben*, or parallel faults, that is, cracks in the *sima*."

Josh Forran made a sweeping gesture with his hand. "By tectonic activity, you mean folding and faulting, do you not?"

"Indeed I do," answered Dr. Wilderstein. "Just imagine giant plates or blocks of rock thousands of miles long and thousands of feet thick, some piled on top of each other, others blending and folding so that they form reverse or thrust faults."

A spark of intution flared briefly in Camellion's mind. "Doctor, in this area are there any particular faults that are unique, geologically speaking?"

Wilderstein turned and surveyed Camellion for a few seconds.

"Odd that you should ask that. Hmmmmm, let me think." Tapping his left cheek with a forefinger, he hurried back to the conference table and rummaged around in his attaché case. He soon pulled out another square of paper, unfolded it, and spread the tectonic map on the conference table. The Death Merchant and the rest of the men gathered around him.

"Yes, yes. This is what I wanted." Pleased with himself, Wilderstein moved his finger from south to north, along a crooked red line. "This fault plane separates two of the largest plates in the entire Caribbean. These plates—or blocks of rock, if you prefer—are so tremendous that many geologists feel they merge with the *sial* of North America. However, there is no way we can be certain."

Frimholtz, Humbard, and Webber exchanged glances. The Death Merchant's next question made them look even more concerned.

"If you're right, then the *sima* of the Caribbean would be under the Gulf of Mexico and, in theory, merge with the *sial* of the southern and eastern United States—correct?"

"Oh yes. I would say the entire Midwest and the East and the South of the United States," Dr. Wilderstein said. "But there isn't any danger of the plates slipping, as far as we know, within the realm of current theory. Quite naturally, anything is possible."

33

The Death Merchant stared intently at the map on the table, his eyes going over every line and swirl and squiggle. Suddenly came the preternatural flash of second sight, the same kind of strong impression which had always served him so well in the past.

"Dr. Wilderstein, would it be possible to superimpose this map with the one on the corkboard? I want to know the exact position of the Russians in relation to the fault."

"An easy calculation," Wilderstein smiled. "Give me a few moments."

He took a pad, a pan, a slide rule, a course protractor and parallel rules from the attaché case. He consulted the map on the table, using the course protractor, after which he hurried to the map on the wall, made more calculations, then came back to the table and mumbled to himself as he worked the slide rule. Once more he used the slide rule, then made a series of lines on the map with the parallel rules.

Wilderstein straightened up. All the men saw the astonishment—and some fear—on his face as he turned to the all-too-calm Camellion.

"This is indeed an amazing coincidence," he said nervously. "As it turns out, the Russian force is practically on top of where the fault is the widest and the closest to the surface. The fault there is only at a depth of seven hundred and eighty feet."

"It is not a coincidence," Camellion said stoutly.

"Damn it, Camellion. Get to the point!" Webber demanded, all ears.

"Dr. Wilderstein, would it be possible for the Soviets to trigger movement of the two plates?" Camellion asked the geologist. "Is there any method known to science that could effect such a shift?"

Wilderstein studied the Death Merchant with curious eyes, all the while rubbing the end of his nose with thumb and forefinger.

"Conceivably it could be done," he said slowly after some moments, "but the power required would be unimaginable. Even so, such an experiment would serve no worthwhile purpose. Just the reverse. A shifting of the plates, even slightly, would cause earthquakes such as modern man has never seen."

"To what extent?" inquired Humphrey Frimholtz.

"The epicenter would, of course, be the position of the explosion, and it would take an explosion to do the job. I would say—"

34

"Would a dozen hydrogen bombs, say of three hundred to four hundred kilotons each, be sufficient, if they were exploded simultaneously?" Camellion asked, sitting down on the edge of the table.

"Probably." Wilderstein's forehead furrowed in deep thought. "The crust of the earth——in this case, the *sima*—is between ten and thirty miles thick. Under the crust is the mantle, extending to a depth of one thousand eight hundred miles. In order to cause a shift, the Soviet technicians would have to drill at least twenty miles, and they would have to widen the passage. I'd say at least six feet, unless they have some very small nuclear devices."

Visibly irritated Frimholtz tapped the floor loudly with the tip of his cane. "The extent of the damage! Tell me, man!"

"It would be the end of the world for the islands in the Caribbean," Wilderstein said. "The island of Jamaica would sink into the sea. So would most of Cuba, Haiti, the Dominican Republic, and no doubt all of Puerto Rico. The Bahamas would vanish. Central America, Mexico, and northern South America would be torn apart by earthquakes. Most of Florida and the entire southern coast would be destroyed, not only by the quake, but by the tidal wave which would be generated by the quake. I can't be positive about the rest of the United States. I would venture to say that terrible effects would occur in cities as far north as Chicago, Detroit, and New York. For all practical purposes, the United States would be demolished." He paused, thought for a moment, and added, "Of course, there would be a tremendous boom in construction for years to follow."

Forran, breathing heavily from excitement, regarded Wilderstein with furious eyes. "How long, Doctor? How long would it take the Russians to drill such a tunnel?"

"They have to drill a minimum of twenty miles," reiterated Wilderstein. "The way things are now, the Russians haven't even been there long enough to start. Take a minimum of three months to prepare the drilling operations. By using lasers to do the drilling, the Russians could do the job in six months to a year. You should be asking engineers."

"Yeah, we can do that," muttered Lt. Commander Norris. "We must have a few engineers stashed somewhere. We've got everything else around here, even a MASH unit."

Commander Webber reacted to Dr. Wilderstein's pronouncements the way a bull reacts to a red flag. "How can you be so damned dogmatic? Isn't what you've said nothing more than an educated guess?"

The scientist's face clouded with displeasure. "Educated guesses about what?"

"The fault, the earthquakes, the whole goddamn nine yards!" Webber's eyes glowed with an anger he was finding difficult to control.

"I don't make 'educated guesses.'" Wilderstein pronounced each word slowly and emphatically. "I am positive that other geologists will evaluate the situation in a manner similar to my own. Now, if there isn't anything else, I have work to do."

"One more question," Camellion said. "What kind of preliminary work would the Russians have to do, preliminary that is to the actual drilling?"

"Oh, there would be a good deal of preparation," Wilderstein said, putting away his instruments in the attaché case. "They'd need a whole orchestra of studies and any number of devices—echo sounders, magnetometers, heat probes, sediment corers, and various acoustic devices needed for making sound pictures. You can bet that their topography maps would be the very best. The Russians are very good at that sort of thing."

He closed the attaché case and started toward the bulkhead.

the Death Merchant glanced at the back of the departing Wilderstein and sat down on the chair previously occupied by Josh Forran, waiting for the comments, for the pros and cons he knew would follow. He couldn't have cared less; he had already made up his mind.

Sitting down, Jason Webber let Camellion have a quick glance.

"I don't buy it. The Russians aren't there because they're trying to cause the earthquake of modern history. They're not fools. They know we would blame them and no doubt launch an all-out strike."

"Agreed," Chris Humbard said, business-like. "The Soviet Union doesn't want to start World War Three."

Silence reigned, no one speaking, most of the men waiting to hear what Camellion might say. Commander Webber and Humphrey Frimholtz sat stolidly, Webber tapping his fingers on the table. Frimholtz, having pushed his chair back from the table, rested his hands on the brass vulture head that formed the handle of his cane.

It was Dr. Mabroless who broke the strange stillness.

"I think you're right, Camellion," he said significantly. "We've eliminated all the other projects in which the Russian could be engaged. That leaves only the earthquake hypothesis."

36

"There isn't anything left but that theory," Norris said firmly, almost glaring at Webber, Humbard, and Frimholtz, as if defying them to disagree. "And it's up to us to do something about it."

Humbard gave a suppressed laugh. "Ha! Another poor soul who believes that the Soviets are going to deliberately start the final doomsday war."

"Gentlemen, gentlemen! Let's be rational about this," Webber said placatingly. "The Soviets are a bunch of lying no-good bastards, but drilling a hold in the ground, stuffing it with H-bombs, and setting them off to cause a quake that would destroy the Caribbean and half of the United States—ridiculous! Can anyone here seriously believe that the Russians would try such a cock-eyed scheme?"

"I can and do," Forran said effortlessly. He knew that from the menacingly look in Humbard's and Frimholtz's eyes that the two were enraged because he, a fellow ONI agent, was not in agreement with them. To their way of thinking, he was betraying the Office of Naval Intelligence. The hell with them. Let them write a dozen negative reports about him to D.C. He, too, had friends in high places.

All this time, the Death Merchant had been doing some serious thinking, and at the same time relaxing by analyzing the people around him. Now, thoroughly annoyed by Webber's and Humbard's pedantic views, he decided to put an end to all opposition.

"The trouble is that some of you are children when it comes to evaluating the Russian mentality. By survival, they mean the next generation and the generations to follow. We in the West think of survival in terms of preserving our own lives and the lives of our children."

"Please get to the heart of the matter," Humbard said tonelessly.

"The Russians aren't drilling the hole as part of any scenario to start a major war. It's to be one of their aces in a pat hand, in case war does break out. They can slip a sub into the Caribbean, stuff the tunnel with nuclear devices, and wreck half the United States. The hell with us and the world knowing who was responsible. By then it wouldn't matter. We'd destroy the Soviet Union and they'd annihilate us."

"Quit talking in riddles!" stormed Webber. "You implied that the Soviets would survive!"

The Death Merchant laughed harshly. "Sure, and a little while ago you agreed with me that it's pipe the Russians have

37

in those long crates. What do you think they're doing with those lengths of pipe?"

"Well, they certainly can't stuff H-bombs down lengths of pipe!" snickered Webber, thinking he had Camellion backed into a corner of cock-eyed logic.

Camellion grinned. "No, they can't. But after they drill the shaft, they can yank the pipe and widen the tunnel—as small as it is—with lasers. But you haven't thought of that."

"And as I recall, you also suggested that it was the Russians who would survive a nuclear holocaust," snorted Webber, still verbally attacking. "That doesn't make sense either."

Frimholtz spoke softly before the Death Merchant could reply to Webber. "Mr. Camellion shares the Soviet conviction that there would be survivors, worldwide, after a nuclear war. The Soviet Union is much larger than the U.S., far more rugged geographically, and is basically a peasant nation. Since the Soviet Union is not a highly industrialized nation, the theory is that Russian survivors could rebuild basic civilization much faster than we. Many of our own analysts have the same opinion."

Lt. Commander Norris said gloomily, "On that basis, the blacks in Africa will come out on top, survival-wise."

Frimholtz surprised every one by agreeing, not only with Norris but with Camellion. "Personally, my own conclusions about the Russians in this area are the same as Camellion's. The simple fact is that we dare not assume that the Russians are not preparing for a man-made earthquake. Our problem right now is what we are going to do about it. Whatever we do, the plan will require a lot of daring and imagination."

Commander Webber summoned up a half-hearted smile and remained silent. Humbard carefully avoided looking at Camellion, who gave a tiny smile, sat back, and congratulated himself. He had been correct about Frimholtz. The man was a realist who didn't permit emotion to color logic.

He said, "We'll know more about a probe after Commander Webber and I talk to Captain McConachie. There is always Factor-X. It is possible that the Soviets are engaged in research that is innocent. We must make sure that whatever their research is, it does warrant our intervention."

"We should discuss the anomalies of the Bermuda Triangle," suggested Dr. Mabroless, somewhat hesitantly. "However, I do realize that the Russians are number one on the agenda of decisions and actions. Yet—"

"Then why bother to discuss such foolishness?" Norris shrugged. He snubbed out his cigarette in an ashtray. "Most

38

of what you hear about the Bermuda Triangle is written to sell books and make movies."

Dr. Mabroless acted as if he hadn't heard Norris. He continued, addressing himself to the death Merchant. "Have you considered the possibility that the Soviets in this area might be experimenting in some way with the Triangle. We do know they've been experimenting in magnetohydrodynamics[2] in the Soviet Union; and they have more of an imagination than Western scientists. They are more realistic. They've proved as much with research into extra sensory perception, or what they call psychotronics. We Westerners are too confined in logic-tight compartments of traditional thinking."

"Much to my regret, I think you're correct," Camellion said wearily. "It's the unspoken credo of the psychologists to refuse to admit that the namesake of their discipline, the psyche, actually exists." He sighed deeply. "In this they resemble other unrealists in some of the other sciences and the arts—musicians who compose only noise, painters who can't draw a straight line, and theologians who insist there is no God."

Josh Logan remarked, "To that you might add 'novelists' who write 'anti-novels,' and philosophers who maintain that philosophy is nothing but linguistics in disguise."

"Ironically, the philosophers might be half-right," Dr. Mabroless said. "I disagree with a lot of modern scientific 'fact.' Space and time, for example. I have always toyed with the idea that the theory of space and time is nothing but a cultural artifact resulting from the invention of graph paper."

Camellion smiled and thought, *He is an original thinker.*

Mabroless continued, "About the time of Descartes, some bright boy popularized the idea of presenting and measuring motions in the form of two axes intersecting at right angles. This is how 'Cartesian' coordinates were born. Ever since, we've been stuck with the idea that if you can draw something on paper, the problem can be solved. When we apply this know-it-allism to the Bermuda Triangle, there is a tendency to say 'Impossible,' or, 'There ain't no such animal.' "

"All those people disappearing!" chuckled Humbard, grinning. "Do you really believe in such bunk?"

"I believe that people vanish with more than usual frequency in the Bermuda Triangle," Dr. Mabroless said seriously. "Or don't you believe in documentation?"

---

[2] The theory that a plasma current or electromagnetic field around a disk-shaped object can move the object without causing shock waves—research in regard to UFOs.

"Entire armies have even vanished without a trace," Camellion said affably. "In 1885, six hundred French troops—all tough legionnaires—disappeared. They were last seen marching in an orderly manner fifteen miles from Saigon. They never reached the city. They never returned to their base. They just vanished, just like the British regiment in 1915 that set off to attack the Turks at a point called Hill 60. This was near Suvla Bay."

"That's impossible," Norris said.

"Not to the observers who watched the regiment up the hill until it became hidden from view in a cloud. Although it was a bright, clear day, there were a few puffy white clouds over the top of the hill. What happened is that the cloud moved away, but there was no longer any sign of the thousand men who had marched into it only five minutes earlier.

"Similarly, three thousand Chinese vanished in December, 1939, after being brought up as reinforcements when the Japs sacked Nanking. It was night and the gooks were spread out along a two-mile front in the rolling foothills. Came morning and the Chinese troops were gone. Investigation proved that they hadn't deserted and they hadn't surrendered to the Japanese. They simply stepped out of space and time."

Christopher said with mock seriousness, "Well, we don't have to worry. We're not in the Bermuda Triangle."

Lt. Commander Norris's gaze jumped to Camellion. "Isn't some of northern Cuba in the Triangle? Not that I take serious stock in any of it!"

"Let's take the west central coast of Florida as a starting point. Go straight southwest for five hundred miles, stop, then move in a straight line slightly to the southeast for two thousand miles. This second line—call it the base of the pyramid—takes in part of northern Cuba, some of the northern part of Hispaniola, all of Puerto Rico, and half of the Leeward Islands. Then—"

"Hispaniola! That's Haiti and the Dominican Republic—right?" asked Norris.

"You got it. About a hundred miles southeast of the Leeward Islands, you stop and go in a straight line fifteen hundred miles slightly northwest. Stop. Turn again. Another line about seventeen hundred miles southwest again. This will take you to the center coast of eastern Florida. That, gentlemen, is the Bermuda Triangle. But just for the record, its malignant influence extends far beyond the imaginary boundary, especially at the base. That's us!"

"There was the British freighter, *Queen Anne*," spoke up

40

Forran thoughtfully. "She vanished only six months ago—and it's not fiction! I was there. She left Kingston and radioed her position a few hours later. All okay. I passed her myself that same afternoon, I and Billy Coopbird, in the *Baby Doll*. The sea was so calm a feather wouldn't have drifted. Then we heard her Mayday. We were close so we answered. No reply. We turned around and hurried right back to her position, the one she had given in the Mayday. She was gone. There wasn't any wreckage. No oil slicks. Nothing but the calm sea."

By now, even die-hards like Webber and Norris were interested.

"What do you and Coopbird do?" asked Webber. He suddenly felt foolish, when it dawned on him that his question bordered on the ridiculous.

"Do?" Forran let Webber have a get-back-into-your-tree look. "What the hell do you think we did? We beat it out of there!"

Lt. Commander Norris slammed his right fist into his left palm.

"Oh boy! Not only do we have to contend with the damned Soviets, we have to worry about being grabbed by whatever is in the goddamned Bermuda Triangle."

"We'll never know until we get started." The Death Merchant stood up and his piercing stare stabbed at Commander Jason Webber.

"Let's go talk to Captain McConachie."

Chapter Four

From where Richard Camellion and Joshus Forran stood on the *South Dakota*—the signal bridge on the port side—they had a full view of the other two ships that comprised the American research force. *Atlantis II*, the finest-equipped research vessel in the world, rested at anchor in an east/west position, her stern only a few hundred feet from the bow of the destroyer. The *U.S.S. Mohawk*, the LCC command ship, was cattycornered to both vessels, her bow pointed toward the bow of *Atlantis II*, her stern a hundred and fifty feet from the stern of the *South Dakota*.

The Death Merchant looked up at the sky. Cloudy, but the barometer was steady. He and Forran could be dead before any rain came. The breeze had quickened to a force 5, moving at between 17 and 21 knots. On land, this would have been a fresh breeze. On water, the result was moderate waves that took a pronounced long form, with quite a bit of foam at their crest.

"I hope they don't wreck the damned thing," Forran said good-naturedly. With Camellion, he watched sailors and technicians, at a large steel V-boom, lowering an odd-looking craft into the water. The vehicle was one of ten "Cubmarines" the Americans had brought with them. A Deep Sea Research Vehicle (although technically it was a diver-lockout submersible), the clumsy-looking contraption resembled a thirty-two-foot-long cylinder resting on four smaller cylinders or pods. The two larger pods, one on each side, were the buoyancy tanks. The pod in the center, betwen the two larger cylinders, contained the batteries. The fourth pod, to the stern, contained the gas storage.

The main compartment, which carried four men, was

43

painted a bright blue, the four pods white. Two skids were underneath the buoyancy tanks. A steel tubing formed a rectangular frame that was perpendicular to the center length of the main compartment. Fastened to the main hull by a series of wide metal braces, this frame supported the auxiliary motor mounted horizontally, with the propeller facing the hull. The second auxiliary motor, with the propeller upward, was mounted perpendicularly to the top of the skid on the port side. The main propeller, driven by an electric motor and surrounded by a ring above the wide rudder, protruded from the stern of the main compartment. The steel tubing frame, three feet from the hull, was also the mount for the bow, stern, port, and starboard sonar scans.

The top of the hull of the main cylinder, or the main compartment, was as unusual as the rest of the Cubmarine. Forward, above the pilot and the diving supervisor section, was the short conning tower, to the outside of which was mounted the underwater communication transducer, the emergency flash and flare, the surface communication aerial, the large spotlight, and the navigation transducer. On the top center of the hull was the big recovery ring, and behind the ring the compass dome.

There were four thick Meganglass ports on each side of the main hull and a large port in the nose of the Control Compartment. This latter port was three feet in diameter and a foot thick.

The diver-lockout cylinder was underneath the hull, situated between the battery pod and the stern pod.

Another gadget was bolted to the top of the hull, just to the rear of the conning tower, a three-foot-square metal box with antenna-like rods protruding from the top and the four sides. To all the sailors and to most of the technicians, except three on board the *Kingfisher*, the box was a total mystery. Two technicians from *Kingfisher* had bolted the box to the top hull of the Cubmarine; they had then connected the mysterious device to controls inside the main compartment.

"This Gf-Mechanism," Josh said in a voice barely above a whisper. "You said it will make us 'invisible.' I suppose it blinds the enemy by sending out a barrage of noise that blankets sonar with 'snow'?"

The Death Merchant, his hands on the railing, quickly shook his head. "No, that's not it. I really don't know how the Gf-M works. I do know that the device doesn't utilize any of the conventional electronic measures, such as the one you mentioned."

"It gives us an edge. That's for sure."

"However it works, it will make the Cubmarine invisible to Soviet sonar and even to their television scanners. The only thing I can figure out is that it generates a warp with some new kind of electromagnetic field. The beauty of it is that while enemy sonar can't get in, our sonar can get out."

"Yeah, but an enemy diver will still be able to see us." Josh flipped a cigarette butt over the side and gave Camellion a quick apprehensive glance. His cheeks looked strangely gray and sunken. "What was that distance again?"

"An enemy diver will have to get within eleven feet four inches of us before he'll be able to see the outline of the craft." Camellion watched with a good deal of interest as the thick steel cable played out over the guide-wheel of the boom, and sailors, on the port side of the destroyer, kept a tight rein on lines to keep the Cubmarine from swinging.

Camellion licked his lips, his eyes narrowing with thought. It had taken several days for him to acquire the use of the ultra-secret Gf-Mechanism. Although *Kingfisher* was protected by a larger version of the device and carried sixteen of the smaller units, Captain McConachie had firmly refused to equip one of the Cubmarines with the device until he had received direct orders from ONI headquarters in CONUS (Continental United States). It had taken another day to equip one of the Cubmarines with the Gf-Mechanism.

"Billy's lucky he's not going with us," pursued Forran, hunched over the rail. "I don't know about you, but the idea of sneaking into the Russian base is about as attractive as going naked into a room filled with angry hornets." His eyes were curious, as if he couldn't quite make up his mind about something. "You're really convinced that the odds are on our side?"

Camellion, realizing that Forran thought of the probe-mission as pure suicide, turned and gave a reassuring grin. "If we didn't have Dame Fate on our side, I wouldn't dare go in. Sure, it's going to be very dangerous. But we have a lot more than the Gf deal on our side."

"The premise that the Soviets won't be expecting us—right?"

"Wrong. The KGB expects anything and everything. However, they're convinced that nothing can get past their network of transponders and sonar and television scanners. Put yourself in their place. Wouldn't you feel secure surrounded by such a network?"

Forran remained silent.

45

"Then there's the bottom, the sea floor." The Death Merchant sounded cheerful. "Topography maps reveal that this entire area of the Caribbean is cut up and filled with little gullies, small canyons and what have you. We'll take the Cub to one and hide out.

Frowning, Forran straightened up from the railing. "Uh-huh, except that we're going to leave the Cub and do a little free swimming investigating. I don't think we'll exactly be welcomed by any Russian divers we might bump into, or should I say swim into?"

"The odds are that we won't be seen," Camellion said reassuringly. "We're not going to be swimming around out in the sunshine. The ocean is a damned poor transmitter of light, the sun warming and illuminating only its surface. Shucks, even in the clearest water the light intensity at a depth of six hundred feet is reduced to less than one percent of the surface illumination. Absorption is so complete that at a depth a little below six hundred feet, there's only inky blackness. We'll stay together by means of a twenty-foot line. The same line will carry our telephone cable. We don't dare use UTEL."[1]

"I'm somewhat confused," admitted Forran, taking another cigarette from the pack. "If we can't use UTEL, how will we get back to the baby sub? We can't go swimming around with lights!"

"A very high frequency homing signal will be pulsed

[1] A device designed to allow a swimmer to communicate with a submarine, a surface craft, or another swimmer. While using UTEL submerged, a swimmer can receive voice transmissions, but if he is to transmit voice, he must be wearing a full face mask with a microphone imbeded in it. However, he can transmit voice while on the surface without a lung mike, by means of a surface mike.

In any event, he can always transmit and receive a homing tone, whether submerged or on the surface. This homing tone can be used either as a vector, i.e. to allow a sub or another swimmer to find the user, or as a means of positive communications, if a code has been previously agreed upon.

There are four major components to the UTEL. Receiver-Transmitter, a lung or surface microphone, headset, and transducers. The transducer output pattern is in the form of a directional beam approximately 100° in width. To make use of its directional response, the transducer must be pointed as a flashlight, directly at the other station. To be used omnidirectionally the transducer is pointed at the ocean floor. The equipment will direct ship noises in the frequency range of 8.3 and 12.0 KC with a limited degree of bearing accuracy.)

46

through the Gf-M," Camellion explained in a low voice. "Don't ask me the how or the why of it. All I know is that any beam or signal sent from a vessel protected by the Gf-M can't be detected without a special closed phase receiver. We—"

"Have special receivers in our helmets, tied into our headsets," finished Forran.

"Affirmative. Let's get down to the main deck. They have the Cubmarine in the water."

Forran finished lighting his cigarette. "Yeah, I see the two tech guys from *Kingfisher* looking up at us. Let's go out and make the Soviets look like fools."

They left the railing and started down the steps of the signal bridge, Camellion saying with a slight laugh, "Well, let's not divide the skin until the lion is shot."

Forran laughed. "Hell, you've got the wrong continent and the wrong people. You mean the Russian bear."

"*Touché!*" Camellion said.

They continued on their way to the main deck, each with his own thoughts. To the Death Merchant, the "invasion" of the Soviet base was a challenge, a problem to be solved, a battle to be won, another victory to be gained. The unknown factor was the Force, the Power, the It in the Bermuda Triangle.

The Death Merchant and Dr. Robert Mabroless's thoughts were similar in many respects, both feeling that UFOs were connected with the deadly effects of the Triangle, their belief based on the numerous reports of Unidentified Flying Objects diving into the water of the area; and they both agreed on the nature of the UFOs' physical characteristics. The saucer shape would allow the craft to move in any direction. They lacked wings, because wings would not permit unidirectional maneuvers. Their glow suggested a plasma-ionized atmosphere. The reported changes of color suggested an electromagnetic field capable of interacting with that plasma.

The true question, in relation to UFOs and UAOs, was: *what kind of minds inhabit the universe.* Camellion wondered, *Are we split personalities unique to our galaxy, or is there something very common in the universe that we are only now coming to comprehend? Ahhh, do we differ or do we resemble? It is too bad we can't hypnotize dolphins, our only captive "alien intelligent species" on this planet.*

Forran's thoughts were not as philosophical. He was not unduly concerned about dying at the hands of the Russians either, although he had not discounted the possibility that he might be ripped apart and scattered all over the Caribbean Sea. The Death Merchant had not said so, but Forran suspected that the "Black Box"[2] was equipped with a destruct device. Should the Cubmarine and the Gf-M be in danger of capture—BANG! Uncle Sam was not going to risk one of his most precious secrets falling into the hands of the Soviets.

There was nostalgia, a wistfulness that made Forran long for the sights and sounds and smells of Kingston. For two years, he had been stationed in Jamaica and he had become accustomed to the easy, relaxed life. *Baby Doll* had become home. Now, ONI had reclaimed the sleek craft. She was secured to the destroyer by means of a line.

The hell with it! Forran told himself. He was letting emotion interfere with common sense. He didn't like that: it meant he was getting soft.

Several minutes later, Forran and Camellion were on the main deck of the *South Dakota*. Thirty-four minutes later, after a conference with Jerome Homes and Walter Atkins, the two electronic technicians from *Kingfisher*, Camellion and Forran were secure inside the Cubmarine, and sailors were removing the cable from the recovery ring on the top center of the hull.

[2] Here the term "Black Box" is used to designate the unknown quality of a device. In reality, "Black Box" is an electronics term used to describe some electrical system that puts out a signal when a signal is put into it. A popular Black Box is the one that automatically turns on a room lamp at dusk.

Chapter Five

The small island of the Pedro Cays group was the most dismal place that Colonel Anatole Bersenko had ever visited. Less than 350 acres, the island was mostly rock with patches of glistening white sand, a tiny blob of nothingness with long beaches over which crawled thousands of land crabs. The entire island was so low that, during a tropical storm, waves washed over the entire area. For this reason, the Soviet solar power station, which was also the living quarters of the Russians on the island and built on steel girders, was 25 feet above the surface of the sand and rocks.

On a security inspection tour, a worried Bersenko and Captain Boris Ruzorkaski stood on the long balcony that jutted out from the south side of the solar power station, protected from the vicious sun by a wooden overhang. With them was Andrew Paasik, the supervisor of the ten men at the station. The bushy-haired Paasik was more than an engineer; he was also a lieutenant in the KGB.

"There isn't any reason why the *Amerikanskis* should even try to investigate this island," Paasik said again. "Frogmen could see there isn't anything of value here, nothing but this station. Sir, in my opinion, it would be a waste of time to ring the island with transponders."

"This new agent, the man named Camellion, makes us think that the United States is prepared to fight," Captain Ruzorkaski said acidly. A hard-faced man, rather heavily built, he always seemed to be on the tense and nervous side. But mentally, he was very tough.

Colonel Bersenko continued to watch the flock of booby birds in the distance. Every now and then, one of the dusky-

49

plumaged sea birds would dive headlong into the sea to grab a fish.

Bersenko suddenly announced, "The three men on the enemy boat, they were a surprise. We didn't expect them to exhibit such ruthlessness. We didn't expect them to have explosives, or to turn on a Jamaican gunboat. Men like that are extremely dangerous."

"There is no way to establish what actually happened?" Paasik inquired casually, secretly wishing that Bersenko and Ruzorkaski would leave.

Bersenko scrutinized Paasik with curious eyes. "How? None of our people witnessed whatever happened, except Major Ivanov's two agents, and they went down with the gunboat. We'll never know what happened."

Captain Ruzorkaski interjected, "It was a miscalculation. Major Ivanov presumed that Forran and the two others would respect the Jamaican flag and permit the Jamaicans to board the *Baby Doll*. The Jamaicans would have taken them to the Coast Guard cutter, and then have sunk the *Baby Doll*. Captain Montroy would have brought them to the *Vitiaz*. We would have had them as prisoners, and no doubt would have learned quite a bit about the American force."

Paasik took off his canvas duck hat and thought of asking what the Center in Moscow might have said about the failure, then decided against it. Better not to become involved.

"Major Ivanov is very upset," Bersenko said with complete frankness. "And with good reason. Not only did he fail to capture Forran and Camellion and that damned *chernozhopy*,[1] but he lost two good agents who were on board, both highly experienced in Latin affairs. To complicate the failure and to compound it, certain highly placed members of the Jamaican government are very angered over the incident, the same officials who permitted Ivanov the use of the Coast Guard cutter. They are demanding one million American dollars for the loss of the ship and its crew—the damned savages."

Bersenko sat up straighter on the crate, while a tiny smile curled around the corners of his wide mouth. "I'd give next year's vacation to have heard the dressing down Ivanov got from the Center. Moscow, of course, will pay the sum. The Center can't afford to antagonize the Jamaicans, any more than we dare take chances with the American force sitting in our back yard."

---

[1] The term used by Russians to refer to black people of all nationalities. A vulgarism, it means "black ass."

Paasik's eyes widened slightly, and he wondered what new security measures Bersenko was about to put into effect. He finished wiping his face and leaned back against the wall.

Captain Ruzorkaski flinched and glanced nervously at his boss. *Damn it! What was the point in being Bersenko's assistant? The pig-faced son-of-a-bitch never consulted him before hand about anything.*

"Comrade Colonel, we have taken every measure possible," he said, careful not to let his voice reveal his resentment. "We have three rings of transponders. Several minisubs are patrolling constantly. The last protective circle has television scanners. The ten capsules are well guarded, and so is the dome in which the drilling is being done. What more can we do?"

Bersenko told him. "From now on we're going to leave the lights burning around the chambers and double the guards inside the dome."

"Surely you don't expect the Americans to attack, Comrade Colonel?" Paasik turned and looked in alarm at the chief of security.

Bersenko looked grave and worried. "I expect the Americans to send reconnaissance teams. They have no choice; they have to know what we are doing. The Center anticipates such action. If and when the Americans resort to this type of deviousness, we are ordered to hold the intruders, and to take direct action against the American expedition."

A chill ran through Paasik. Genuine surprise ran all over Captain Ruzorkaski's sunburned face.

"Colonel Bersenko, direct action implies . . ." He let his words dangle off into the silence of dark implication. All the while he stared at Bersenko. Direct action meant an all-out attack, and a confrontation, especially this close to the continental United States, could very easily lead to World War III. The thought of the annihilation of world civilization was too horrible to contemplate. Those old men in Moscow—mad, they were all mad!

"We have air-to-air and land-to-land missiles," Ruzorkaski said, his voice strained, "and the Americans have the same kind of weapons. Or will we make only a punitive strike using conventional weapons?"

Bersenko's gaze swept angrily over Ruzorkaski. "We first capture any Americans who attempt to invade our underwater space," he said in measured tones. "We then report to Moscow and await instructions."

Ruzorkaski said, with uncharacteristic bluntness, "It would seem that the Central Committee is determined to even the

51

score with the Americans for the Cuban missile fiasco in the Khrushchev days. It is a mistake. The Americans did not back down then. They won't now."

"Captain, that is very dangerous talk," warned Colonel Bersenko in an ominously soft voice. "You are fortunate that you are among friends . . ."

Ruzorkaski's face remained impassive. He stared up at the sky, watching a frigate, or man-o'-war, bird ride the upper air currents. He envied the bird. It had a freedom he could only dream of.

Chapter Six

The sound of the electric motor driving the main propeller was a steady hum within the cramped confines of the Cubmarine, a kind of background symphony for the louder hissing of the air regenerators. The main hull was 9 feet in diameter, but because there was conduit and other equipment inside the compartment, space in which to move was at a minimum.

Richard Camellion and Josh Forran sat behind Jerome Homes, who was piloting the Cubmarine, and Walter Atkins, who was listening to the sonar impulses. In their thirties, both men said little, did not exhibit fear, and gave the impression of being very efficient. They had to be because the Cubmarine would travel the last seven miles in total darkness, guided to the Soviet base strictly by sonar which would function as its "eyes." Sonar impulses would warn Homes when the vessel was approaching any kind of a barrier or obstruction. Depth was not a problem. The reinforced hull of the Cubmarine made it possible for the vehicle to submerge to a depth of 450 meters, nearly 1,500 feet. At maximum depth the hull would be subjected to a pressure of 46 atmospheres—45 of water, plus one for the air above it. Such a pressure is equivalent to more than a third of a ton on every square inch of the body.

The Cubmarine moved slowly through the water, at 8 knots per hour. At a depth of only 55 feet, it cut silently through the wetness without lights, the hum of its motor silenced on the outside by the Gf-Mechanism. Inside the craft there was only a faint green glow from the instrument panel in front of Homes, whose hands were steady on the two "joy sticks" that controlled the rudder and the four diving planes.

At this minor depth, the underwater world possessed a ghostly, unearthly beauty that made even the Death Merchant reflect on man's smallness in relation to the planet on which he lived and hoped and died.

Through the wide and thick Meganglass of the round window in the nose of the vehicle, and through two of the much smaller ports in the rounded hull, one could see schools of fish swimming parallel to the Cubmarine, and, here and there, bright silvery angel fish, darting crazily like silver streaks.

"Pretty eerie, isn't it?" muttered Forran.

"And deceptive," Camellion said. He didn't elaborate, but he had meant color. At 40 feet red changes to green, yellow to brown—all because visible light is composed of electromagnetic radiation, ranging from the longer wavelengths of red-colored light through orange, yellow, green, to the shorter wavelengths of blue color. However, the various wavelengths are not absorbed in water at the same rate, with light of the colors with longer wavelengths, such as red and orange, being absorbed most rapidly. For example, the red portion of the visible spectrum is reduced 10 percent of its surface intensity at a depth of 15 feet; the remaining wavelengths of visible illumination penetrate further. The blue colors of short wavelengths are the last to be extinguished.

Clad in navy blue coveralls, Camellion studied Homes and Atkins, and the instruments in front and on either side of the two technicians. There was far more than the control panel of the Cubmarine. There were the various controls and sets of the Gf-Mechanism, as well as the panels of the complicated inertial navigation system, and the gadgets, the dials and switches and buttons, of the acoustic positioning system—all of it tied together by an electronic computer.

"I trust the two of you can guide us to the target," Camellion said with a sudden show of candor. He was confident that Homes and Atkins could; yet he wanted to analyze any replies they might make.

Homes gave a wry smile. "Well, if we can't, we'll be in deep trouble with you guys—if the Soviets can find the pieces. Do I have to tell you what our orders are if this bucket of nuts and bolts becomes trapped by the Russians?"

"You don't," Camellion said easily, mollified by Homes's attitude and respecting him for his flippant frankness. *He probable would have enjoyed Pearl Harbor!* the Death Merchant thought. "How much explosive is contained in the Box, and what kind is it?"

"Sorry, that's classified," Homes said, then laughed like a small boy putting the end of a girl's pigtail into the inkwell.

54

"Tell you one thing though. If it comes to that, it will be a good way to go. You'll never hear it or feel it. A blink of the eyes and that's it."

Forran made a face. "Homes, did anyone ever tell you that you'd made a damn good undertaker?" He reached into one of the top pockets of his blue coveralls, then remembered that smoking was forbidden on the Cubmarine.

Walter Atkins didn't remove his eyes from the sonar scan screen.

"Don't mind Jerry," he laughed. "He's always been a pessimist. An optimist wouldn't be worth two ounces of lead in hell on a job like this. He'd assume all his luck was good and get knocked off within five minutes."

"We take the opposite view," Homes announced happily. "We know that luck doesn't have anything to do with success, so we're twice as cautious from the beginning. We'll get you guys to the Soviet base, and we'll get you back. Just one thing: once you leave this contraption, you're on your own. Our first concern must be the Gf-M."

"Fair enough," grunted the Death Merchant. He leaned back against the padded seat and looked at his wristwatch—13.00 hours—one o'clock in the afternoon. They were on schedule to the minute.

Forran, familiar with only surface navigation, was curious as to how Homes and Atkins could navigate with such precision underwater. Homes calmly explained that the entire business was comparatively simple once you had the hang of it.

The fore, aft, port, and starboard sonar sent out waves to detect any obstruction, a fail-safe system that made it impossible for the tiny submarine to collide with any object.

"There's more to it than sonar," Homes said. "Our navigation transducer is tied in with the compass. To keep us on course, all I have to do is watch the compass heading and the secondary sonar readings which 'Edgar' the computer—feeds to my instruments. At the same time he's giving the same readings to Atkins. Then there's this." He pointed up at a long graph posted above his head and angling outward. Very slowly a tiny red light, no larger than the head of a pin, was flashing on and off, and moving very slowly across the graph to the right.

"This is the Sonoprobe of this part of the Caribbean, furnished by GEBCO.[1] It's scaled to 1:12,000,000, which makes

[1] General Bathymetric Chart of the Oceans.

it one of the best. By consulting the graph, I know exactly where we are and what's on the bottom. I guess you know the red dot is us."

"Yeah, but how will you know when we're close to the Soviet base?" asked Forran in an almost businesslike tone. "By sonar?"

"Sonar, plus infrared television scan. And the signals from the Russian transponders will be picked up by our navigation transducer when we come within range. The signals will be analyzed by Edgar and fed instantly into the sonar scan screen. The screen's scaled to 1:25,000,000." Homes turned around and grinned. "I'll know within three feet where the first Soviet transponder ring is."

Forran nodded understandingly, his long face conveying that it was a pleasure to be in the hands of men who were experts, who exhibited utter confidence in their ability to do a vital job.

Homes's voice was suddenly brittle and authoritative. "One more mile and we'll be at the seven mile limit. I'm closing all side ports. Another three minutes and I'll take her down to five hundred and we'll start edging along the bottom."

"Time to suit up," Camellion announced lazily. He and Forran left their bucket seats and, hunched over and bracing themselves, made their way to the diver-lockout chamber. Within this cramped space they struggled into their special deep-dive suits and began checking their equipment, item by item. These diving suits were the most modern in the world, the Neoruperine suit so constructed that a diver could descend to almost one thousand feet. This was accomplished by means of a special tank containing compressed oxygen, which flowed through the first two layers of the suit and acted as a pressure wall against the intense squeeze of the water.

The plastic back pack of the dry suit contained not only the two tanks of breathing gas, stored at a pressure of 300 atmospheres, but all the equipment necessary for the closed-circuit breathing system with electronic gas-mixture controls.

Another innovation was the large waterproof pocket on each leg of the suit, located on the outside of the thigh. Camellion and Forran carried a stockless Ingram submachine gun in one pocket, a deadly little chatterbox that was only 11.5 inches long. In the other pocket of each electrically heated suit were four magazines of special ammunition—cartridges of .25 caliber, with bullets of soft lead that would explode on impact. Each magazine contained 50 cartridges.

The Death Merchant and Forran tested the 25-foot Plastoperene line that would link them together after they left the small sub. They closed the square face plates of their helmets, and tested the telephone communications setup. The mikes and the speakers in the helmets worked perfectly.

Forran unsnapped the Plastoperene line and opened the face plate.

"At least we're lucky that neither of us suffer from claustrophobia. How do we test the return impulses?"

"We'll have to wait until we're outside," Camellion said. "If we don't get any impulses, we won't go. We'll be at seven hundred feet, maybe lower. At that depth it will be darker than the inside of a pig's gut."

He and Forran could feel the sharp forward slant of the craft as Homes moved it down into the lower depths of the Caribbean.

"What about the back packs?" asked Forran. He was highly experienced in shallow scuba diving, but deep operations were completely new to him.

"We'll wait until we're ready to flood the compartment," Camellion said. "The packs are too uncomfortable unless you're in the water."

The speaker in the compartment wall suddenly became alive with the voice of Homes. "We're approaching the perimeter of the first Soviet warning circle. The signals are coming in as clear as a whore's wink."

Feeling like an intelligent sardine encased in Neoruperine, Camellion leaned closer to the round grill-covered opening in the wall.

"How is the Box working?"

"Perfect." Homes suddenly sneezed, then added, "The only problem the two of you will have is not letting the Russians see you once you leave this contraption."

The Death Merchant nodded to himself in satisfaction. "At this point, do you have any areas in mind for the put-down?"

Homes answered, "Sure I have, based on what I see on the Sonoprobe graph. First we have to see where the Soviet base is situated. I've activated the two bow television scanners and we'll know within the next five minutes. Right now, we're hugging the bottom, as close as we can get."

"I'm coming forward," Camellion said somberly, and turned from the wall. Already he was beginning to perspire within the diving suit.

"I'll wait here," Forran said resignedly. "In these clown suits, there's not room for two of us up front."

Camellion gave Forran a reassuring look and began the short crawl to the control compartment.

Entering the compartment, the Death Merchant saw that the two television screens were filled with pictures. At full maximum, the infrared cameras could penetrate only 700 feet ahead. Within that range the two monitors, to the left of Homes, revealed a landscape that could have been the surface of an alien world from another galaxy. In some places, the bottom was sandy and smooth. Other sections were scarred, marred, and cut up, ditches of various sizes crawling over the floor of the sea. On the right-hand side a ravine extended as a gentle depression, with barely a hint at first of its sharp drop to over a hundred meters, where it divided into branching chasms between narrow canyon walls. Dead ahead were several small, flat mounds covered with dark basalt. These *guyots*, or tablemounts, were the remains of a volcano that had been extinct for millions of years.

"We just passed over the first ring of Soviet transponders," Walter Atkins announced. "We'll cross the second in a few more minutes."

"My God! Look at that!" The words jumped out of Homes's mouth. Automatically, he switched off the electric engine and brought the Cubmarine to a stop. Slowly the small craft began to settle to the bottom. The Death Merchant also saw the strange object ahead.

Walter Atkins, who was sitting with his back to the right of Homes and Camellion, swung around and looked at the two television screens, fear and fascination clouding his face.

"It's . . . it's one of the OINTs!" whispered Homes, his breath quickening. "Just look at the size of that thing!"

Preoccupied, the Death Merchant studied the long, cylindrical object 600 feet ahead. Smooth and of a light blue color, the craft—or machine, or whatever it was—rested perfectly motionless in the water, although it appeared to be rising slowly upward. A delusion—Camellion and the two other men realized. It was the Cubmarine's settling to the bottom that made it appear the cylindrical object was rising.

With a slight thud, the Cubmarine touched the sandy top of a tablemount.

"The damn thing is four hundred feet long if it's an inch!" Homes said hollowly. "There's no sign of a conning tower, no diving planes, no rudder, no prop, nothing! Man, whatever that thing is, it wasn't made on earth!"

Atkins made an odd noise with his mouth. "How can it stay

like that without settling? It's against the laws of physics—
look!"

Ever so slowly, the alien craft began to turn to its port, the
nose—for all the three men knew it might have been the
stern—swinging around to face the Cubmarine.

Forran, in the aft compartment, sensing that something was
wrong, used the intercom, calling out, "We can't be there yet.
Why have we stopped?"

Homes's eyes never left the television screens. He called
back, "We've spotted something that belongs to the OINTs, a
craft of some kind. It's turning toward us."

"What are OINTs?"

"What we in the sub service call 'Other Intelligences.' The
Navy boys refer to them as the 'Invisibles.' "

By the time the alien craft had very slowly executed a
quarter of a turn and its front was directly facing the Cubmarine, Forran had crawled into the control compartment and,
leaning over Camellion's shoulder, was staring increduously at
the two television screens.

"It looks like—I don't know what it looks like!" Forran
muttered. "Did you see its length?"

"Four hundred feet," Camellion told him. "It made its turn
before you got here. As you can see, its full length has the
same circumference; otherwise, we'd see some curvature,
lengthwise, in the hull."

"I'd say it's about thirty feet in diameter," Atkins said in a
nervous voice.

"I got the feeling that whatever is inside is sizing us up!"
Homes said fearfully. "I've heard a lot of talk about these
things, but it's the first time I've ever seen one."

Forran whispered, "What are we going to do, just sit here
and wait?"

No one answered. No sooner had Forran spoken than the
vehicle began to turn once more, to swing back to its original
position. Finally, its long length was once more horizontal to
the Cubmarine.

"I'll be triple damned!" exclaimed Forran, now that he
could observe the full length of the whatever-it-was. "I see it,
but I don't believe it. It doesn't have a rudder or propeller. No
ports of any kind. It's—by God! It's starting to move again."

At first the strange craft of blue metal moved ahead at no
more than several knots. At the same time its stern turned
slowly to port. There was no churning of the water behind the
craft, the stern of which was equally as rounded as its bow—
or it might have been moving backward.

59

Jerome Homes reached up with his left hand, pushing a button that would permit the two infrared cameras to move at a wider angle.

Abruptly, the craft increased speed until it was moving at *several hundred knots per hour*. Within seconds it was gone, having disappeared in a southeast direction, moving faster than a bolt of blue lightning.

For a long moment, the four men stared at the empty water. They had just witnessed the impossible. They had just seen something that should not be, but was . . . something that should not exist, but did. It was similar to sleeping and dreaming of a beautiful garden, then waking up with a freshly cut rose in your hand.

Homes's voice broke as he said, "When we report what we saw, we'll be questioned for days by the CIA and the ONI. They'll ask the same questions over and over, and then try to tell us that we saw an overgrown whale."

"No, they will not," Forran announced firmly. "I'm ONI myself, and *I know what I saw*. Whatever it was, it was a machine under intelligent control, a device that could not have been produced by any technology on earth."

"Let's say any technology on the surface of the earth," Camellion said in an offhand manner. "What might be under the surface, say in the depths of the sea, is a different matter. Anyhow, it's all a matter of sheer conjecture. The OINT is gone. Let's get underway. We've lost six minutes."

Homes, swinging his seat around, reacted infinitesimally, but very quickly regained control of himself and gaped at the Death Merchant with disbelieving eyes. "Get underway!" he exclaimed. "You've got to be kidding! With that thing moving around out there?"

Forran said quickly, but calmly, "If the Soviets saw it, they might have divers out in force. It's something to think about, Camellion."

The Death Merchant stood firm, his lean face a mask of determination. "Unless the Soviets have infrared cameras out there, they didn't see the OINT. They're not going to have their TV monitors out this far. They'll have them close to their base." His eyes shifted to Atkins. "Did sonar pick up the alien craft?"

Atkins blinked rapidly and looked surprised. "Come to think of it, it didn't."

"Then the Soviets couldn't have detected the craft with their sonar," Camellion said. "As for the OINT we saw, it's not going to harm us. It could have destroyed us a little while ago.

It didn't. I don't know what it is, where it came from, or who made it, but I think we're as safe down here as we would be on the surface, or even twenty thousand feet in the air."

Homes's lower jaw fell slack.

Atkins looked at the Death Merchant with an amazed expression. "Are you saying that the damned thing can fly, too?"

Camellion, moving a finger across his upper lip, wiped off sweat.

"Well, it's obvious from what we saw that the craft operates on a principle other than F equals MA. That leaves electromagnetism or magnetohydrodynamics. Call it anti-gravity. Now let's get moving."

He motioned for Forran to back out of the control compartment, and watched Homes switch on the electric engine. The Cubmarine was once more moving by the time Camellion, following Forran, was easing himself carefully into the aft compartment.

"We're approaching the second line of Soviet transponders," Homes called out over the intercom, his voice tight.

Forran glanced at Camellion, but neither man spoke.

Camellion and Forran waited. They had strapped on their back packs filled with air tanks and the closed-system controls, and had triple-inspected their closed-breathing systems, as well as their spear guns. Each spear gun contained twelve "spears," each three and a half inches long and about the thickness of a lead pencil. Powered by highly compressed CO_2, every dart could pierce a shark, or a man, with the velocity of a high-powered bullet. The maximum range was 65 feet.

The Cubmarine passed over the second barrier of Soviet transponders, soon came to the third and final ring and, cloaked by the cover of the Gf-Mechanism, crossed over it, while Homes kept the Death Merchant and Forran informed over the intercom in the aft compartment.

"There's a narrow gully ahead," Homes voice came nervously over the speaker. "I'm going to put us down there. We're just twenty yards beyond the third ring, but I can't get closer. The Russians have their underwater base lit up like a friggin' Christmas tree.

Walter Atkins said, "We'll give you the green when it's time for you to flood out."

All set except for the final closing of their face plates and the switching on of air, the Death Merchant and Forran could feel the small craft tilt downward. For a few minutes it leveled off. Finally it touched bottom with a slight thud.

A green light began flashing in the front wall of the compartment.

"Floor-out time," Homes called out. "Good luck out there."

Camellion closed the forward bulkhead, spun the lockwheel, and sealed the round steel door. He looked at Forran, who nodded and turned on his air valve. Camellion closed and secured his own face plate, turned on the air, and carefully checked the mixture. The gas they breathed had to be perfect.

Pure air would act as a poison. The nitrogen, pressed into the blood by extra pressure, would knock a man's mind off balance and turn him into a helpless victim of the "rapture of the deep." For that reason most nitrogen was removed from the breathing mixture and replaced by helium—a physiologically harmless gas. Oxygen, too, was reduced and carefully metered out to compensate for added pressure.

The Death Merchant looked at the meter attached to the tube at his waist. The mix was 2 percent oxygen, 4 percent nitrogen, and 94 percent helium.

Satisfied that he and Forran were ready to become a part of the watery environment outside of the Cubmarine, Camellion pulled the "Flood" lever. With a rush, cold Caribbean water poured into the compartment and splashed around the feet and ankles of the two men. Quickly the water was up to their knees and waists, then their chests. In a few more moments, the water completely filled the compartment.

Camellion spun the wheel of the hatch in the floor. He opened the hatch and eased himself through the circular opening into the open sea. There was little room in which to maneuver, for this bottom of the aft section, supported by the stern braces of the two larger pods, was barely 7 feet above the sea floor. Careful of the spear gun in his right hand, Camellion did a half-roll to the left, swam underneath the vehicle, straightened up, and waited for Forran, who appeared almost immediately in the gray-blackness, swimming with easy strokes.

Camellion removed the 20-foot line from his weighted belt, clipped the ring of one end to a snap at his waist, and plugged in the end of the telephone cable to the receptor pack, which was also on his belt. After Forran had connected his line and cable, Camellion said, "Either you hear me or you don't, old buddy."

"I do, loud and clear," Forran said, as calm as a sleeping sponge. "I also hear the homing signals from the Gf-M. How about you?"

"We'll have no trouble getting back," Camellion said. "Our

62

difficulty might be getting there. Notice the faint glow up front? The whole damn base is ablaze with lights." Camellion looked at the MK-1-Mod-0-depth gauge on his left wrist. They were at a depth of 580 feet; therefore, the Russian complex had to be situated lower on the sea floor.

"We won't know until we try, will we?" Forran commented.

They swam through the sea ferns from the stern of the Cubmarine and, keeping toward the uneven contour of the bottom, headed for the Soviet underwater base, several miles away.

All around them, the Caribbean was a mysterious litany of life, a community of algae, corals, sea fans, sponges, sea anemones, tunicates, mollusks, barnacles and an immense variety of fish—angler fish, damsel and squirrel fish, parrot fish, triggerfish, wrasse, grunt, grouper, snake eels and scorpion fish—an exuberance of colors and shapes that was matchless in nature.

Swimming toward the Soviet base was different for one reason: Camellion and Forran had to swim very close to the bottom, thrusting themselves through sea ferns and other tangled growths. Several times their connecting line became tangled in the mass of plants, and they had to work carefully to dislodge the lines.

Their advance was gradually downward, on a slant; and all the while they drew closer and closer to the Soviet underseas installation.

Within half a mile of the base, they saw the high-penetration iodine-vapor floodlights mounted to the top of 40-foot steel poles placed strategically around the ten buildings made of silvery-gray metal.

The Death Merchant nodded to himself. It all was very logical.

Titanium constructed to withstand the pressure!

Camellion and Forran, concealed within a thick mass of porphyra plants, studied the amazing structures before them. Nine of the modules resembled Quonset huts, only much larger—50 to 60 feet wide, and 150 long. These nine buildings, connected to each other by means of metal tubes, were arranged around the tenth structure, an enormous dome that was 400 feet in diameter and, at its apex, at least 125 feet high. Projecting from the dome—to Forran and Camellion's right—was a box-like rectangular structure, its outside end supported by a massive pillar at each corner. The metal overhang was at least 100 feet long, 60 feet wide, and 30 feet high.

This projection was the "swimming pool," by which divers, small submarines, and equipment could enter the dome. This "foyer" did not have a bottom, i.e. a floor. Inside, the surface would resemble a large swimming pool. The pressure of the dome, equal to the outside sea pressure, kept the water from bursting in. It was this "swimming pool" that formed a "door" between the dry world inside the dome and the vast wetness of the Caribbean on the outside.

Camellion was hot inside his dry deep-dive suit. He said, "If the Soviets are drilling into the fault, they have to be doing it inside the dome."

Forran's voice was metallic over the wire. "They have to be drilling sideways. It would work just as well with the fault. You wouldn't have to drill straight down. They can't have a conventional derrick. The dome's not high enough."

"We can't be sure at this point," Camellion said.

"I know." Forran's voice was weary. "The only way is to have a look inside. I'm sure we don't have the good sense to leave well enough alone."

In spite of the gravity of the situation, Camellion had a good feeling about Forran. The ONI agent talked like a gloomy pessimist, but his verbal dolefulness was only a facade.

"We don't have a choice," Camellion remarked cynically. "We must go inside the dome. But sit tight. Do you see the yellow ahead, to our left, several hundred yards in front?"

"It's some kind of mini-submersible," Forran said. "The light is moving too straight horizontally to be in the hands of a diver. It makes sense. The Soviets are using security measures similar to our own, patrolling their perimeter with mini-subs."

"But they're not looking; they're listening," Camellion said coldly. "They can't conceive of anyone or anything slipping past their transponder lines."

In the darkness it was impossible for them to see even a vague outline of the Soviet vehicle. All they saw was the dim white-yellow light. For a minute or so, the light moved parallel to them; then it became smaller and smaller, dimmer and dimmer, as the craft, moving in a large circle, kept turning to starboard.

The Death Merchant moved slightly, his feet sinking a foot into the silt, disturbing a sea eel, which instantly slithered rapidly away, its frantic movements creating a slight underwater dust storm.

"Any special ideas for getting inside?" Forran asked.

"All we can do is keep toward the bottom and swim for the entrance," Camellion said. "Watch your line and your air mix.

On the surface you often get another chance. Down here, there isn't any second round."

"Well, we can't build a reputation on what we're going to do," Forran said. "So let's do it."

Like some strange species of fish, they swam toward the dome. As much as possible, they kept close to the bottom, yet were careful not to let their life line become entangled in kelp or the thick, matted seaweed called Wakame.

They were 300 yards from the dome's pressurized pool entrance when they saw the first Soviet divers—four of them, 50 feet to the right and 25 feet above them. The four Russians were dressed in black dry suits, and carried closed breathing system air tanks enclosed in back packs. The only difference between the suits of the Americans and the Russians was that the back packs carried by the Soviets were of a deeper gray. All four Russians were linked together by a life line, and all four carried conventional spear guns, for there was always danger from sharks and the vicious great barracuda. The Russian in the lead carried a hand-held strobe lantern.

It was the third Russian in line who spotted Forran and the Death Merchant. He did a half-loop in the water, tugged at the line securing him to the next comrade, and pointed at Camellion and Forran, who, knowing they had to get within range, were swimming toward the four Soviet divers. The second, first, and fourth Russians stopped, kicked water to maintain equilibrium, and turned and looked toward Forran and the Death Merchant. Forran and Camellion could see that the four enemy divers had not yet time to realize the danger confronting them. For now, the Russians were only curious, surprised at coming across what they assumed to be fellow members of the Soviet expedition.

The Death Merchant also knew that if one of the enemy divers managed to cry out an alarm to the surface ships above, or to the KGB security in the dome, he and Forran would have to fold their tents and run like hell for home.

"Kill them," he said calmly into the mike to Forran. He turned his spear gun toward the nearest Russian and pulled the trigger. There was a short *whoosh*ing sound, then another as Forran aimed and pressed the trigger. Two of the Russians, taking three-and-a-half-inch darts in the chest, jerked, went limp, and started to sink toward the bottom. The last two Russians, now being pulled down by their two dead companions, reacted quickly. One kicked sideways, and at the same time fired his spear gun at the Death Merchant, who again fired. A *whoosh* and the Russian's slim shaft of steel cut the water and

65

knifed by the Death Merchant's right side, the deadly point missing him by only a few inches.

The last Soviet diver fired at Josh Forran only a moment before Forran fired. Paul Nogov's spear would have caught Forran high in the chest if Josh hadn't twisted to one side. Nogov's spear missed Forran's left side by 15 inches and the rear of his back pack by several inches. Nogov was not as lucky. Forran's dart caught him in the stomach and lodged against his backbone. The Russian sagged and the strobe lantern slipped from his hand.

Alexandyr Pottin's luck was also bad, as rotten as it would ever get. The Death Merchant's little 3½-inch missile stabbed him high in the right arm and tore through the biceps muscle. Pottin was holding back a scream, trying to dive to the cover of sea ferns and turn on his UTEL, when Camellion's next dart buried itself in his chest, the tip touching his heart and switching off his life.

Slowly, silently, the four dead Russians sank to the bottom of the Caribbean.

"You think any of them was able to get off a warning?" Forran asked, swimming with Camellion toward where the Russians lay in a mass of Wakame.

"I doubt it." Like an enormous catfish, Camellion jerked his body to where the strobe lantern lay, its bright beam pointing sideways. "It all happened too fast. The pig farmers were too busy trying to kill us and save their own lives. Just the same, we'll wait and see what happens. If one of them did get off an SOS, this general area will soon be as thick with divers as fleas on a hound dog in Texas. Switch off their air tanks. I'm going to slit their suits."

The Death Merchant picked up the strobe lantern and turned it off. He then pulled a Mark-I Gerber knife from a sheath on his left leg and, as Forran turned the valves of the air tanks, slit the rubberized suit of each Russian. The faster the water poured in, the more weight would be added to each corpse. Now the four corpses would be discovered only by accident. There were no telltale air bubbles.

Camellion and Forran swam to the right, snaking their way over landscape dominated by coral mounds and castles decorated with brightly colored fauna.

"Over there in that tangle of sea ferns," Camellion said. "If we don't see any divers soon, we can assume we're safe."

"Those four clowns either came from the surface," commented Forran, "or else they were on patrol from the dome or one of the other buildings."

"Yeah, I'm wondering, too, how soon they'll be missed. Careful, the minisub is back. Three hundred feet behind us and a hundred overhead."

Forran snorted. "They won't see us unless they change course. That's not likely. That sub seems to travel on a set course. Man, it's cold as hell. I don't think the Commex batteries are working at full strength.

They waited, snuggled down within the weaving sea ferns, their feet sinking into calcareous mud. Within several minutes the small underwater craft was gone. Around Camellion and Forran was only deep twilight, the light that existed made possible by the glow from the iodine-vapor floodlights."

Forran stared around, straining his eyes. "I don't see anything."

"Now's as good a time as any." Camellion's voice was steady. "Swim straight for the southeast corner of the dome's entrance hatch."

Calling on extra strength, they swam the 500 feet to the dome, the structure assuming more massive proportions as they drew closer to it. Suddenly they were edging under the long rectangular pressure hatch, the open "swimming pool."

The Death Merchant paused, unsnapped the safety line, and swam forward to the southeast underside corner of the tremendous open hatch through which light shone from above.

The Death Merchant waited until Forran caught up with him. Forran had pulled in the safety line, and had attached the loop to his belt.

Slowly, the Death Merchant swam upward and poked his head out of the water.

From now on, it's up to Fate.
And to God. . . .

Chapter Seven

Lady Luck, I could kiss you ten times over!

His head above water, the Death Merchant looked all around as Forran popped up beside him. On either side of them was a Russian mini-submarine, the port side of one craft only six feet away, the starboard side of the second sub not more than ten feet away, the bows of both vehicles pointing north.

Camellion and Forran shut off their air flow and opened the square face windows of their helmets. To the north was a 40-foot-wide stretch of water—the "swimming pool," the open hatch. To the north, next to the water was a 25-foot section of concrete—the dock. As the Death Merchant and Forran watched, several lift trucks went by, their forks loaded with boxes. Both fork lifts were headed in an eastern direction, toward the interior of the dome.

Behind Camellion and Forran, to the south, was another section of concrete, much of it filled with boxes, wooden crates, and metal drums. Some of the boxes and crates were marked V-VALVES in Russian. Others were stenciled: CONNECTORS: 1"-D. On the various drums was painted CASING LUBRICANT. *And casing lubricant means drilling!* Camellion told himself with triumph.

On each side of Camellion and Forran, the gray mini-subs towered only five feet above them, vessels that were slightly larger than the American Cubmarine, but similar in design, except that the conning tower was toward the stern.

Camellion kicked water, moved to the side of the bow of the Soviet sub to his left and looked around the slanted prow toward the west. The northside dock was filled with supplies, and there were dozens of Russians on the west strip of concrete. Some were working on two deck decompression chambers. Four of the Russians, in deep-dive suits, were strapping on back packs.

The Death Merchant looked in the opposite direction, to the east. From this vantage point, he could see the edges of the thick doors that, when tightly closed, sealed the dome from the enormous open pressurized "swimming pool" hatch. Past the doors lay the immensity of the interior of the dome. But in order to see the interior, Camellion and Forran would have to leave the water.

"Josh, we can go behind some of the crates in back of us and hide our back packs," Camellion said, his voice resembling a weird squeak, causing Forran to give him an odd look.

"Are you all right?" Forran did a double take when his own voice came out heavily sprinkled with various kinds of squeals. Alarm flashed all over his face. A heavy smoker, he had always worried about cancer of the larynx.

"Yeah, we sound like midgets approaching puberty," Camellion said. "It's the air mix down here. Helium and pressure raise the pitch of a man's vocal cords and alter the acoustics of his mouth."

"You mean we're going to walk right into the dome and look around?" Forran asked, an incredulous look on his sweaty face. He then answered his own question. "I suppose we could. Our suits are similar, except for minor details and the color of the packs. There's only one minor problem: I don't speak Russian."

"But I do." Camellion started swimming toward the edge of the southside dock, which was now less than 20 feet away. When Forran reached him, they pulled themselves up slightly, put their hands on the edge of the concrete, and looked in either direction around the stern ends of the two small submarines. More crates, boxes, and cartons, many stacked neatly on wooden pallets, would soon be hoisted by the double prongs of a fork lift.

"Those crates in the southeast corner are just right," the Death Merchant said, pulling himself out of the water onto the concrete dock. "It will be days before the Ruskies get around to moving them."

Forran didn't say anything. Feeling as uncomfortable as an armless poker player, he didn't like to think about what would happen should the Russians discover their air tanks. There would be no leaving the dome; they would be prisoners of the Russians. Well, a bullet through the roof of the mouth would prevent capture—if it came to that.

70

Forran hoisted himself out of the water, looked from the left to the right, from the east to the west, and followed the Death Merchant through a maze of stacked boxes to the southeast corner of the dock. Here were a dozen large crates, large enough to have contained refrigerators. These crates faced the north. Smaller crates formed the west end of the enclosure.

Camellion and Forran edged sideways between the back of one large crate and the side ends of smaller boxes. Quickly, they unscrewed the hose connections, removed their back packs, and placed the air tanks close to the east wall.

"What about these flap pockets bulging with the Ingrams?" Forran said. He unzipped the front of his diving suit, reached inside, and unsnapped the strap holding a Mossberg Military Combat .45 in a shoulder holster over his coveralls.

The Death Merchant, checking an 18-round P-18 L.E.S. in a shoulder holster, said morosely, "You're an old poker player like me. How do you like the odds?"

"They're not worth a damn, but thinking of the pot keeps me going." He paused and thought for a moment. "Shouldn't we take off our helmets?"

The Death Merchant had taken a small high speed Millax motion picture camera from his pocket and was testing the lens. "We might have to make a run for it. It would take too long to put them back on. Life is a great thing and I intend to save a lot of it for four or five thousand tomorrows." He looked curiously at Forran who had a wistful expression on his face. "This is not the time for any nostalgia, my friend. Or you might get us kicked into the next world."

"Would you believe it, I was thinking that we might not get home for Christmas."

"Who gives a damn? Christmas is only the time when you get homesick—even when you're home. Let's go take some pictures."

They moved from behind the large crates and started walking leisurely toward the dome's enormous entrance, 40 feet to the east. Four times, empty fork lifts on their way to the docks passed them. Three times, lift trucks with pallets went by, going in the opposite direction into the dome. None of the drivers so much as glanced at them. Neither did the blue-uniformed guards at the entrance. On the left side were four Russians; five were on the right; and all nine carried AK-47 automatic rifles slung over their shoulders.

Camellion and Forran, with fork lifts going back and forth on either side of them, walked down the center of the passage

71

and very soon found themselves on the west side of the dome. Several times other Russians passed, but none seemed suspicious. It was only logical that the Russians shouldn't be. The mere fact that Camellion and Forran were in the dome was indicative that they were members of the Soviet force and belonged there.

Listening to the pounding of their own hearts and to the many noises of construction going on inside the dome, Camellion and Forran moved to the right, to where three Gvidons[1] rested in a row. To one side of the Gvidons were dozens of medium-sized crates marked OXYGEN GENERATING CANDLES[2]. Not far from the crates was an electric-powered crane, its 70-foot boom extending upward at a 60-degree angle from the cab, which stood on a mount of wide caterpillar treads 6 feet off the ground.

Camellion whispered, "Let's get to that crane. We'll be able to get a good view of the entire dome from inside the cab."

As if they had every right to be there, Camellion and Forran ambled in the direction of the crane, passing four Russian construction workers on the way, one of whom nodded and said, "You two ought to get out of those suits. It's already eighty in here and getting hotter."

Forran, not understanding a single word the Russian had said, only nodded.

Camellion answered in perfect Russian, "We're going out into the water again soon. It's too much work getting these suits on and off."

The four Russians went on their way. Without a backward glance, Camellion and Forran walked the rest of the way to their destination. They went between the three *Gvidons* and the crates, walked to the crane, climbed into the cab and

---

[1] A Russian underwater apparatus for studying fish shoals and fish tackle. It can submerge to a depth of 250 meters, is extremely maneuverable, and has an air regeneration system that can support two divers for three days.

[2] Chemical candles containing sodium chlorate and iron filings are widely used in modern submarines for providing breathable air by means of an oxygen-generating device. The candle is inserted into a burning chamber through a loading door. A plunger fires a cartridge that ignites the candle. The emitted oxygen passes through a double filter—first slag wool, then charcoal—that extracts traces of salt. The air is then diffused into the sub's atmosphere through perforated holes in the outflow chamber. Because a candle's life is only 90 minutes, a supply of hundreds must be carried.

snuggled down in front of the seat. Camellion was quick to notice that there was a small, two-door, battery-powered car on the other side of the crane. *No doubt a supervisor's runabout,* he thought.

"Stay down, Josh." Camellion took the Millax camera from an inside pocket of his coveralls. "Some wise ivan might wonder what two divers are doing in a crane."

"Just in case, I'm going to be ready," growled Forran, who pulled the Ingram submachine gun from one long pocket, and a magazine for the weapon from the other pocket on the thigh of his deep-dive suit.

The Death Merchant reared up and looked over the bottom rim of the cab's right window, feeling nothing but admiration for the Soviet engineers who had constructed this fantastic dome. To the northeast were rows of high-pressure membrane compressors, through which gases were pumped to air cylinders the pressure of which needed to be restored or whose gases needed replenishing. Close to the compressors were a dozen, large gas-mixing units, each one ten times the normal size of a regular unit. From here an operator controlled the combination of pure gases in the mixing banks, and also checked the pressure of the stored mixtures. Close by, lined up in long rows, were hundreds of gas cylinders—pure oxygen and helium stored at high pressure. Camellion could see that the entire system was a combination of SDC and DDC, or submersible decompression chambers and deck decompression chambers. *Pretty neat!* Camellion congratulated the Soviet scientists. *The dome is self-sufficient. It does not have to depend on air for breathing and for pressure from the ships above.*

To the north was a bank of fourteen generators, which furnished the electric power for the half-dozen cranes and other equipment. Sighting through the viewfinder of the camera, the Death Merchant directed his line of vision to the center of the enormous dome, to where there was a 20-foot-square opening in the metal floor—bare rock, bare basalt.

A square framework of steel girders was being erected in the center, with one end of the 60-foot-long section over the middle of the bare rock. While one end of the framework was only 5 feet over the rock, the opposite end was 60 feet above the metal floor, the entire structure braced by large girders forming four inverted *V*s. There was a large platform at the end of the highest section of what the Death Merchant knew was a special kind of derrick.

He didn't need an announcement from *Pravda* to know that the Russians were getting ready to drill through the basalt of the seabed. For one thing there was equipment that, when assembled, would be hydraulic controls for blow-out preventers. For another, there were large mud pumps and drawworks, the latter being the winch that would raise and lower the drill pipe and casing loads. To put the head on the beer, there were those long crates, dozens and dozens of them, that the Russians on the platform had handled with such tenderness. But the contents were no longer a secret. Workers were taking long sections of pipe from the crates. Some of the pipe was conductor pipe, casing through which the drill-string would be run. Other workers were removing drill-string from long boxes—long sections of hollow pipe smaller than the casing.

A short distance from the rigging were hundreds of sacks of cement. The cement would be used to secure the casing in place. And there were the drums of "mud"—a drastically oversimplified term for a complex mixture of chemicals, the composition of which would be carefully formulated. In addition to keeping the hole open, the "mud" would also keep the drill bit cool, displace cuttings, and return them to the surface—to the floor of the dome—via a pipe known as a marine riser.

"How much longer?" asked Forran, who was looking up over the bottom edge of the cab's middle window.

"I have enough proof right now that they're preparing to spud-in," the Death Merchant said.

" 'Spud-in'?"

"A drilling term, getting the hole started." Camellion turned off the camera, slipped his hand through the unzipped front of his diving suit, and placed the camera in the left breast pocket of his coveralls. "Now all we have to do is get back to the pressure pool."

"That won't be easy!" Alarm rang in Forran's husky voice. "We've been spotted. Some of the yokels by the drill rig are pointing up at us. Oh boy! Now some of the jokers in blue uniforms are running this way. We've got big trouble."

"Terminate them," Camellion said without hesitation. Then he actually laughed, a low, amused chuckle, as his hands darted to the long pockets of his swim suit. For a split second, Forran regarded him with some amazement, the thought crossing his mind that Camellion actually seemed happy that they would have to fight their way past the Russians. Or perhaps it was because Camellion hated the Soviet Communists, and realized that if he and Forran were to die, they would take a lot of commies with them into eternity.

The hell with Camellion and what his reasons might be. Forran raised the special-chambered Ingram submachine gun and cut loose with a line of .25-caliber projectiles that struck three of the blue-uniformed KGB guards. The slugs exploded instantly on impact, the tiny blasts tearing out chunks of flesh and bone and sending up tiny clouds of pulled-apart blue cloth.

Hundreds of Russians dashed for cover, getting behind any machine or object that could provide protection from the deadly hail of slugs raining down on them from the cab of the crane. By now, the Death Merchant was firing short, sporadic bursts through the right side window, his chain of projectiles putting to sleep forever three KGB guards and a dozen workers who had been taking casing pipe from long crates.

But the Russians were not helpless. Highly trained KGB guards immediately returned the fire, with literally hundreds of 7.62mm missiles from AKM assault rifles and PPS submachine guns zipping through the open windows and glancing off with loud whines from the steel sides of the cab.

All Camellion and Forran could do was keep down, although now and then they reared up to fire off quick bursts, or else got off shots from the openings on each side of the cab. Both men were well aware of the risks involved. Not only was there the very real danger of being tagged by a Russian bullet, but there was always the chance that a slug would graze one of the Neoruperine diving suits. Even a slight cut would weaken the one-inch thick suit. A graze that left a half-inch cut would be fatal, weakening the suit to the extent that, once the diver was submerged in the water, the oxygen would rupture the suit and burst through the cut. In effect, the suit would explode. The diver would die within seconds, not only from lack of breathing gas but from the big "squeeze," the tremendous pressure of the depths.

The Death Merchant, firing from the right side opening, spotted the Russians approaching from the northeast. Using a large fork lift to protect themselves from slugs, they had elevated the fork, loaded with crates, to a height that put the boxes between them and the Death Merchant's line of fire. He couldn't see them. By the same token, they had to drive using only a general sense of direction.

To the screaming of projectiles glancing off the sides and front of the cab, Camellion turned and looked up toward the panel of the crane, at the row of red buttons which controlled the rotation of the cab, and the raising and the lowering of the boom. A 7.62mm bullet hit the metal rim of the crane operator's seat, glanced off, and narrowly missed Forran's right shoulder, as it sped out the left side window. Several other Russian projectiles smacked the back of the operator's chair with loud rings, flattened out, and ricocheted, one clanging against the stubby barrel of Forran's Ingram and almost knocking it from his hand. The other blob of copper-coated lead zipped past the Death Merchant's head, zinged against the control panel, then rocketed out the left side window.

"It's time we get the hell out of here!" Forran yelled, turning toward Camellion. "This is worse than Saturday night in a Greek bar." Without knowing it, he had turned in time to avoid another ricocheting slug that, had he not moved, would have struck the glass of the helmet's open face plate. Instead, the bullet buried itself in the plastic handle that opened and closed the left side cab window.

"They're coming at us in a fork lift," said Camellion. "Scoot over here and let me know when they're underneath the boom. We'll flatten them, then make a run for it in that electric car."

"You've got to be nuts!" protested Forran, crawling over to the opening on the right side. "We'll never make it to that pressure pool."

"We're both candidates for the rubber room, or we wouldn't be here." Camellion shoved a full magazine into the already hot Ingram, then reached up and put his left hand close to the row of buttons on the control panel.

"Can you swing the cab?" called out Forran, who was watching the Russians in the fork lift and calculating distances in advance.

"Which way, left or right?" Camellion put the tip of a finger on one of the red buttons.

"Twenty feet to the right, then drop the boom."

Camellion pressed the button and slowly the cab of the crane rotated on its turntable, Camellion mentally gauging the distance by looking up through the middle opening and watching the large hook on the end of the boom.

That should be just about ten feet, he thought, and removed his finger from the button. The cab stopped its movement to the right.

"There, right there!" yelled Forran. "Now bash the bastards."

The Death Merchant pushed in on another button, holding it down firmly with his finger.

The long boom fell. The heavy metal girders dropped down like a gargantuan anvil, the weight crushing the crates on the

76

raised fork as though they were made of paper. The driver and the five KGB guards hanging on behind him never really had time to know what was happening. Sitting in the seat, the driver was higher than the other men. He was the first to die. The bottom girders and cross-braces crashed down on him, turning his head and upper torso into a bloody hash of crushed bone, flesh and blood, the entire mess splattering over the five KGB guards a thin slice of a moment before they died.

The 150-pound hook, swinging from the end of the boom on 4 feet of steel cable, pulverized their heads the way a sledge-hammer would splatter an egg. Skull bones exploded, and gray-white brain matter shot in every direction, at the same time the bottom girders made pulp of their shoulders, backs, and chests. The six Russians had not even had time to scream. Now, all that remained of the men was a conglomeration of bones, blood, chunks of flesh, and shredded uniforms—a gluti-nous mixture of foulness that caused other Russians to turn their heads and vomit.

Stunned, the Russians stopped firing for several moments, an interlude that Camellion and Forran used to good advantage. Ingrams and pistols in their hands, they jumped from the cab of the crane and started dodging and weaving toward the electric car—a cream-colored vehicle with a sloping front, two wheels in the rear, and a single guide wheel in the center front. A roof of white plastic covered the electric car, the bat-teries of which were underneath the front hood.

They were halfway to the car when they ran smack into a group of KGB guards, who had slipped around from the south side of the dome in an effort to come in behind them. Not expecting to see Forran and Camellion, the startled Russians hesitated and tried to reshift their thinking, the slight pause giving Camellion and Forran the edge.

The Ingrams, minus their stocks, were small enough to be held in one hand and fired like auto-pistols. That's how Ca-mellion and Forran used the vicious little submachine guns, while in their left hands they held their regular autoloaders, Forran his Mossberg .45, Camellion the 9-millimeter P-18 L.E.S.

Ducking low to the left, Camellion cut loose with the In-gram. The compact chatterbox jumped in his hand while the short barrel spit out a dozen .25-caliber slugs that ripped across the chests of three KGB guards—a dozen tiny explo-sions that threw out sprays of flesh and blood, and patches of blue cloth. A fourth Russian, Leonid Goripukin, jerked back

77

to avoid the whirlwind of slugs, firing a Stechkin machine pistol on fully automatic as he tried to duck behind a large centrifugal pump still in its crate.

But the Death Merchant had spotted Goripukin earlier, guessed the pig farmer's intention, and jumped to one side a split second before the Russian fired. The stream of 9mm Stechkin projectiles flew past him and chipped a cloud of splinters from another crate, at the same time Camellion triggered off another burst with the Ingram, the *duddle-duddle-duddle-duddle* of the automatic weapon sweet music to his ears. The sound was a requiem for Comrade Leonid Goripukin. Three of the Death Merchant's projectiles missed. Two did not. One caught Goripukin in the right shoulder, exploded, tore out five inches of his clavicle, and left his arm hanging by several strands of muscle fiber. The second bullet smacked the Russian just below the right nipple, and sent jagged pieces of ribs, and chunks of blood, flesh, and cloth flying outward. Stone dead, Goripukin twisted around, fell flat on his face, and lay still.

Josh Forran was also having his share of trouble. Right off he proved that Camellion's original assessment of him had been one hundred percent correct. Simultaneously with the Death Merchant, he terminated two KGB men with a burst of Ingram slugs, worried when he heard the firing pin hit an empty chamber. A third Russian, swinging the barrel of an AKM A-R toward Forran, cried out in agony when Josh's hollow-nosed .45 bullet stabbed him in the chest, and knocked him back against another Russian who was pulling back the cocking lever of a PPS submachine gun.

By now, the Russians were all around the two Americans, closing in from all sides.

"Otchet po v tylu armii!"[3] yelled Vasily Grusha, the senior KGB officer of the group. The sinewy Grusha, only seven feet to the left of the Death Merchant, had spoken his last words. As he attempted to rush the tall American, Camellion snarled, *"Idyi k chortoo"*[4], ducked to the right to avoid the butt of a Stechkin machine pistol being swung at his head, and shot Grusha in the face with the L.E.S. auto-loader. The 9mm metal-jacketed bullet, striking the Russian an inch above the nose, made a nice round hole in his forehead, and snapped his head back as though his neck were made of rubber. With an

---

[3] "Take the swine alive."
[4] "Go to hell."

78

astonished look on his hate-filled face, he fell to the metal door.

Concurrently with Camellion's action, Forran—more angry than a penned bull—slammed the barrel of the empty Ingram against the skull of Yuri Berzin, who was coming at him with a PPS submachine gun, in an attempt to brain him with the frame stock.

"Son-of-a-bitch!" growled Forran, a feeling of immense satisfaction running through him when he felt Berzin's temporal bones shatter under the force of the barrel. Just as quickly, he swung the Mossberg .45 toward Andrei Kravchenko, Josef Chevsky, and Anatoli Botarev, all three of whom were attempting to rush him and pull the weapons from his hands.

Josh became somewhat startled when he saw and heard Chevsky jerk, cry out, and put both hands to his throat, from which thick blood was spurting. Camellion had shot Chevsky; at the same time he had kicked in the scrotum of the cockroach who had tried to smash him with the butt of a Stechkin, the toe of the Death Merchant's weighted Neoruperine boot flattening the man's testicles like a pancake. Shock slid over the man's face. A gurgling sound came from his throat, and he dropped unconscious to the floor.

To save ammo in the P-18 L.E.S. pistol, Camellion chopped another Russian across the side of the neck with the weapon, then used the Ingram as a club to smash in the face of still another unlucky KGB guard, breaking the Russian's nose and upper jaw. A jab to the throat with the barrel of the empty Ingram sent the dazed man choking into an unconsciousness from which he would never awaken.

Andrei Kravchenko and Anatoli Botarev almost reached Forran. But "almost" wasn't good enough. The game of Life vs. Death does not allow for half-successes. Botarev cried out in agony when a Mossberg .45 silvertip hollowpoint stabbed him in the pit of the stomach and sent him reeling against Kravchenko, who had been trying to grab Forran's left wrist. All Kravchenko got for his effort was a .45 slug in the lower left chest, the dynamite impact twisting him around so that Josh's next bullet caught him in the middle of the left side. The Russian was dead by the time he sagged to the metal floor.

In the meantime, Camellion had snapped the Ingram to the built-in weight belt of his diving suit, and had picked up a PPS submachine gun dropped by one of the dead Russians.

"Grab another PPS and let's get to the car," he yelled to Forran, jumping to one side to avoid a spray of slugs from one of three KGB men creeping in from the west. The stream of missiles missed, although he felt one bullet barely nick the Neoruperine suit along the left rib cage. A punch in his stomach and another bullet buried itself in one of the lead weights around his waist. Worried about how deep the cut in the suit might be, Camellion triggered the L.E.S. as, thrown off balance, he fell on his left side. One 9mm hit the Russian who had fired the PPS in the chest and tumbled him against one of the other men who was trying to level down on Camellion with a Czech vz/23 submachine gun. The first of the Death Merchant's nine-millimeter slugs hit at the same instant that Forran triggered off a short burst with the PPS he had snatched up from the floor. The seven high-speed projectiles made the third Russian dance a quick, final jig before he followed the other two corpses to the floor.

The Death Merchant got to his feet and was soon with Forran, who muttered, "We're going to have wall-to-wall blood if this keeps up!"

"And a lot of it will be ours if we don't get out of here," said Camellion, worried about the cut in his diving suit.

With a few slugs zipping around them, they zigzagged to the electric car and Camellion jerked opened the door on the left-hand side. "You drive," he said. "I'll ride shotgun." Glad that the car did not have any glass in the openings, Camellion slid over, turned, and looked out the back window. Forran got in, shoved the PPS next to Camellion and looked at the dashboard. He saw that the car was started by pushing a button and that the speed was controlled by gripping a small handle on the steering wheel. He pressed the starting button, gripped the steering wheel, and the car started to move forward, going faster and faster as his left hand squeezed the handle.

There had not been too many trained KGB personnel inside the dome, Colonel Bersenko's reasoning being that if the Americans did attack they would do it in force, in which case the majority of guards would be needed to protect the surface ships. The dome was too huge and too fragile to be saved under any attack conditions. A single underwater missile could destroy it. In his wildest fears, Colonel Bersenko had never even considered the possibility that only two Americans might be able to penetrate the underwater warning system and gain entrance to the dome.

But the Death Merchant and Josh Forran had gotten inside the dome and they had killed most of the KGB guards. Nine guards were left, the nine stationed between the dome and the east end of the "swimming pool." These nine were very much alive and very determined to stop the two maniacs, who, within the short space of ten minutes, had turned the dome into a slaughterhouse.

Three of the KGB guards were in a large fork lift truck with a top enclosure. They had first raised the fork prongs to the height of the electric car's windshield space, and then had wired a length of sheet steel over the front of the cab, leaving just enough space so that Mikhail Koloviev, the driver, could see where he was going.

The other six KGB agents had positioned themselves behind various crates and cartons, a short distance southeast of the double doors. The mammoth doors could not be closed without decreasing the air pressure above the "swimming pool," in which case the Caribbean would pour in through the pool and flood the entire compartment, trapping the personnel inside the dome.

The three Russians on the fork lift came at the electric car at an angle from the northwest, at a top speed of 25 m.p.h., Koloviev determined to pin the vehicle with the two prongs of the fork lift.

While the fork lift was rolling toward the car, the Death Merchant spotted one of the KGB men waiting in ambush to the southeast, to the left of the electric car. At that same moment in time, he had also seen the fork lift coming toward the car at an angle that would bring the prongs crashing into the little vehicle in another 60 feet. Camellion glanced again at the crates where he had seen the Russian. *Only a hundred and fifty feet* he realized.

"Dodge that fork lift," Camellion said calmly to Forran. "Either cut across it or try to outrun it."

"We can outdistance the damn thing, but you'd better take out the driver when we pass him." Forran's hand gripped the handle on the steering wheel and the car speeded up to maximum—40 m.p.h.

The Death Merchant reared up slightly and triggered off a long sweeping burst to the left, using the Ingram which he had reloaded with the last magazine of .25-caliber explosive cartridges.

Camellion didn't know it, and the commie cockroaches at the corners of the tall wooden crates hadn't taken time to think about it, but the crates contained cylinders of liquid air and cylinders of liquid ammonia. Dozens of .25-caliber slugs exploded all over the crates, the numerous concussions not only filling the air with sprays of jagged splinters, but also loosening valves on five cylinders of liquid air and four cylinders of liquid ammonia. Instantly there were loud hissings and clouds of a pale blue color mingling with the slightly opaque vapor of the escaping ammonia.

There was not a single cry from the six Russians. The liquid oxygen, at a temperature of 197 degrees below zero on the Centigrade scale, had frozen them instantly. Their hair, skin, and clothes the color of chalk, the frozen stiff corpses toppled over, their clothes cracking like panes of glass, the arms of three of the "statues" breaking off when the solid bodies struck the floor.

The snarling of the Ingram was still echoing when Camellion dropped the empty Ingram to the floor of the car, grabbed the PPS beside him on the seat and, in one quick motion, jerked back the cocking lever and swung the weapon through the open window to the right. Just as quickly, Forran had swung the electric car to the left, the small vehicle tilting dangerous. It took only an instant, an instant in which Forran managed to dodge the fork lift. Mikhail Koloviev had come within a few feet of the car, and had tried frantically to turn to the right in order to pierce the open side with the end of the fork prongs. But he missed the target. The Death Merchant didn't. The PPS in his hands roared, the muzzle flashing fire. Koloviev jumped on the driver's seat, and his hands left the steering wheel of the fork lift as his head exploded like a melon hit by buckshot. Bits of shirt and blue uniform coat cloth popped from his right shoulder. Standing on the single long step on the back of the fork lift truck, Sorge Uritsky and Lavrenti Abt were flooded with "Made-in-the-USSR" slugs. With muffled cries, they fell from the back of the fork lift, their corpses looking as if they had been jammed through a rusty sausage grinder. The fork lift, now out of control, cut to the rear of the electric car which, by now, was almost to the double door entrance. The lift truck, like some mindless monster, continued on its blind way, and crashed into more of the crates filled with cylinders of liquid air and liquid ammonia. This time two cylinders of air and three of ammonia exploded outright, creating an instant cloud that began to spread and rise slowly. Seeing the ballooning fog, the several hundred engineers, scientists, and technicians to the north and the east sides of the dome began putting on industrial respirators, and grabbing portable tanks of chemicals that could neutralize the ammonia and render it harmless. The liquid air was not all that dangerous. Within a ten-foot radius the liquid air would normalize. Within five or six seconds after leaving the cylinders, the temperature would be harmless.

The electric car shot through the entrance, Forran skidding the vehicle to the southeast, while the Death Merchant sprayed with machine-gun slugs a group of ivans at the northwest end, whose curiosity was more powerful than their common sense. Four men sprawled backward against a stack of crates. Three others—two of them women—were severely wounded. They cried out, dropped, and lay still, except for one woman who had taken a slug in the left leg. Moaning, she tried to crawl between two large boxes, trailing blood behind her. She failed. Getting out of the electric car, Camellion stitched her behind with three more slugs. The Russians woman cried out in agony, jerked, fell to her side, and died.

"You never give a sucker even a fourth of a break, do you?" Getting out of the car on the driver's side, Forran secretly envied the cool precision with which Camellion killed . . . without any regrets, the way most men light a cigarette.

"Busy hands are happy hands," Camellion said cheerfully, sniffing the air. Even through the burning smell of ammonia, there was that nootarous, cloying scent of death. How often he had smelled it before!

"Hurry up and get your tanks on," he said. "I'll stand watch. We won't link up with the line until we're in the twilight zone, past the vapor lights downstairs."

Forran hurried off, and Camellion got to one corner of a crate, a position that gave him a clear view of the west, the north, and the east. He put the tip of a finger to his left side and gingerly felt of the cut in the Neoruperine suit. *Not more than an inch long and maybe a quarter of an inch deep*, he thought. *But suits have exploded over less. Well! Either it will explode or it won't!*

Forran soon reappeared, his back pack strapped securely, his face plate still open. Spear gun in hand, he went over to Camellion, and leaned the spear gun against a crate.

"Watch yourself," Camellion warned and handed him the Soviet machine gun. "The average pig farmer is so dumb he runs around his bed to catch up with his sleep. But he's like an animal. He keeps right on coming."

Camellion turned and went to the southeast corner of the "swimming pool" to put on his back pack. By the time he returned to Forran, the smell of ammonia was so strong that Josh had closed his face mask and was breathing the divers' mix. Forran raised his left hand and made a circle with thumb and forefinger, indicating that it was safe for them to go into the water. The Death Merchant closed his own face plate, securing it tightly, and pulled the small lever on the back pack that activated the automatic mixture controls.

Forran dropped the submachine gun. With spear guns in their hands, Camellion and Forran jumped feet first into the water, alert for any Soviet divers who might be waiting for them. There were none.

Desperation giving them the needed extra strength, they swam at a measured pace, gradually increasing the distance between themselves and the silvery gray dome. The water, illuminated eerily by the iodine-vapor lights, pressed against their bodies with a vengeance. Not that the sea was an enemy. It wasn't. It wasn't a friend either. The sea is always neutral.

By degrees, the water changed from gray to light purple and, as Camellion and Forran swam farther and farther from the dome, the smaller modules and the lights, from light purple to a purplish black. When the two men found themselves in that narrow zone where the very deep purple began to blend into inky blackness, they connected the line to their suits and plugged in the telephone cable.

"How's your signal from the Cub?" asked Camellion. "My own is loud and clear, and the beeps are becoming longer."

"Mine's okay," Forran said, relief in his voice. "We're on course. I doubt if the pig boys on the surface have had time to organize a search. Whoever was in charge in the dome wouldn't have called for help to capture only two men. How would it look to those in command?"

"Just let the beat of the heat get to your feet and keep swimming," said Camellion. "We don't know what little surprises those Neanderthals might have waiting to use, but I suspect we'll find out in the next couple of days." He looked at his depth gauge. *Yep, we're swimming with the rise in the terrain,* he thought.

Very suddenly, the light from the patrolling Soviet mini-sub appeared. *In front of them!* Within a few seconds the pale yellow eye had become a glowing white shaft of brightness.

"Dive—to the left," Camellion said, his tone more savage than anxious. "The bottom is only forty or fifty feet below us."

"I don't think they've seen us." Forran felt the connector link pull against him, as Camellion dove quickly downward to the left. Afraid that Camellion might think he was tiring, Forran took extra powerful strokes, which took him skimming across tall eel grass growing between weaving fan ferns. Almost immediately he was at the bottom, in a half-horizontal position with the Death Merchant.

Forty feet above them, the shaft of light began to fade, growing dimmer and dimmer with the churning of the water behind the mini-sub's propeller.

"I was right," Forran said, relieved. "They didn't see us."

"I wish they had," responded Camellion. "They might have tried to follow and entangled their propeller in seaweed. Let's get with it."

A short time later, they reached the Cubmarine and lost no time in swimming through the bottom hatch into the flooded diver lockout chamber. His body soaked in sweat, Camellion swung shut the hatch cover in the floor, spun the lock-wheel, reached out and pulled the Air-release valve. A loud hissing began as the intense pressure started to force the water through the vents and out of the chamber.

The water was down to Camellion and Forran's shoulders when there was a subdued popping sound and the water began bubbling with air.

The cut on the left side of the Death Merchant's Neoruperine suit was now a six-inch-long rip, a complete tear that had gone all the way through the inch thick material. But now it didn't make any difference. Camellion was safe inside the lockout chamber. He was not being subjected to the terrible pressure of the outside water.

He and Forran opened their face plates as the water very rapidly fell away. Quickly it was at their waists, then down to their knees, ankles, and feet. Finally there was only the empty chamber, except for the wet steel floor and the two objects that had not been there when the Death Merchant and Josh Forran had left the chamber.

"Man, were you lucky," Forran said, cold sweat on his own forehead. "If your suit had ripped five minutes ago—thank God it didn't!"

"I thought you were an atheist," Camellion mocked, his face breaking into a satisfied smile.

"In cases like this I always give it up for Lent," Forran shrugged. "I've gotten kind of used to your being around." It was then that he noticed the two objects, but before he could call Camellion's attention to them, Jerome Homes's voice came over the intercom.

"Are you guys all right back there? We can't stay here all day, you know."

Not only had Homes and Atkins heard the water being pushed from the chamber, but once the chamber had been totally emptied and the air pressure normalized, a green light had flashed in the control compartment.

"Affirmative," Camellion said in a loud voice. "Get us out of here. We had a bit of difficulty back there, and the sooner we get home and report what happened, the safer we'll all be."

"Hang on," Homes said.

Forran touched Camellion on the shoulder. "Look in that corner. There's a pyramid and a box. They weren't there when we left."

Hunched over because of the low rounded ceiling, Camellion turned his head and his strange blue eyes raked the compartment lit by a single riton tube. In the southwest corner of the area were a cube and a pyramid, both of a light reddish color, the latter resting on top of the former, the cube fitting snugly into the corner so that two of its sides were flush to the walls.

"What are they?" whispered Forran curiously. He reached out and grabbed a handhold as the Cubmarine, getting underway, tilted upward and slightly to starboard.

Camellion stepped over to the corner, got down on his haunches, picked up the pyramid, and examined it. He estimated that it was six inches square at the base and five inches from base to point. He handed it to Forran, who was beside him, commenting, "It's light and made of metal. But it's not aluminum, and I think it's solid. And not a mark on it."

"But who put them there and why? And what are they?" Forran glanced at the Death Merchant, then turned the pyramid over in his hands, a worried expression on his face.

Camellion picked up the cube and studied it.

"I'd say about six inches on all sides," he said professionally. "No openings. Not a trace of a seam."

He turned the cube over once more, then set it down on the floor. Forran carefully placed the pyramid on top of the cube and, along with the Death Merchant, stared at the strange objects.

"Plastic. Could they be red plastic?" Forran suggested.

"No. I'm not a metallurgist, but I'm certain they are not made of steel or aluminum."

"How can you be so sure?"

"Just a hunch." Camellion pulled the M-1 Gerber from its sheath on his left leg and, holding the pyramid with his left hand, moved the sharp point of the blade along one side of the metal cone. There was no mark. He tried again, harder this time.

The metal pyramid could not be scratched.

86

Forran suggested, "You don't think those two oddballs up front are playing a joke, do you?"

Camellion shook his head in the negative.

"I'll tell you what I think. I think that the OINTs have left us their calling card. . . ."

Chapter Eight

The Death Merchant did not like the uncertainty. This was the night of the fourth day since he and Josh Forran had battled the Russians in the dome only ten miles to the east. The Russians had not responded by attacking, nor had they complained to the United Nations about U.S. "piracy" on the high seas. Coded radio transmissions had increased enormously, and American Intelligence had learned that a Soviet vessel, docking in Havana, had brought enough Red Army officers to command a brigade. However, the arrival of the officers in Cuba was not a direct result of the fight in the dome. The ship carrying the officers had left the Soviet Union days before Camellion and Forran had gained entrance to the dome.

Camellion made sure the two Auto Mags were in place, then closed the special attaché case, and placed it under one of the bunks in the stateroom he shared with Josh Forran and Billy Coopbird. *This whole business is one big mess*, the Death Merchant thought. *Not only is the nose of the camel under the tent, but the hump as well.*

He didn't feel any better after he had taken a shower and was putting on one of his own black gabardine jumpsuits, especially when he reflected on the general conference that had been held that afternoon in the planning room of the *Mohawk*. Besides Webber, Humbard, Norris, and Frimholtz, two newcomers, who had flown in early that morning from Guantanamo, had been in attendance: Cullen Torway, a CIA man from the Company's Science and Technology Division, and Philip Meadows, a high-level analyst from the Defense Intelligence Agency.

Torway and Meadows had brought firm instructions from Washington: "Take no further action against the Soviets."

89

And, should the Soviets attack the three American ships, the Americans were to use only "conventional weapons" in retaliation.

"But, suppose the Soviets decided to use a small nuclear warhead in, say, one of the smaller missiles in their SS class?" Camellion had asked, controlling his temper. "Put another way, how does one retaliate after one has become part of a radioactive cloud?"

Torway and Meadows didn't know. "Blame it on a 'Mom and Pop Presidency' mentality," Torway had said. Nonetheless, the orders from the unrealistic peanutheads in D.C. were firm: Let the Russians attack first. Then use only non-nuclear weapons.

Cullen Torway had also brought the Death Merchant a special message from the company's DD/O (Deputy Director of Operations) office, which had been countersigned by the chief of the Covert Action staff. It had taken Camellion several hours to decode the message: SHC = SPONTANEOUS HUMAN COMBUSTION. WORLDWIDE. REPORT TO CENTER AFTER CARIBBEAN PROBLEM RESOLVED. A final touch of irony had been added: UNLESS WE'RE IN WORLD WAR III, IN WHICH CASE IT WON'T MAKE ANY DIFFERENCE.

Buttoning the last button of his jumpsuit, Camellion debated whether to remain in the state room and practice Yoga breathing or join Forran, Coopbird, and some JGs who would be—(as Forran had put it) "holding prayer meeting with the Devil's prayerbook"—playing poker!

A light knocking on the door interrupted his thoughts. He opened the door and found a sailor standing there.

"Mr. Camellion, Mr. Meadows, and Mr. Torway would like to see you on the observation deck of the signal section. I'll take you if you don't know where that section is, sir."

"I can get there. Thanks."

Ten minutes later, Camellion was on the observation deck of the signal section and found Torway and Meadows on the starboard side, leaning against the solid railing and looking out over the moonlit water. They both turned when they heard the Death Merchant approaching. Even in the half-darkness, he could see that both men, dressed casually in civilian clothes, were in a serious mood.

"Glad you came," Torway said matter-of-factly. "It's a beautiful night, isn't it?"

Philip Meadows came bluntly to the point. "We wanted to

talk to you in private, without the others sticking in their two cents worth and cluttering up the conversation."

The Death Merchant leaned against the railing, his back to the sea. "Here I am—talk."

"We want your assessment of the Russians," Meadows said. "I told you this morning that the Soviets will attack."

"You're convinced they will," said Torway, "but you don't think they'll use nuclear weapons."

"They have to attack, or pack up and move out." Camellion's manner was firmly distant. "They saw me taking photographs. They know those photographs are being studied in Washington right now. They know we're wise to what they're doing in that dome. The Kremlin realizes also that Uncle Sam might fight when he's shoved around in his own back yard. Then again, as I said this morning, the Soviets might be gambling that we'll back down in this part of the world just like we've been doing in Africa—blowing a lot of hot air about Cuban and Soviet intervention, but doing nothing about it."

"Unfortunately, we have vote-conscious politicians making decisions that should be made by only the military," Torway said bitterly. "Plus morons in the State Department who judge every foreigner by American standards."

Camellion saw Meadows smile thinly in the darkness. "Our people in the Pentagon have made the same appraisal as you, Camellion," the DIA agent said. "We want you to give us a better reason why you are convinced that the Russians will attack these three ships, a reason or reasons we can code back to D.C."

Added Torway quickly, "A better reason than you gave this morning. You see, should the situation here develop into a full-scale confrontation, our people will need hard facts to give the politicians."

The Death Merchant took a deep breath. "Western sociologists have been making cultural evaluations of the Russians for the past thirty years." He laughed somewhat mockingly. "My own speculations at this late date would be of little value."

"Not necessarily," countered Torway. "You've fought the Soviets, particularly the KGB, all over the world. Such experience is worth more than the combined opinions of a hundred Kremlinologists."

Camellion gestured with his right hand. "What can I tell you that the Intelligence community doesn't already know? In order to deal effectively with the Soviets, we must work at an analytical level that even most diplomats aren't aware of. The basic difference between us and the Russians is that they are

91

products of a high-context culture. They examine all the circumstances in which events are happening in order to understand them. It's the same with the Arabs. This is why we don't understand the Arabs anymore than we do the Russians."

"I don't understand you." Torway, annoyed, rubbed the end of his small chin. "Exactly, what do you mean?"

"Basically, I'm talking about the context of a statement and its actual meaning. Applied to the various cultures of the world, this means that they are placed on a continuum, or based on the amount of communication that's in the verbal message as compared with the amount in the nonverbal context. We Americans are low-context. We have a tendency to put more emphasis on the verbal message and less on the context. For that reason, we get down to business very quickly, without a lot of ceremony. It's different with the Russians and the Arabs. Their high-context culture demands that they know all about us before they can do business. They know no other way. They take time and have patience. We don't. We hurry at a dizzy pace. It's the patience on their part that gives them the advantage."

"Then you mean there's a lot of preliminary in a high-context culture?" said Cullen Torway. He snickered. "Within that frame of reference, it's like sex."

Camellion smiled. "Let's say courtship. Without all the proper procedures—the foreplay—sex becomes synonymous with rape."

"But there's more to a high-context culture than that—right?" said Meadows.

"It's all the tiny differences that count. For example, the Ruskies are very good at reading your eyes to judge responses to different topics. But they're not as expert in the art as the Arabs."

"I guess that explains why many Arabs like Arafat wear dark glasses, even indoors," commented Torway.

"The pupil of the eye is the indicator of how you respond to any given situation," continued the Death Merchant. "When you're interested in something or enjoying yourself, your pupils dilate. If you don't like the topic, your pupils contract. It's because of this 'eye talk' that we have conversational distances in various cultures. Watch two Americans talking. Generally, they'll be about five feet apart. As a rule, Arabs use about two feet, Russians about three. Another thing is that the Arabs and the Russians will look you straight in the eye. They're not taught that it's staring or hostile or too intense to do so. This doesn't mean, however, that the Russians and the Arabs have

92

the same type of culture. For one thing, the Arabs do a lot of touching when they talk to you."

"I know." Meadows sounded impatient. "In the Middle East, you can see two men holding hands even. Yet they're not queer."

"The Russians don't touch when they talk," Camellion said. "They will watch your eyes and read other body language, but they're not a people who touch. Of all races, the Japanese are the least 'handy.' "

"Look, this is all damned interesting," Meadows said wearily, "but how does it tie in with the situation here in the Caribbean? What do we tell the Big Brass back home? That's what we want to know."

Camellion stood up straight. "You're asking the impossible. You're asking me to predict the future. I will tell you this: The Soviets have studied the situation from every possible angle. On this basis, we can conclude that they're prepared to fight, determined to stand their ground—if you'll pardon the pun—against us."

Cullen Torway was not convinced. "You will admit there's the possibility that they might back down."

The Death Merchant's blue eyes twinkled. "Yes, I'll concede the possibility, though I don't think it's very probable. The Soviets would lose too much face in Africa and the Middle East if they let us chase them out of the Caribbean. It would prove to the world that they're all bluff. Nor are they prepared to resort to nuclear warheads. If they were—"

"If they do, we'll never know it!" said Meadows with unabashed candor. "It wouldn't make any difference to anyone in our area."

"If the Russians wanted to start World War Three, they wouldn't have had to come to the Caribbean to do it. They wouldn't have begun a project that will take at least a year, maybe longer, to complete. I've seen all the equipment in the dome. I'm convinced they intend to drill."

As Camellion talked, his eyes wandered upward to the immense signal tower amidships. A hundred feet in height, the tower contained a complicated array of radar sensing devices. There were HSA S-band height-finders, navigation and target-indication scanners, HSA LW02 L-band surveillance radars, and a TACAN dome for homing and navigation signals, plus HSA radar and GS1-Y pickups for in-read signals from satellites.

After a short pause, Phil Meadows said, "All we can do is report to the brass in D.C. that you're convinced of an attack,

93

your conviction based on your knowledge of the Russian mentality." He looked from the Death Merchant to Torway. "You compose the report, Cullen. You're much better with words. Do you have anything to add?"

"Negative." Torway sighed. "We'll report it as a wait-and-see situation."

Ever since he had met Torway and Meadows, the Death Merchant had studied the two men, an analysis that made him feel rather guilty, guilty over his comparisons. While the two men thought alike, they were very different physically. Camellion compared the tall, narrow-chested Torway to a spindly stork in a bed of leaf lettuce; the broad-shouldered, muscular Meadows to a wild pig in a turnip field.

"I have something to add," Camellion said. "In your report, I want you to include a request from me. I want to know the CIA's evaluation of the cube and the pyramid we sent back to the U.S. before the two of you arrived. You might include that I'm well aware of *HORSEHIDE-U-O-A-W,* the company's study of unidentified objects in the air and in the water; and I know the conclusions reached—intelligent life not of this planet. Aliens! The company arrived at that conclusion ten years ago. The only unanswered questions are: who they are, what they are, where they come from, and what they want."

"Okay, we'll include your request," Torway said, "but don't blame me if the home office doesn't comply. *H-U-O-A-W* is such a top secret that not even the President is kept up to date. Presidents lose elections and that knowledge is too dangerous to trust to any ex-President. But how the hell do you know about *Horsehide?*"

"Sorry, I can't tell you," Camellion said.

Torway took Camellion's refusal as a matter of course, saying, "That's another aspect of the situation between us and the Soviets. Since we know there are aliens on earth, so do they—in theory, anyhow. It's possible that part of their project out there is concerned with the extraterrestrials. Frankly, this whole goddamn area gives me an extra case of willies. Far too much is happening that can't be explained."

"Camellion, you are positive of what you and the others saw out there when you were approaching the Soviet underwater complex?" the cautious Meadows said undiplomatically.

The Death Merchant let the DIA agent have a look that would have made a king cobra drop dead of fright. "As positive as I am that there are twice as many feet as there are people in the world—*dummy!*"

Never one to take an insult, Meadows drew back and made

an angry face, but before he could start trading backhanded compliments with the Death Merchant, the scream of a loud electric siren, mounted amidships, split the air. Sirens also screamed from *Atlantis II* and the *South Dakota*, sirens that meant only one thing: the underwater sensing devices, the transponders and much longer range sonar at the first five-mile warning line, had detected intruders. And as far as Camellion and the two other men knew, surface radar had detected craft on the water.

"We have no more than twelve minutes at the maximum!" yelled Torway just before he, Camellion, and Meadows dashed for the stairway.

"Or we'll all be radioactive dust within one minute!" Camellion said with a barely perceptible laugh.

And if we are, he thought, *Death will be the greatest adventure of all!*

Chapter Nine

Trained personnel do not panic over anticipated emergencies. Ever since the Death Merchant and Forran had returned from the dome, the American force had expected the attack and had prepared accordingly. Not only were automatic rifles, submachine guns, grenades, small arms, and other equipment kept ready in convenient locations on all the decks, even in the engine rooms, but the hundred SEALers were kept on 24-hour alert. Deployed throughout the three ships, 50 of the SEALs were on the *Mohawk*, the LCC command ship, 40 on *Atlantis II*, the floating lab of oceanography, and 10 on the *South Dakota*, the DD-type destroyer.

"Emma" was turned on—a special jamming device[1] that, operated from *Mohawk*, "moved" the three vessels several hundred yards to the east from their actual positions as seen on Russian radar. Had the ships been moving, "Emma" could have "moved" them several miles. However, this maximum deception was not possible when the vessels were stationary, at anchor.

Now that the Russians had actually been detected, everyone was relieved. The waiting was over. The agony of expectancy would not produce any more tension. Nervousness was replaced by rage and a determination to defeat the enemy.

The Death Merchant was rushing to his cabin when the

---

[1] This is not fiction. Such a jamming device actually exists. In Uncle Sam's arsenal there is also a "magic circle" that totally blinds enemy radar. This "circle" is formed around attacking units of fighter-bombers by an EF-111 jaming plane. There even exist special artillery shells that explode above enemy formations to black out communications with a blast of electronic noise.

Soviet missiles struck—seven SS *Lzumrud*, "Emerald"[2] which knifed into the calm water and exploded with crashing roars, the savage concussion creating mini-tidal waves that smashed against the three American vessels, rocking them violently, as though they had encountered wild waves whipped by a typhoon. Without "Emma," the Soviet missiles would have blown all three vessels out of the water. However, all seven Emeralds had exploded 600 feet east of the three vessels.

On the main control bridge of *Mohawk*, Commander Jason Webber, wearing headphones and mike, cursed to relieve anger and barked orders to the operators of Emma in the control dome; "Change to the west—maximum range." Instantly, buttons were pushed in the horizontal reference panel and coordinates changed by computer, in 1/40th of a second, in the junction command unit. Should the Soviets launch a second wave, the missiles would hit 600 feet west of the three American ships.

"Damage control report," Webber spoke into the mike.

There was some damage but it was minor. The huge waves had slammed the starboard bow of *Mohawk* against the port bow of *Atlantis II*, the smash buckling some plates in *Atlantis II*. Some water was seeping into the fore peak of *Atlantis II*, but the pumps could handle the water; and the bulkhead was closed.

Camellion, almost thrown to the floor by the rocking of the ship, finally reached the cabin where he found Josh Forran and Billy Coopbird, both men barefooted and wearing only Navy poplin trunks.

"We haven't been vaporized," Forran said, with a crooked grin. "Be damned if you weren't right, Camellion. The Russians don't want to start the Big War."

"This isn't over yet," Camellion said, and reached for the attaché case underneath the bunk. "Anything might happen."

By the time Camellion and Forran and Coopbird had buckled on sidearms, grabbed Ingrams and ammo bags, and had made their way to assembly area two on the boat deck, all readings from the underwater sensing devices had been tabulated and radar scans verified.

Five Soviet underseas craft were coming in at a depth of 20 fathoms from the west. The Americans assumed that the vehicles were *Sumov* SDVs, roughly the same as the American

2 The SS-D *Lzumrud* is a ship-to-ship missile that carries 1,200 pounds of TNT and has a range of 20 miles.

SEAHORSE-10, a SEAL swimmer delivery vehicle that carried ten divers, including the driver.

Cross-line radar had detected ten blips to the east, ten fast troop-carrying ships. The Soviet tactics were very clear: while the surface ships attacked from the east and took out the two weakest ships, the enemy SDVs would take out the *South Dakota*, which from the west, could be called the "base" of the American defense wedge.

The Americans were more than ready for the attackers. The side loading hatches in the vessels had been closed. Men waited behind heavy machine guns in turrets on the *Mohawk* and the *South Dakota*. Five-inch guns and braces of 20MM and 40MM Bofors were depressed. Divers, armed with dart "spear" guns went over the sides of the *South Dakota*. Seven of them carried Darsher-6H electronic mines that could be placed against the sides of the SDVs.

After giving the Death Merchant a rundown on the Soviet forces speeding toward them, Lieutenant Commander Red Norris suggested that Camellion, Forran, and Coopbird slip into Kevlar bulletproof chest-and-back packs and put on helmets. Camellion had already noticed that Meadows, Torway, and a dozen other men in the area were wearing Kevlars and busily checking their automatic weapons.

"Where are Humbard and Frimholtz?" Camellion looked at Norris, and put the heels of his hands on the butts of the two Auto Mags protruding from the holsters on his hips.

"The last I heard—"

A voice, coming over the loudspeaker, interrupted Norris. It belonged to one of the technicians in the radar compartment. The voice was crisp and professional: "Enemy surface targets six miles east, point four by south, and increasing speed."

"The last I heard, they were with Webber in the main control bridge. By God, they had better stay there. If those two know-it-alls come down here and try to tell me how to fight, I'll toss their asses to the Ruskies."

Half-smiling, Camellion went across the room to the long table filled with Kevlar outfits.

Red Norris looked at Forran and Coopbird with a mixture of amazement and disgust. "You two going to wear nothing but trunks?"

"Yeah, we're going to wear nothing but trunks," Forran replied with some asperity. Then he and a grinning Coopbird walked over to where Camellion was dropping a Kevlar chest and back pack over his head.

"Are these vests any good?" Forran asked Camellion and picked up one of the outfits.

Coopbird, slipping one of the packs over his head, said in a worried tone, "I was under the impression we'd knock out the Russians before they could board us. Now I'm not so sure."

Tightening the Velcro straps, the Death Merchant explained that Kevlar was layered material fiber and that the bullet-stopping capability of the vest was determined by how many sheets of material was placed in the "sacking."

"A bullet's difficult to stop because of its speed and shape. Sharp-pointed rounds push the fibers aside and have a tendency to work their way through more layers of the material. A big .45 ACP or .44 Magnum slug will bounce right off. But a sharp 9mm Luger, .38 Super, or even a .22 Magnum round will bore right through. These vests aren't foolproof."

"And not bulletproof either!" growled Forran.

The expression on Coopbird's black face was grim. "Russian handguns use 9-millimeter stuff and most of their automatic weapons are chambered for 7.62-millimeter rounds. Where does that leave us?"

"About fifty percent safe," Camellion said. "We're wearing suits that have forty-two layers of Kevlar. They'll stop any slugs fired from a handgun, even from an Auto Mag. They won't completely stop the standard Russian 7.62 by 39mm. A lot depends on the distance and angle. A 7.62mm might not bore all the way through. But at a short distance and point blank—forget it. You'll end up a big bag of cold cuts."

Forran, adjusting and tightening his vest, glanced over at Camellion, who had just cocked the Ingram and was now switching on the safety. "Billy boy and I are going with you, wherever you might be going. We know you're not going to stand around up here and wait for the pig boys from Mother Russia."

Camellion laughed harshly. "You might be safer away from me."

"Mon, we be twice safe with you," Coopbird said, going into his dumb black Jamaican act. "Old man rattle-bones, he no git close to you. Old man Death, him and you drink from the same cup of blood."

Overhearing the conversation, Lieutenant Commander Norris said in an authoritative voice, "My men and I will be on the main deck. Civilians can't go lower than the upper deck, the deck below this one. That's an order."

Torway and Meadows didn't protest. Neither man was anxious to get his head blown off. Camellion, quick to detect their

100

emotions by watching their eyes, didn't blame them. Torway and Meadows were not fighters. Their world was the world of the desk, of analysis, of intrigue on paper.

"The upper deck is fine with me," Torway said.

"I, too," seconded Meadows.

Forran and Coopbird locked eyes; then they looked at Camellion.

The Death Merchant gave Norris a long, pitying look.

"Norris, you're forgetting who's top honcho around here," he said complacently. "I go where I please, and I'm going to the main deck. If Mr. Forran and Mr. Coopbird wish to accompany me, they're welcome. Oh, yes—one more word out of you and you'll end up a Seaman First Class . . . if the Russians don't make more pieces out of you than a kid taking apart a tinker toy."

Conscious that some of his men were watching him from the corner of their eyes, Norris was too disciplined to lose his temper. Besides—whoever Richard Camellion might be, whoever he really was—the son-of-a-bitch was in charge. No wonder the nation was going to hell in a hand basket!

"Jump in the fuckin' sea if you want, Camellion!" Norris sounded cool and unperturbed. "Forran and Coopbird"—he gave them an icy stare—"can jump in with you. Just don't get in our way. We'll step on you. Got it?"

"We'll take this up later. Just don't slip on the deck." Cradling the Ingram under his right arm, Camellion walked out the door. Forran and Coopbird followed him, marching like proud peacocks.

Time had almost run out. The waiting Americans could see that the attacking Russian ships were fast patrol boats, craft that NATO had designated as "Hop Toads," slightly smaller but faster than an American PTF, a swift U.S. Navy patrol boat. Each Hop Toad could carry thirty men. The thought was not exactly comforting: Skimming over the moonlit water were 300 men. . . .

Camellion and Forran stood on each side of an air duct. Six feet forward from Camellion, Billy Coopbird was to the left of a 3-inch gun's armored shield. Norris and his men were spread out behind the solid railing on the port side of *Mohawk*.

Forran made a snickering sound. "If you ask me, I think the ivans are trying to have intercourse without getting screwed," he said as a joke to Camellion. "We're thirty feet

101

above their decks. What the hell? Do they think we're going to help them aboard?"

"They'll get aboard," Camellion said. "Those who do had better give their hearts to God, because their butts will belong to us."

The gunners on *Mohawk* opened fire when the Hop Toads were three miles away, the 5-inchers and the 3-inchers lobbing explosive projectiles at the slim, darting enemy patrol boats. Huge geysers of water began blooming all around the craft, tons of water shooting upward, some of the explosions rocking violently the now zigzagging boats, but none doing any serious harm.

When the Russian patrol boats were within a mile and a half of the bows of *Mohawk* and *Atlantis II*, the 20MM and 40MM Bofors and the 20MM Oerlikon guns began firing, their roaring crashing against one's ears, the weapons expending hundreds and hundreds of rounds of fixed ammunition. Every third round was a tracer, so that light-bright lines crisscrossed, each line filled with hundreds of steel-cored projectiles.

On the forward deck of *Atlantis II*, a mount with four 20-millimeter Flak cannon had been installed, and it too threw lines of steel at the approaching Hop Toads, each cannon firing 180 rounds per minute. Many Americans found it incredible that any vessel could continue to "live" through such a curtain of flying steel.

Not all of the Hop Toads did. Four of the patrol boats had broken away from the main line and were speeding to the southwest when the gunners on the *Mohawk* got lucky. One of the four Hop Toads exploded with a crashing roar, and a brief flash of red and orange fire. For a blink of a second, there was a rolling fireball, then nothing but a lot of twisted, burning metal, parts of bodies and blazing corpses, the whole mess flying upward as if to collide with the full white moon. None did. The ripped and twisted metal, and the broken bodies, slammed back into the Caribbean and sank quickly beneath the water.

The three other patrol boats continued to slice to the southwest; then one cut sharply, its sharp prow pointing east, directly between the starboard bow of *Mohawk* and the port side of *Atlantis II*. The other two Hop Toads made a much wider swing to the right and, at a distance of 700 feet from the starboard side of *Atlantis II*, began to race in toward the vessel, zigzagging in wide sweeps, from side to side, to escape the rain of 50-caliber Browning slugs sweeping down on her from the midship housing of the vessel. But the projectiles were ineffective against the armor. Moments later, braces of KPV machine guns, mounted on turrets of the two patrol boats, began firing streams of 14.5mm projectiles, which raked the decks and side of the oceanographic vessel, many of them piercing the non-armored walls of the midship housing. The 14.5mm cartridge, comparable to the U.S. caliber .60 cartridge, was a round that could also be used in an antitank rifle.

The crew of the Flak mount on the bow of *Atlantis II* concentrated their fire on the Russian patrol boat, which was only a few hundred yards and half a minute from darting between the bows of *Atlantis II* and *Mohawk*. Four streams of 20-millimeter missiles raked the sleek Soviet craft. Several hundred zipped through the stern deck, killed 14 Cubans, and found the fuel tanks of the twin Diesels. In an instant it was all over. A tremendous roar, a brief fireball, and the Hop Toad and its cargo of human beings ceased to exist, some of the twisted wreckage even landing on the bow decks of *Mohawk* and *Atlantis II*.

The six other enemy patrol boats, concentrating on *Mohawk*, zigged and zagged to the northwest, while the gunners in the bow, center, and aft turrets raked the port side of the LCC command ship with streams of KPV heavy machine gun projectiles, most of the 14.5mm glancing off. Those that didn't find armor plate shattered glass and zipped through other material. A sailor in the observation tower, above the main control bridge, yelled when wooden splinters and pieces of aluminum struck him in the face, one fragment of aluminum striking him in the left eye. Three sailors in engineering, on the main deck, died instantly when they were foolish enough to open the armored slides across the wide ports and look out. Steel-cored projectiles literally exploded their heads.

The Death Merchant and the rest of the men couldn't do a thing but keep down and wait. As the enemy machine gunners continued to fire, the six Russian patrol boats glided to a full stop, their bows pointed northwest. All six vessels were 40 feet from the port side of *Mohawk*.

On both the port and starboard sides of each Soviet attack vessel were three large tubes, each tube 6 feet high and 7 feet in diameter. All the tubes were mounted on swivels so that they could be tilted complete horizontal to complete vertical. Now they were tilted at an angle of 60 degrees.

Down on one knee behind the air duct, the Death Merchant analyzed the probability of casualties. *We'll be lucky if*

*half of us aren't wiped out. But we'll win this round. We'll lose
round two unless we attack the Soviets at their base.*

With only six patrol boats, the Russians would not be able
to conquer the *Mohawk*, nor could a mere sixty of the enemy
take over *Atlantis II*. At the present time, it was the *South
Dakota* that was in the most danger. Being at the base of the
American defensive triangle, the destroyer had not been able
to turn her guns against the patrol boats, or she would have
hit *Mohawk* or *Atlantis II*.

The real danger to all three American vessels was the divers
on the Soviet SDVs. Should the Russians succeed in planting
mines against the hulls of the vessels, defeat would quickly
come. Camellion knew it was a matter of luck, or Fate. He
personally could not resolve the problem. *Kingfisher* could not
help either. She had sent several dozen of her best divers to
assist the divers from the *South Dakota*. Then Captain
McConachie had moved the nuclear submarine five miles to
the north to await developments. Should the Russian submarine launch missiles, or come in close to fire torpedoes, *Kingfisher* would respond in kind.

World War III would then become a reality. . . .

An IMP[3] in his right hand, Lieutenant Commander Norris
was at the southwest corner of the midship housing. He had
ordered all the men back from the port side railing, and now
the Death Merchant heard him call through a bullhorn, "Get
back and down. They'll be coming over the side any moment.
Brace yourself for grenades."

Camellion nodded to himself in satisfaction. Norris was a
go-by-the-book crud, but he knew the business of killing.

The enemy kept to the schedule. While the bow and stern
KPV heavies continued to fire and rake the side of *Mohawk*
with a deadly tornado of projectiles, the midship heavy machine guns of each patrol boat were suddenly silent. It was
time for the Cubans to board. There were very loud *whoosh*es
as the ends of the three tubes on the port side of each Soviet
attack craft opened and telescoping ladders, impelled by compressed air, shot upward, their ends coming to rest against the
top of the enclosed railing on the port side of *Mohawk*.

Cuban soldiers poured up the eighteen ladders, Cubans

[3] Individual Multipurpose Weapon, the only true U.S. machine
pistol. Developed by Colt, the IMP is one of a series of survival
weapons for the U.S. Air Force. It uses 5.6-mm (0.221-inch)
Remington Fireball ammunition. The weapon can be fitted with a
40-round clip, the magazine being behind the forehand grip.

dressed in light brown tropical fatigues, and wearing side arms, cartridges pouches, and submachine gun magazine bags. Each man carried a PPS Russian submachine gun. The first man up each ladder also carried a fragmentation grenade.

The gunners in the patrol boats set up a furious cover firing as the Cubans poured up the ladder, three of the Hop Toads concentrating on the American machine gunners high up on the midship housing, the Cubans in the other three patrol boats centering their ring sights a foot above the railing of the *Mohawk*. All twelve gunners ceased firing when the first soldier up each ladder was only six feet from the top of the enclosed railing and pulling the pin from his grenade. Moments later, eighteen grenades exploded along the entire length of the *Mohawk*, the concussions, sounding almost like one single explosion, accompanied a split second later by the *ping-ping-ping* of chunks of shrapnel. By the time the Americans reared up, the first Cubans were coming over the railing. Those first Cubans died, riddled with slugs, but more were behind them. It took only ten seconds to dirty up the wide deck with three dozen Cuban corpses. Yet time was not on the side of the Americans. Not only did they have to pause to reload, but many of the Cubans, who followed the first wave, came over the railing firing short bursts with their PPSs, the chain of slugs forcing the Americans to duck back. During those moments, the Cubans gained ground, and within a very short time, scores of the enemy were on the deck, firing to cover the men coming up behind them and jumping for any cover that was available.

Methodically, the Death Merchant went to work with his Custom Model 200 International Auto Mags, each stainless steel autoloader sounding like a mini-cannon each time he pulled the trigger. Each time, a Cuban jumped and died from the terrible force of a .357 Magnum bullet.

Within such a comparatively small field of combat as the main deck of a LLC, the battle quickly became a hand-to-hand shoot-out, an eyeball-to-eyeball confrontation that only the luckiest could win. Much of this depended on ability and training, and in these departments the Americans were way out in front. Each SEAL was worth three Cubans, the latter of whom would just as soon have stayed at home. But now that they were here, they had to fight for their lives, a task for which—compared to the Americans—they were ill-equipped.

The Death Merchant, moving from the corner of the air intake duct, ducked and fell flat to avoid a line of 7.62mm projectiles from a bearded Cuban cutting down on him with a

105

PPS sub-gun. Camellion fired the left AMP the instant he hit the prone, then pulled the trigger of the right Auto Mag Pistol.

The first flat-nosed Jurras .357 hit the Cuban in the pit of the stomach, bored a bloody tunnel all the way through his body, and struck another Castro halfwit in the left side, just above the hip. The first Cuban, doubled over from the impact and dying, was flung against the second man who was going down with a .357 Magnum slug sizzling in the center of his liver when the projectile from the right-handed AMP chopped a third man in the left shoulder, going in sideways. The man's arm flew upward as if jerked by a string. The bullet pulverized the shoulder bone, broke the clavicle, and broke the backbone in back of the neck. The Cuban dropped faster than a cannonball, his head wobbling from side to side.

Glancing first to the left, then to the right, Camellion scampered to his feet, and noticed that Forran and Coopbird were more than holding their own. Wearing a Mossberg Military .45 on each hip, each man was triggering off three-round bursts with his Ingram Model 11.

Another sight caught Camellion's eye, and this one he didn't like. Three Cubans were climbing up to the turret that, only 20 feet astern of the bow's warping winch, housed a brace of 20MM Bofors. They were halfway up the turret when one of Red Norris's boys stitched all three with a burst of M7 submachine gun slugs, the big .45s from the grease gun tearing off bits of flesh and pieces of shirt. What was left was bloody hash.

Dan Sullivan, the SEALer who had killed the three Cubans, got it next. A fierce-eyed Cuban raked him across the chest with a burst of PPS slugs, only two of which penetrated the Kevlar bulletproof vest, and then only half an inch past the layer of material closest to the skin. Less than half an inch of the Spitzer-shaped projectiles were in Sullivan's chest, and he wasn't in any danger from the comparatively slight wound. But he died, died when the Cuban first raked him across the thighs, then sent a burst into his head as he was falling. Sullivan dove into eternity with parts of his brain soaring up to the wild blue yonder.

In hand-to-hand combat, the Cubans were no match for the better trained and more determined Americans. Billy Coopbird, his black body glistening with sweat, had backed up against the rounded side of a turret, the back of a frantically struggling Cuban pressed against his chest. Coopbird had his hands around each end of a PPS machine gun and was pulling the weapon tightly against the man's throat, strangling the Cuban, who was clawing at the weapon with both hands, a look of utter horror on his face. He didn't claw very long. As if switched off, he suddenly went as limp as a soggy strand of spaghetti. Coopbird let him fall to the floor, turned to the left and, got the first full-blown shock of the day. Another Cuban, only five feet away, fired at him pointblank with a Tokarev auto-pistol. Two blunt-nosed 7.62mm bullets hit the front of the bulletproof vest. The first slug landed high in the chest, the second bullet just below the breast bone. Feeling as if he had been stung by hornets, Coopbird was surprised to find himself still standing. The Cuban was even more surprised, too stunned to fire at either Coopbird's head or legs or arms. Coopbird immediately flipped the PPS over in his hands and sent the last four slugs in the magazine into the Cuban. Dying, the man crashed against Roberto Calcines, another Castroite, and in doing so inadvertently saved the life of Lieutenant Commander Norris, who was using a brass-knuckled knife in his left hand and the empty individual multipurpose weapon—as a club—in his right, swinging, ripping and stabbing.

Roberto Calcines, aiming down on Norris with a PPS submachine gun, was about to pull the trigger when the corpse of the man shot by Coopbird fell against him and knocked him off balance. The PPS chattered off a dozen rounds, but instead of hitting Norris the projectiles raked across another Cuban and the SEALer who was about to cut his throat. Cuban and American went down in a spray of blood and cloth, falling into each other. Roberto Calcines attempted to straighten up, but the long burst, while not warning Norris, had alerted the Death Merchant, who snap-aimed and pulled the trigger of the right Auto Mag. Calcines' head exploded, parts and portions of skin, skull and brain making like shooting stars.

There were several reasons why the Death Merchant had lived through so many firefights, one being that he had developed visualization into a fine art. In a sense, this meant that he could see not only the picture as a whole, but also the fine details. In a practical sense, this meant that he was constantly watching his flanks as well as the area in front of him. The second reason was instinct, that preternatural "second sight" which all survivors possess to a high degree, that intangible something which automatically warned him when an enemy was coming in at him from the rear.

It was this visualization that enabled the Death Merchant to notice a large group of Cubans detach themselves from the fighting on the foredeck and edge toward the starboard steps on the side of the main deck midship housing. At first, Camellion thought the group was retreating because the Cubans were losing the battle. If that had been the case, the Cubans would have headed toward the ladders resting against the port side.

Instinct supplied the answer. Should the Cubans be able to gain access to the boat deck, they might succeed in making their way up the "tower" to the main control bridge. *That's what the trash is after,* Camellion thought, *the main control bridge.*

Yet something was not right about the group, about the men who were darting first one way, then another. That was it. One of the men didn't look "right." Somehow he was out of place. The answer stabbed at the Death Merchant. *His features aren't Latin. They're Slavic. The crud's a pig farmer!* Sure, it made sense. While nothing more than cannon fodder to the realistic Russians, the Cubans were being led by Soviet officers.

However, for the moment Camellion had other problems. At sight of the two *Fidelistas* swinging sub-guns in his direction, he jerked to the right, mentally aimed at the two Cubans and, with his arms extended in a broad *V,* fired both Auto Mags. Practically at the same time, one of the SEALers—the man looked like Radar on the television program "MASH"—triggered off a line of Gwinn Bushmaster projectiles at Julio Gutiérrez, the man at whom Camellion had fired with the left AMP.

The other Cuban, Andres Fonseca, took the .357 Magnum slug from the right AMP just below the hollow of the throat, the impact of the dynamite-powered slug opening a hole in him the size of a lemon and slamming him back with such force that he was almost lifted off his feet. As for Gutiérrez, he might as well have been in the center of an H-bomb explosion. The Death Merchant's big bullet banged him in the upper left chest and was spinning him around when "Radar's" stream of 5.6mm Fireball slugs ripped him first across the right side, then across the small of his back, the burst almost cutting him in two.

Again the Death Merchant had to give Norris credit, this time for his choice of weapons for his men. The SEALs were using not only IMPs but Bushmasters, Ingram Model 11s, Colt CAR-15s, and various kinds of "grease guns."

Camellion ducked low to the left and once more searched for the group of Cubans led by the Soviet officer. By now they had reached the starboard side of the midship housing and were busier than ever. One Cuban was running up the gang-way to the boat deck, a small brown package in his hands. *Yeah*, Camellion thought, *they're going to blow the bulkhead and go in from the chart room side. What a shock Torway and Meadows are going to get.*

Another Cuban, a brown package in his hands, was running around to the port side of the main deck. *He's going to blow the door to engineering. Damn!*

Looking all around him, and almost slipping on the deck thick with blood and gore, Camellion managed to get close to Forran and Coopbird who had developed the technique of fighting back to back. This "Odd Couple," as Camellion had privately dubbed them, had just put to sleep four Cubans who had been stupid enough to try to charge them. The four Cubans now lay sprawled on the deck, Mossberg .45 slugs in their bodies.

"Cover me while I reload," Camellion said. "The Cubans are trying to get to the main control bridge. Norris and his boys can handle this fracas."

As if to defy the Death Merchant, two explosions crashed against his ears. The Cubans had blown the bulkhead doors.

Chapter Ten

The Cubans and the dozen Soviet officers leading them were definitely having a bad day. Slowly, the Cubans on *Mohawk* were being cut to pieces. The fifty-six Cubans and the two Russian officers who had attacked *Atlantis II* met with instant failure.

The scientists on board the research vessel had lined the top of the port and starboard railings with packs of thermite. The two Soviet patrol boats had shot their six ladders to the starboard railing and the Cubans had began to crawl upward. The first Cubans had tossed grenades and were about to crawl over the top of the railing when the scientists detonated electronically the packs of thermite.

Caught in an instant hell of white molten metal burning at a temperature of 4,000 degrees, the first Cubans became human torches that, shrieking hideously, fell back against the other horrified men coming up the six ladders.

Just as much of a disaster was that the thermite quickly burned through the ends of the six aluminum ladders. With a loud creaking and groaning, the ladders crashed downward and fell into the water, taking the Cubans with them.

There was more in store for the surprised and angry Cubans. Although much of the enclosed railing had been eaten away by the thermite, reduced to a foot high in places, sailors crawled as close as possible to the still red-hot railing. They had to stop a dozen feet from the railing, not only because of the intense heat, but because of the machine gun slugs the gunners on the two Hop Toads were tossing at *Atlantis II*. Each sailor carried a bottle filled with a mixture of gasoline and oil, to which had been wired an electric detonating timer. Carefully each sailor turned the timer on each bottle to 60 seconds, then tossed the bottle over the smoking railing, as other sailors, who had inched forward on their bellies, began to throw sand on the wooden decking ignited by the thermite.

The bottles landed among the Cubans in the water and exploded, tossing flaming gasoline and oil over the trapped Cubans. Screams rang out from the trapped Castroites, shrieks that were a dirge to the men on board the two Soviet patrol boats, but a song of victory to the Americans on *Atlantis II*.

To make matters worse for the Cubans, the six collapsed ladders made it impossible for the two Soviet Hop Toads to flee. Under normal circumstances, electric motors would have automatically retracted the ladders into their tubes. In falling, however, the six ladders had damaged the control mechanisms so that now reversal was impossible.

From the viewpoint of the Cubans and their Russian officers, they were faced with disaster of the first magnitude. Forty feet from the starboard side of *Atlantis II*, their bows pointed west, the two Soviet patrol boats tilted heavily to starboard, each vessel off balance from the wrecked ladders in the water. Working as quickly as possible, Cubans with hack saws attempted to cut the ladders from the tubes. Vitali Losev and Pavl Ryndin, the Russian officers on the two Hop Toads, cursed and hurried them to greater speed. Between the two attack boats and *Atlantis II*, the blazing water continued to spread, drawing closer and closer to the two Soviet vessels, until finally Losev and Ryndin had no choice but to order the helmsmen to move the two crafts farther away from *Atlantis II*.

Clumsily, the two Soviet boats moved to the southwest, away from the side of *Atlantis*, once more stopping dead in the water when they were three hundred feet away from the floating laboratory, the six ladders still tilting them to starboard. It was a fatal mistake on the part of Losev and Ryndin who, in an effort to keep the fire from spreading to the Hop Toads, had forgotten about the Flak mount on the bow of *Atlantis II*.

All this time, the American gunners had not been able to fire, had not been able to depress the four cannon to an angle that would enable the 20MM projectiles to hit the close-in patrol boats. But now, at a distance of 300 feet, the two Hop Toads were sitting ducks.

The gunner on the Flak mount opened fire, the four cannon throwing out hundreds of 20MM projectiles that raked the two attack boats from bow to stern. Cubans on deck screamed, died, and fell into the water. Missiles cut into the small deck house and killed the helmsman, the navigation officer and Pavl Ryndin. Ten seconds later the Hop Toad exploded into a fireball tinged with oily black smoke, much of the blazing wreckage crashing onto the deck of the other patrol boat, which was only 30 feet to port.

Vitali Losev and six Cubans jumped overboard only moments before the vessel dissolved with a thunderous roar, and turned into thousands of pieces of burning junk that rained down on the helpless men struggling in the water. Screams of fear! Screams of intense agony! Loud sizzling and steam as fire reached water.

The jubilant Americans on *Atlantis II* saw a rounded stern sticking up out of the water, the rudder and twin propellers reflecting flickering shadows from burning wreckage that water had not yet reached. The stern slid under the water and was gone. And so were most of the Cubans who had been in the two patrol boats. Those still alive in the water kicked furiously to keep afloat.

The divers in the *Sumov* swimmer delivery vehicles were all Russians, the Cubans being too stupid to be dependable—all first rate frogmen who had received extensive training in both frigid and tropical waters. The Americans who had dived down to engage the Russians were more expert, better trained, and with greater motivation of purpose. Their method of attack was also superior to the Russians.

Fourteen American divers, power lanterns in their hands, swam toward the Soviet SDVs at the same level as the underwater vehicles, at 120 feet. Dozens of other divers dove deep into the darkness 100 yards west of the *South Dakota,* some staying at positions which would enable the Russians to pass directly over them, others diving just as deeply but swimming to the north and the south.

The Soviet SDVs stopped several hundred yards west of the *South Dakota* and discharged their divers—45 professional underwater demolition experts, each carrying a spear gun and ten 3-foot "reloads." Each diver also carried a mine filled with 6 pounds of cyclonite, more than enough to blow a 6-foot hole in the hull of any vessel, even a heavily armored battleship.

Commander Venyamon Antipin, the Russian officer leading the divers, suspected that there were more Americans than the divers with lanterns in the distance, the 14 coming straight at him and his men. Nonetheless, his orders were clear: swim to the American vessels and plant mines underneath their hulls. The 14 Americans should be easy to dispose of.

113

Antipin and his 44 divers swam straight into the cleverly designed trap. When the Russians were 25 yards from the Americans with the electric power-beam lanterns, the American divers pulled out underwater flares, jerked the igniter strings, and let the bright blue-white flares sink downward.

A worried Antipin suspected that the flares were a signal of some sort, and began debating whether he and his men should change course and try to swim over or under the Americans. But it was too late. All too quickly, Antipin and his men realized that they had been cleverly "suckered" in—boxed in, surrounded. Not only were enemy divers swimming toward them, but coming up at them from both flanks and even from the rear.

Antipin and his men could not see the fourth group of American frogmen who were swimming up toward the bottom hulls of the SDVs, all seven preparing their Darsher-6H firing tubes.

"Destroy the Amerikanski ships!" Those were the orders. And those ships were straight ahead. Antipin and his men didn't hesitate. They fired at the Americans with the power lanterns. Slim, 3-foot spears found three of the American divers. Their deep-dive suits exploded, the men went limp, died, and slowly started to sink to the black depths.

The Americans fired. A barrage of 3½-inch darts made hissing sounds as they cut through the water and punctured five Soviet divers, who jerked and flopped violently, like fish stabbed with a frog-gig.

The Russians who were reloading their spear guns didn't have time to complete their work, and those who had not fired were too surprised by the small size of the darts to react with a speed greater than that employed by the Americans.

By now the Americans were all around the Russians, and they were very fast in getting off another underwater cloud of darts. This time the Soviet frogmen were both enraged and horrified to see seven of their number struck by the vicious little missiles. Rage turned to fear and fear to dread when the Soviets realized that the enemy was carrying spear guns that didn't have to be reloaded, that fired off darts the same way an auto-pistol fires bullets. . . . Their fear increased when they heard a series of hollow explosions behind then, as though someone was beating on hollow drums. Other American divers had succeeded in coming up underneath the SDVs and were shooting Darsher-6H mines against the bottom hulls of the small vehicles, each mine exploding 20 seconds after

114

contact. . . . a small explosion, just large enough to make each swimmer delivery vehicle unusable.

One American diver missed the target and the mine missed. The diver-driver of the Russian SDV didn't wait to see what would happen next. *He knew!* Gloved hands shaking, he started the electric engine, turned the SDV around, and headed away from the area, dreading that he would have to report total failure. The attack was a disaster!

Three hundred feet to the east, many of the Soviet frogmen succeeded in reloading and firing off spears at the American frogman who were looping, diving, and barrel-rolling all around them. Three Americans caught spears and died quickly, their corpses sinking slowly, air bubbles streaming upward from where the steel shafts protruded from the Neoruperine suits.

The Russian divers, disorganized and sick with the knowledge of failure, did their best to survive. They ducked, and dodged, and wavered back and forth. In one final attempt to save their lives, they tried to dive to the safety of the dark water toward the bottom, some five hundred feet down. None succeeded. One by one they died from American darts, which stabbed into various parts of their bodies.

Swimming for his life, Commander Venyamon Antipin headed for the depths, using long powerful strokes. He was almost to the purple twilight zone when several dart-spears zipped into him—one in the back of his left shoulder, one in the right side of his neck.

Whooooshhhhhhhhhhhhhhhhhhhhhhhh!

The deep-dive suit collapsed and the air began bubbling away. The dart in his neck had barely pricked the skin. It had lost much of its penetration power in first going through an air hose; yet it had punctured the rubberized suit at the neck. Air was pulled from Antipin's lungs and an overriding sense of nightmare and unreality became his entire world, symbolic manipulations of consciousness no longer functioning. The Russian knew he was dying, not only being squeezed to death from water pressure but rapidly suffocating. Blackness dropped over his brain and his mind ceased to exist. So did he! His suit filling with water, he sank silently to the bottom— like a statue, arms and legs not moving—and came to rest among some sea ferns.

The American divers regrouped, reloaded their spear guns, and put together sections of electric shark prods. With all the fresh meat in the water, it would be Christmas and Thanksgiving all rolled into one, for the killers of the deep.

Led by Lieutenant Carmine Molina, the Americans headed east. There were Soviet attack boats that demanded their professional attention.

Richard Camellion, Josh Forran, and Billy Coopbird had managed to work their way close to the starboard side of the housing amidships, a lifeboat, swung inward to the deck on its davits, protecting them. The Cubans had blown the bulkhead to engineering on the port side of the main deck, but Camellion realized that in order for the enemy to reach the boat deck above, they would have to demolish the inside bulkhead. Such a project would require time. First the Cubans would have to overcome the sailors and officers inside Engineering.

The Cubans had also used explosives against the bulkhead to the chart room on the boat deck, on the starboard side of *Mohawk*. That the Cubans had gained entrance and were fighting it out with Cullen Torway, Philip Meadows, and a handful of technicians was in evidence from the roaring of automatic weapons.

From the end of the lifeboat, Forran looked dourly up the long stairway. The bulkhead had been blasted inward and the ragged doorway was still smoking.

"Charging up that stairway would be tantamount to suicide," the ONI agent said. "And if we went on the main deck, portside, we'd be stuck by the locked bulkhead at the top of the steps inside."

The Death Merchant carefully measured the distance, one part of his mind thinking of the real distinction between human beings and that which they considered their most deadly enemy—Death. The true distinction was between those who were willing to live at any price and those who suffered anything, come what may, in order to live with dignity, with their own pride as free human beings.

"Cover me," Camellion said to Forran. "After I go in, you and Billy can go up back to back and cover each other. The faster you and Billy do it, the better off you'll be."

"Let's get on with it," Forran said with a touch of grimness, and cocked the Ingram.

Coopbird sighed. "Old man Death, he gonna sit down on us for sure. We already taking in breath on borrowed time."

"Eventually we'll all be dead," Camellion said suavely. "But it won't happen today, not to us. See you guys later. Don't get your pants wet."

"Or bloody," added Forran. He raised the Ingram and pointed it at the top of the stairs.

An Auto Mag in his right hand and an Ingram in his left, Camellion moved from the side of the life boat, dashed to the bottom of the stairs, raced up them, and paused just before he came to the landing that sagged slightly from the force of the earlier explosion.

Do it! He took the final two steps in one leap, reached the landing, tore through the blasted bulkhead, and, listening to intuition, darted to the right. He saw in that lightning flash of a second that the Cubans were down behind overturned chart tables and chairs, and were firing at the two doorways inside the chart room — the door in the northeast corner that opened to the junior officers' wardroom, and the door to the east that was between the chart room and Assembly Area Two.

Momentarily, the Cubans and Major Ryurik Bogachiev, the Soviet officer in charge of the group, were taken off guard by the Death Merchant's unexpected appearance. Ramon Prendes and Raphael Roja, the two Cubans behind the overturned table to Camellion's right, had time only to turn their heads to the left and look up at Death—a blink of the eye before Camellion smashed them to the floor with a short burst of 9mm Ingram slugs, then leaped over the two corpses, got down beside them, propped up the still bleeding Roja, and wriggled behind the dead Castro chilipepper.

Major Bogachiev, down behind an overturned chart file across the room, raised a Stechkin machine pistol and triggered off a long burst, some of the nine-millimeter projectiles skimming over the table, but most cutting through the metal top, a few even thudding into the corpse of Roja. While other Cubans continued to fire at the two doorways, Armando Acosta, Jose Matar, and Eliseo Torriente concentrated on Camellion. At positions to the right of Bogachiev, they raked the table top with streams of PPS projectiles, the high velocity 7.62mm's punching scores of holes in the thin sheet metal. Six slugs struck Roja and tore off more pieces of his shirt, shredding the dead flesh of his chest. Another 7.62mm, most of its power spent in tearing through the table top, smacked the Death Merchant high in the chest on the right side. Wincing from the sharp sting, from the "trampoline" effect, he knew he had to do something—and quick—or the Cubans would eventually cut him up into little pieces. *And where were Forran and Coopbird?*

He fired off the entire magazine of the Auto Mag in his right hand, carefully spacing out the .357s along the underside of the metal table top, each big *Berroommmmm* ringing throughout the chart room. In spite of the loud roaring of machine guns, there were loud high-pitched *clangs* as the large, flat-nosed projectiles struck metal chart files, ripped through the metal, and buried themselves in paper or other items in the drawers. Four .357s, however, cut through the chart table top behind which were Bogachiev, Acosta, Matar, and Torriente. One bullet tore between Acosta and Torriente. Another brushed the top of Major Bogachiev's helmet in its passing. The third cut a burn mark on Matar's shirt, close to his neck. The fourth struck the barrel of Acosta's PPS, ricocheted, pinged against the wall, and came close to giving the three Cubans and the Russian officers a case of instant diarrhea.

The four men, wondering what kind of weapon the lone enemy was using, were hugging the floor with greater effort when Forran and Coopbird stormed into the chart room, their Ingrams firing short three-round bursts as they moved the weapons in horizontal motions.

Camellion's booming AMPs had given Forran and Coopbird his position and now, as they darted to the right, Forran yelled, *"Hold your fire! It's us!"*

Machine gun and pistol slugs zipping around them, Forran and Coopbird jumped behind the table, in that instant realizing that they were in a very dangerous position—no cover but the table, which already looked as if it had been attacked by a madman with a giant can opener.

While Camellion reloaded the Auto Mag, Forran bellycrawled to the end of the table, and got off a short burst of 9mm Ingram slugs. Billy Coopbird, borrowing from Camellion's imagination, struggled to prop up the bloody corpse of Ramon Prendes and use the dead man as a shield.

During the interim, Torway, Meadows, and seven sailors in the next room had heard Camellion's AMPs, Forran and Coopbird's Ingrams, and Forran call out to the Death Merchant. Correctly they deduced that the Cubans were now in a kind of narrow pincer trap. They also knew that sooner or later the Cubans on the main deck below would somehow reach Assembly Area Two, no doubt by blowing the bulkhead at the top of the inside stairs. To help Camellion, Forran and Coopbird, Torway and the others intensified their firing from the doorway, except for four sailor-technicians who kept watch over the bulkhead on the north side of the room.

Old pros, Major Bogachiev and the Death Merchant were aware of why the firing had intensified from the next room. The two men came to the same conclusion at the same time

There was one chance for success: take the fight to the enemy—*charge!*

"Oh, my my," exclaimed Forran at Camellion's suggestion of a charge. "But I suppose it's better than hiding behind a couple of Castro's spics."

"Thank God for these vests," Coopbird said.

As it came about, Major Bogachiev and the Cubans jumped up and rushed out from behind chart tables, files, and other pieces of furniture at the same time that the Death Merchant and his two men stormed out from behind the overturned chart table. From the doorway to the east, Torway, Meadows, and three sailors darted in with their hands filled with 9mm Hi-Power Browning auto-pistols.

Two Cubans raised their PPS submachine guns, but neither man had time to pull the triggers. Torway put two 9mm Browning slugs into the Castroite who was trying to cut down on Camellion, and Meadows killed the optimist who would have placed a dozen projectiles into Forran's Kevlar bulletproof vest and back protector.

The chart room was 10 feet by 15 feet, yet because of overturned furniture and the number of men involved, the shootout developed into a face-to-face confrontation, with some Cubans and Americans only 6 feet apart, such close contact making it impossible for either side to stop and reload once their weapons were empty. To torture both sides, the roaring of gunfire, beating against one's ears, was the worst kind of concussion. Breathing was difficult because of the fumes of burnt gunpowder.

Savagery took over. As the Cubans on the east side of the chart room clashed with Torway, Meadows, and the sailors, another group of stringy-bearded Cubans went after Forran and Coopbird, who had also emptied their Ingrams and were pulling their Mossberg Military .45s.

Detecting that the Death Merchant was somehow special, Major Bogachiev and the Cubans around him went after Camellion, aiming not only at the broad portion of his body protected by the Kevlar vest, but also at his legs and head.

Camellion ducked low, darted to his right, and, all in the same quick motion, fired the Auto Mag and the Ingram subgun, the latter of which he was using like an auto-pistol.

Major Bogachiev's stream of 9mm Stechkin M.P. bullets missed Camellion's left side by only a few scant inches. Armando Acosta's chain of 7.62 PPS projectiles went over the Death Merchant's head, several so close to the crown of his helmet that they came within a fraction of scraping the metal.

Jose Matar and Eliseo Torriente had not had time to shove fresh magazines into their PPS Soviet machine guns. They fired at Camellion with Tokarev and Tula-TT pistols. Torriente's three projectiles came close to Camellion's legs, but the Death Merchant had moved with lightning speed. One bullet did rip through the right pant leg of the jumpsuit, passing through the material several inches to the right of his knee. Matar's four T-TT slugs came very close, two buzzing by on either side of Camellion's head, the third and fourth 7.63mm shorts smacking the Kevlar vest high in the chest. The Death Merchant became more angry and snarled, "*Yeeeaaahhhhhhh!*" from the two sharp stings.

All his slugs from the earlier bursts with the AMP and the Ingram had missed, but the blasts had done the job of throwing off the aim of the Russian and the three Cubans. A second chance was out of the question for Major Bogachiev and the three Castroites.

In a low crouch, the Death Merchant fired the AMP and the Ingram. A swarm of 9mm Ingram projectiles erased Jose Matar's face and popped open his skull like a lemon hit by a blast from a double-barrelled shotgun. A massive heart attack couldn't have killed him quicker. Nor Eliseo Torriente! A .357 Magnum AMP projectile chopped him in the chest and punched him all the way back to the northside wall.

Very quick thinking saved Major Bogachiev and Armando Acosta's lives. They knew they couldn't retreat from the *Amerikanski*'s slugs. They didn't have time to reload either. Bogachiev's Stechkin was empty, and so was Acosta's PPS. The two men did the only thing possible under the circumstances. They threw their weapons at the Death Merchant and, at the same time, charged him.

Major Bogachiev's Stechkin machine pistol struck Camellion in the left shoulder, and he had to duck—almost falling—to keep the PPS from hitting him in the face. By the time he regained his balance, Bogachiev and Acosta were on him, each man grabbing his wrists and tossing blows.

The Death Merchant ducked a left fist jab by Costa and twisted away from Bogachiev's right-handed Sambo chop, which, if it had landed, would have cracked his neck. Yet the Death Merchant couldn't free his left wrist from the steel grip of the Russian's left hand. Armando Acosta now gripped Camellion's right wrist with both hands and forced him to drop the Auto Mag, as a very fast Major Bogachiev put his right hand on Camellion's left wrist and, with both hands, twisted.

120

The Death Merchant's fingers opened and the Ingram fell to the floor.

Trained in Sambo,[1] Major Bogachiev was too experienced to stoop and try to pick up either the AMP or the Ingram. Instead, he tried to stomp the Death Merchant's left instep and aimed a three-finger-and-thumb stab at Camellion's throat. Expecting such a common-sense move from the Russian officer, Camellion jerked his head to one side, brushed aside the right-handed spear-finger stab with his left forearm, and rattled the Russian by laughing in the startled man's face. Major Bogachiev's foot smash missed because, while the Russian was bringing down his right heel, the Death Merchant's left leg was coming up at Acosta, who had been stupid enough to try to pick up the Auto Mag. Camellion's knee connected with the bottom of Acosta's chin, the blow bringing a strangled cry of agony from the Cuban as his teeth broke off, but only after they had bitten off the end of his tongue. Acosta's mouth filling with warm, salty blood, his mind began to skid, and he sank to his knees, overcome by nausea.

The Death Merchant instantly kicked the poor slob full in the face, driving shattered frontal bones into the man's brain, and staggered Major Bogachiev with a *Furi Uchi Ken* crack, a Goju-Ryu swinging knuckle blow that landed on the Russian's upper lip and sent him reeling back, spitting out teeth and blood. Now on the offensive, the Death Merchant went after the pig farmer with a cold and vicious vengeance.

Close by, Josh Forran and Billy Coopbird were fighting like wild men to stay alive. While Forran used the last .45 cartridge in his right Military Mossberg auto-pistol to blow away a Cuban, he kicked another coming at him with a knife, the tip of his foot flattening the man's testicles. As if hit by the explosion from a stick of dynamite, the Cuban collapsed from sheer shock, his eyes two round saucers, his mouth wide open in a soundless "O."

With both Mossbergs empty, Forran began swinging alongside Coopbird, who had slipped a massive pair of brass knuckles on his right hand, and had his left hand wrapped around a Mossberg so that its butt protruded outward. The Jamaican broke one Cuban's jaw with a well-connected right cross, the brass knuckles hitting with the force of a hammer. Coopbird then cursed over his own carelessness as Salvador Bárcena

[1] The Russian version of karate. All KGB officers are trained in Sambo.

made the fatal mistake of trying to stab him in the chest with a knife that had a large Bowie-like blade. Bárcena paused in surprise when the blade failed to penetrate the Kevlar material. Bárcena was amazed. Coopbird was damned lucky. An ice pick might have penetrated the vest.

Bárcena tried to draw back, now genuinely afraid. But he was too slow.

"Mon, you be dead!" hissed Coopbird with a fake Jamaican accent.

He slammed the butt of the Mossberg .45 down on Bárcena's wrist and chopped him in the temple with the brass knuckles, feeling the metal cave in the thin temporal portion of the skull. Bárcena dropped as if his legs had been sawed off at the hips.

Death was having a feast at the east end of the chart room. Torway, Meadows, and the three sailors, motivated by the biological imperative of self-preservation, fought with a fury that even they found incredible. All five held Hi-Power Brownings in both hands, and they triggered the ten autopistols with terrible efficiency. But not all of the Americans were lucky.

Lieutenant Manuel Pazos stitched Dave Arbornott perpendicularly with a stream of PPS slugs, ripping open the sailor from belly to brain. Arbornott didn't even have time to wish he had put on a Kevlar vest. He died instantly and fell back through the doorway.

Pazos next turned his attention to Billy Coopbird, but before the fat Cuban could sight in on the Jamaican and pull the trigger, Wally Robbins raised both Brownings and punched several holes in the man's chest with 9mm projectiles. The double impact knocked Pazos against the left side of Anselmo Guerra, a collision that destroyed Guerra's sighting in on Josh Forran. The Tula-TT in Guerra's hand cracked. But the bullet missed Forran and hit a Cuban trying to come in behind Josh, the bullet going across his right shoulder and boring through the side of his neck. Drowning in his own thick blood, the Cuban melted to the floor, a widening pool of blood slowly spreading from his mouth.

There were five Cubans on the north side of the room, all five wearing black berets. On the left side of each beret was a red metal triangle, point downward, a white star in the center, the badges indicating that the men were special commandos of the Fidel Castro Brigade, the best Cuba had to offer.

Three of the Cubans turned to meet the attack from Tor-

122

way, Meadows, and the sailors. The other two turned to assist Major Ryurik Bogachiev, who now realized that, in Camellion, he was confronted with an expert.

Too busy staying alive to be afraid, Torway and Meadows darted to one side, both to the right, both firing the four Brownings as they sought the safety of the floor. Jackson Napier, one of the sailors, fell flat where he stood, triggering off several shots as he "hit the prone."

In contrast, Wally Robbins stayed put and fired in a crouching stance, his two Browning slugs catching Carlos Luzardo in the stomach. With a loud cry, Luzardo started to go down, a shocked expression on his face. So did Robbins, blood gushing from where his head had been. Alberto Ortiz had triggered off a short burst of PPS slugs, which had exploded Robbins's skull, getting off the shots a split second before one of Cullen Torway's 9mm projectiles popped him in the right side of the chest, and Phil Meadows's two bullets struck Cirilo Vizoso, the latter of whom had fired a final burst with a Stechkin machine pistol on full automatic. All six nine-millimeter slugs went wide of their mark, except one which cut through the fleshy part of Meadows's right arm, the hunk of lead tearing through the lower part of the deltoid muscle and breaking the humerus. Meadows cursed and found the Browning slipping from his broken, bleeding arm. Damn it! It was his tennis arm, too!

The Death Merchant had just employed a *Kake Uke* to block Major Bogachiev's high, right legged snap-kick aimed at his chest. The Russian had walked into the trap. In this case, he had "kicked" himself into a fatal error. Off balance by the kick that missed, his defenses for the moment were down. The Death Merchant speared him in the solar plexus with a *Nukite* spear hand. But the Russian officer had edged back and the thrust had lost much of its power. Yet it did have enough force to make the Russian wince with pain.

Alert as always, Camellion sensed that two Cubans were about to attack him from the rear. Turning slightly to his right, he let Bazan Zayas have an *Empi* smash in the stomach, Camellion's right elbow practically tying Zayas's stomach in a bow around his backbone.

Simultaneously, Camellion executed a high, left-legged backward *Kakato Geri*, the heel of his foot crashing into the abdomen of Francesco Suarez, who had been about to stab him in the back of the neck with a short-bladed bayonet. Zayas was already down on his knees and in agony, his arms hugging his stomach. Now it was Suarez's turn. Retching, bile running out of his mouth, Suarez let out a long *"Ohhhhh,"* collapsed, fell on his face, and began to squirm like some kind of gigantic worm.

Major Bogachiev was like a man who had a choice between being hanged or shot. He couldn't run and he couldn't win. He tried a sword-ridge hand strike at Camellion's neck and, with his left hand, a spear thrust to Camellion's throat. The Death Merchant was too fast for the Russian. He jerked to one side, jumped back, and countered with a very high *Mae Geri* snap-kick. The ball of his foot smashed into Ryurik Bogachiev's face, a grand slam that broke both jaws, made mush of the Russian's nose, and broke off most of his teeth. His face a bloody, broken mess, Bogachiev wilted to the floor—the Death Merchant right behind him, scooping up the Auto Mag and the Ingram and listening to a series of hollow-sounding underwater explosions to the north, just off the port side of the *Mohawk*. The American divers had succeeded in planting mines under the Soviet patrol boats. There was also the sound of automatic firing from directly below. Lieutenant Commander Norris and his men had stormed into engineering on the main deck.

The chart room resembled the crust of hell. Overturned chart tables and other furniture! Corpses lying at grotesque angles! The floor slippery with blood! The air so thick with blue fumes that breathing was difficult and one's mouth tasted bitter.

Breathing heavily, Josh Forran and Billy Coopbird looked all around them, amazed. Robinson Crusoe must have worn a similar expression when he discovered Friday's footprint in the sand!

His mouth a tight line, Cullen Torway was shoving fresh magazines into his Hi-Power Brownings. Meadows, holding his right arm with his left hand over the right wrist, leaned against the wall while Jackson Napiler cautiously pushed himself up from the floor. He jumped slightly when he heard Richord Camellion's Auto Mag roar. Turning, he saw Bazan Zayas jerk from the impact of the .357 bullet. A final shudder, and Zayas lay still. Napiler stared at the tall American in the black jumpsuit, his feelings a mixture of admiration and revulsion. Napiler had never spoken a word to Camellion. He didn't know anything about him and had only listened half-heartedly to the whispered rumors of other sailors on board *Mohawk*. Now, watching the Death Merchant, Napiler felt that the rumors were true. Richard Camellion was not only the most cold-blooded man he had ever seen, but he was the twin brother of catastrophe, a man whose natural habitat was the bleak and dark landscape of Death.

Camellion proved it by dropping the muzzle of the Ingram toward Francesco Suarez, who had rolled over on his back and was attempting to sit up. He quit trying when he saw the dark muzzle of the Ingram and the intense blue eyes staring down at him. Yet a part of the Cuban whispered there might still be a chance for life.

"No tire más, no tire más," he mumbled. He gave up all hope when he read the finality of decision in the blue eyes. *Sí,* die bravely.

"Viva Cuba Libre!" he croaked, hate in his eyes. *"Viva la Revolución! Viva—"*

"Adiós, estúpido," Camellion said and pulled the trigger.

A short burst of 9mm slugs silenced Suarez forever.

"Damn it, don't kill the ivan," Torway called out in an angry voice. "The son-of-a-bitch might be able to give us a lot of valuable information."

Forran, who had moved closer to Camellion, glanced reproachfully at the Death Merchant. "It's possible those dimwits might have known something important. You shouldn't have terminated them."

"They're only excess baggage." Camellion jerked the empty magazine from the Ingram, pulled a full one from his ammo bag, thrust it into the butt of the weapon, pulled back the cocking bolt, and sprayed all the Cubans on the floor. Never assume an enemy is dead. Always be positive.

Lieutenant Commander Norris's loud voice came from Assembly Area Two, *"Don't fire! It's us!"*

"Come ahead," Camellion called back. Once more he shoved a full magazine into the Ingram and glanced at Norris who stalked into the chart room, followed by five of his men. All six had smoke-smudged faces, and their fatigues were dirty and torn.

Norris put his hands on his hips, looked around the fume-filled room, and slowly nodded, satisfied with what he saw, until his hard eyes came to rest on Phil Meadows. "How bad is it?"

"The bullet's still in. The bone's broken and it hurts like hell," Meadows replied, gritting his teeth in pain. "I won't be doing handsprings for a while."

Norris jerked a thumb toward one of his men and snapped, "Get him down to the infirmary." Then he blinked rapidly at the Death Merchant. "The Cubans are cold meat, except for

125

five who surrendered. I wish we had gunned them down, like these cruds." He pushed a foot against the corpse of Bazan Zayas. "They're only Russian stooges. I doubt if they could give us the correct time of day."

"He can," said Camellion. He pointed at Major Bogachiev, who, starting to regain consciousness, had begun to make groaning sounds. "He's an ivan. He'll have to write his answers to our questions. I think that maybe both his jaws are broken." Camellion turned to several of the SEALS with Norris. "Haul him down to the hospital and stay with him."

The two men glanced at Norris, who nodded. They then went over to Bogachiev, picked him up by the armpits and dragged him from the chart room.

"Those explosions," started Forran, wiping his face. "Our boys got to the Hop Toads with mines?"

"Every damned one." Norris gave a suppressed laugh. "All six blew up. We're tossing the dead Cubans overboard, and you should see the water! There's enough moonlight to see the sharks. They're gorging themselves."

"We could toss flowers on the water," commented Cullen Torway, his face revealing amusement, "if we had some. Flowers cover everything, even graves."

"What the situation on *Atlantis* and the *S.D.*?" Camellion asked.

Norris patted the walkie-talkie on his belt. "I received the reports before I came in here. The *South Dakota* didn't even get her paint scratched. Seven were killed on *Atlantis*. Four of them were my guys. But the Cuban trash didn't even get aboard. Hell, some of the scientists got the idea to use thermite on the railing. It worked beautifully." He paused for a moment, then added bitterly, "We lost fourteen on this tub. Three are wounded and in pretty bad shape. Four, counting Meadows. Another dozen have some cuts and bruises, but nothing serious."

Billy Coopbird said thoughtfully, "We Jamaicans have a saying that a man's alive as long as he's remembered, that he's killed only by forgetfulness—a rather ridiculous saying in my scheme of things."

"Dead is dead," Forran said flatly. "When consciousness goes, you go. You're gone, nonexistent. What good is being remembered if you're not aware of it?"

Norris moved a step closer to the Death Merchant, who was brushing off his jumpsuit. "I guess we won't argue about the next step. We've got to counterattack immediately, hit the Ruskies with everything we've got. And we have plenty. This

126

tub and the *South Dakota* are loaded with missiles—Sky Flashes, Shrikes, Lynx-4s, and Sea-Demons, all tied in to an Asroc System. In one salvo, we can slam several hundred missiles into those Soviet ships. *Bang!* End of mission. *Kingfisher* can take care of the dome and the other buildings below the surface."

"Nope, we can't use missiles. We'll attack, but missiles are out," said Camellion, watching Norris's eyes. The pupils expanded rapidly, indicating that his emotional barometer had risen to very stormy weather.

Norris appeared stunned, his face livid with anger and frustration.

"No missiles! Do you realize what you're saying?" he raged. He made a motion with his arms, his right hand forming a fist. "Our orders are to retaliate. The Russians used missiles. We have every right to hit 'em with everything non-nuclear in our arsenal. You're not going to tell me otherwise."

"I just did," Camellion said in a calm voice. "We are not going to use missiles because that is what the Soviets are expecting us to do. We know damn good and well they have anti-missiles. We didn't have to use ours because of 'Emma.' The Russians won't have a choice; they'll use anti-missiles, then toss bigger stuff back at us."

Anger slowly faded from Norris's face and his expression became serious and as grim as the other men's.

"I don't want to risk developing a MAD [Mutual Assured Destruction] situation. One nuclear warhead, just one, and the whole world explodes! A miscalculation and World War Three becomes a reality. There's a better way to attack the Soviets, and missiles play no part in it."

Forran spoke up, "It seems to me that any move we make entails some risk. But I agree in regard to missiles. World War Two started because of a miscalculation on Hitler's part. He didn't believe that France and England would declare war when he attacked Poland. Let's not make the same mistake."

"Us and Hitler," snorted Torway. "I don't think that's a valid comparison."

"Perhaps not, but a miscalculation knows no time. One now would be just as valid as one thirty years ago—and just as fatal."

Red Norris grimaced. "Okay, we don't use missiles," he said irritably and gave the Death Merchant a long, demanding look. "We have less than a hundred fighting men, and we don't have time to fly more in from the States. We can't use sailors in an attack. To top it off, the Russians have the Cubans to draw on. Damn it, there's no telling how many Cuban soldiers might be on their way to defend those Soviet ships. Tell me, Camellion. How do we attack?"

The Death Merchant's brow furrowed in thought; then he drew in a long breath and sighed. "The second thing we do is haul up anchor, head west, and make the pig farmers think we're turning tail."

"I'll be damned," Coopbird said. "Such a method seems rather strange."

"What's the first thing we do?" asked Norris acidly.

"We go to the main control bridge and have a pow-wow with Webber," Camellion answered. He then turned and headed for the starboard side doorway, his thoughts gloomy, but not because of the present situation with the Soviets in the Caribbean. Conditions with mankind had already gone too far. What might happen in the Caribbean was of little consequence. The physical earth was entering a new vibratory field, with new frequencies weaving a web over the affairs of man. Camellion was positive that a very mysterious esoteric phenomenon was lurking in the very near future. The new decade, the 1980s, would not be one of peace, but of hunger, pestilence, and death . . . years of Orwellian nightmares. The thought of SHC, Spontaneous Human Combustion, burned in Camellion's mind.

It might very well be that the New Age of Horror has already begun. . . .

Chapter Eleven

The sense of urgency in the planning room of the *Mohawk* was only part of the general tension. The other half was the acute awareness that "PINK INK" could explode into World War III. Or as Forran called it, "The War of the Mushrooms." The only consolation, shared mutually by the Americans, including Richard Camellion, was that the Joint Chiefs of Staff had—by radio—given their blessing to the plan. There had to come a time to stand firm against the gangsterism of the Soviet Union. That time had come. That time was now. There was only one problem: how to attack the Russians with the most possible speed and with a minimum of loss, and yet sink the *Vitiaz*, the *Mikhail Tukhachevsky*, and the *Suarez Guyol*, the Cuban ship that had brought the brigade of Cuban soldiers to the Soviet expedition.

Commander Jason Webber was more annoyed than tense. The hell with World War III. It was only a matter of time before World War III became a reality. It might as well be now as later. It was the thought of moving in a direction away from the Soviets that was abhorrent to him, an ice pick chipping away at his pride—even if the west heading was only a tactical maneuver. By 10.00 hours, when the men were entering the planning room, the three vessels had reached a distance of 68 miles west of the three Russian vessels.

The Death Merchant was annoyed for another reason, one for which he couldn't blame the Soviet Union. Josh Forran was eating a sandwich and making noises like a pig. Intolerable to Camellion (*Next he'll be talking with his mouth full!* he thought), who was a firm believer in three principles, come hell or high water—love of one's country, respect for the elderly, and good manners. Those three would never go out of style.

Concealing his annoyance with Josh, Camellion listened to Humphrey Frimholtz, who, with his usual aplomb, had jumped ahead of the immediate discussion and was already rattling off statistics and fighting World War III.

"In an all-out nuclear conflict, we wouldn't be too bad off," Frimholtz was saying. "At this point I'm referring to our nation, not to us here in the Caribbean. The Titan and Minuteman missile systems comprise our fixed ICBM system. We have a thousand Minutemen in silos. They can be fired in an instant, although they are believed to be potentially vulnerable to a first-strike attack. The third side of our deterrent triangle is our force of Polaris submarines. If my memory serves me correctly, and it always does, we have 41 P-subs, with approximately 650 SLBMs and 5,400 warheads."

Cullen Torway grinned happily. "More than enough to make the Soviet Union a radioactive wasteland for the next hundred years."

"The latest report is that the Soviet Union has 950 SLBMs," Frimholtz droned on. "On our debit side, too, is that the only Soviet threat to our SLBMs is their ASW forces, a rather weak defense against our Polaris-Poseidon system, and probably an even weaker threat to our Trident class of submarine. Best of all, the consensus is that Soviet technology on the high seas lags five to seven years behind ours."

Captain Claude McConachie, immaculate in his white uniform, took the briar pipe out of his mouth, all the while nodding. He glanced in agreement at Frimholtz. "There's truth in what you say, I know that our attack submarines are superior to the Soviet Union's. Our submarines—"

McConachie quickly explained that American nuclear attack submarines carried the SUBROC system, an underwater launch missile that maintained a rocket trajectory until it reached the vicinity of the target, when it released a depth charge. The charge would then follow a ballistic trajectory into the water and descend to a predetermined depth, from 1,500 to 2,000 feet, and explode. The depth charge could either be conventional or nuclear. Another excellent feature is that SUBROC could be launched from a submarine's torpedo tubes. This method allowed carrying interchangeable numbers of SUBROC missiles and torpedoes. Another advantage to the system was that it did not create any wake. Enemy subs could not detect it by sonar, since in its final approach it became an air-to-water missile.

"But it's our Raytheon BBQ2 sonar system that has it all over the Russians," McConachie said. In response to questioning looks from Torway, Forran, and Meadows (whose arm was in a sling), McConachie explained that the BBQ2 sonar system employed the BQS6 active sonar with transducers in approximately 15-foot diameter at the bow—a total waste of time on McConachie's part since no one but Commander Webber and the Death Merchant knew what he was talking about.

"We also have BQR7 passive sonar with hydrophones mounted on the forward side of the hull," McConachie said.

He said that while active sonar is ideal for fire-control purposes, it has a much shorter range compared to the passive sonar, and also provides the enemy with easy detection. "You see, the passive sonars have been so improved that contacts are obtained at long distances. That is how we know the Soviet sub is behind us at nine miles, trailing us. And a lot of improvement has been made in determining bearing with sufficient accuracy to provide continuous inputs to the fire-control system."

"I take it you fellows no longer look through a periscope and say, 'Fire!' " Coophird said, smiling.

"Hardly," McConachie said stiffly. Patiently he explained that the submarine's fire control was a central computer that received input from all the sensors and translated this data to the weapons positioning on potential targets. The operator would select the target and mode of attack, and the computer would transmit the information to the designated weapon—in short, taking over the continuing problem solution.

"As you might expect, the Soviets have the same kind of on-target firing system, but theirs is less sophisticated and much less accurate."

All this time, the Death Merchant had sat quietly, his hands folded on the green felt of the table, his patience rapidly dwindling. Now, he had had enough. *Frimholtz is an impractical 'Dr. Strangelove,'* he thought, *and McConachie must think he's on a lecture circuit. Time to put an end to it.*

He spoke with a quiet firmness, his eyes stabbing from Captain McConachie to Humphrey Frimholtz. "Gentlemen, we're not here to discuss World War Three, or how the firing system of *Kingfisher* works. My only interest is the three Soviet vessels."

"I second, third, and fourth the motion," grunted Red Norris. Since the Cuban attack, his attitude toward Camellion had changed from one of resentment to one of respect, his manner showing that he considered Camellion an equal. His eyes jumped across the table to Camellion. "My only concern is our going through the hull of the *Mikhail Tukhachevsky.* I can understand your reasoning, but the odds against obtaining any real information—is the risk worth it?"

"I've been thinking along the same lines," Forran said, somewhat reluctantly. "I'm not afraid of the ship going down with us on board. Bulkheads will close automatically and seal off the flooded compartment, but swimming into the flooded section, then blasting the closed bulkhead or going straight upward—it's one enormous gamble."

"I'm counting on surprise," Camellion said. "The Russians certainly won't be expecting us to come on board from below the waterline. By the time they realize what has happened, I intend for us to be on dry decks and have the advantage."

Captain McConachie cut in, "There won't be any difficulty in sinking the other two ships. Two SUBROC missiles will blow them out of the water. A couple of pounds of regular explosive will blow a hole in the side of the *Mikhail Tukhachevsky.* We still have to work out the coefficients. One thing we don't have to worry about is detection. With the Box cloaking the boat, the Russians won't even know we're there."

"Until they hear the explosions!" laughed Cullen Torway.

"There should have been some kind of fail-safe included in the overall plan," Commander Webber said. He looked deliberately at the Death Merchant. "It's a damn poor game plan in my opinion—destroying the dome and the smaller buildings below, in advance of sinking the two ships and blasting the *Mikhail Tukhachevsky.* Why not hit the ships on the surface first?"

"Pressure for one thing," Camellion said. He moved back slightly to avoid a shaft of sunlight slanting through a porthole and hitting the table. "The pressure generated by those underwater detonations would crush us like eggshells. All the blasts below have to be over and done with by the time we leave *Kingfisher.*"

Phil Meadows looked and sounded doubtful. "Synchronizing the chopper attacks with the surface hits is going to be tricky, but the timetable can be worked out."

"Two or three minutes either way won't make any difference," Camellion said. "Surprise is the key element."

Forran tapped ash from a cigarette into an ashtray. "What assurance do we have that the Russians won't see us transfer from *Atlantis* to *Kingfisher*?" he asked with feeling. "You know that I mean *hear* and not *see*? The ivans would have to

132

have divers under the hull to see us leave the observation chamber in the bottom hull."

Commander Webber said offhandedly, "It will take another few hours to convert the observation chamber to a diving chamber."

The Death Merchant started to speak, but Captain McConachie beat him to the explanation. "It's simple, Mr. Forran. *Kingfisher* is five miles ahead of us. The Russian submarine is nine miles behind us. With the Box cloaking our boat, she's 'invisible' to the Soviets. Her radio float antenna is too small for the Russians to pick up on either radar or sonar. Even if they did get a read-out, they wouldn't associate it with a sub that 'isn't there.' "

"The Russians are not stupid," Christopher Humbard said emphatically. "They might very well get the idea we're waltzing them around with some kind of cloaking mechanism."

"You'd better believe it!" Camellion's voice dripped pure venom. "We'll waltz them in a final dance of death."

Humbard, who privately considered Camellion a brilliant psychopath, glanced distastefully at Camellion. "Fate has always been a tricky bastard. The affair could turn out to be your own funeral."

"Very possibly." Camellion was cheerfully. "If it does turn out to be my funeral, I won't know about it, will I?" He scratched the top of his head. "Then again, maybe I would. Wouldn't that be interesting?"

Commander Webber turned his head toward the Death Merchant. "It's agreed then, as we discussed earlier." He glanced at his wristwatch. "We'll proceed another thirty miles—roughly that—then come to a full stop, and put men over the side and fake work on the propellor of *South Dakota.*"

"Agreed," Camellion said. "If anyone has a better idea, now is the time to put it on the table."

"I think your plan will give us the edge, Camellion." Cullen Torway said. "Hell, with thermite and vomit gas, the Russians and their Cuban stooges won't have much of a chance. But I do think it's going to be a waste of time. What's his name—Bogachiev? That son-of-a-bitch swore he didn't even know about the drilling going on at the dome. You could tell he was speaking the truth. Anyhow, I think he was."

"So do I," agreed Commander Webber. "With God's help, we'll win and do it without starting another world war." Noticing the broad smile crossing Camellion's lean face, Webber's eyes narrowed, and the lines around his mouth tightened.

"That wasn't meant to be funny, Camellion. Or could it be that you don't believe in God?"

"Commander, I wasn't laughing at you," Camellion said, half-seriously. "I was only thinking that if I were God, I'd chuck the whole damn human race and start over again."

Josh Forran smiled, then lit a cigarette.

Billy Coopbird roared with laughter. "Ah, mon, the Good Lord, he done do that," he said, using his fake accent. "He made it rain, mon. For forty days and forty nights, He make it rain. The world, it fill with water. It say so in de Good Book!"

"This go-around He gonna use de fire!" Camellion cracked. "He gonna use like nuclear warheads. It say that too in de Good Book."

"Like hell it does," laughed Forran. "It says only fire."

"Okay, so the old prophets didn't have a tape recorders or stenographers," Camellion said lazily. "They should have said hydrogen bombs."

No one smiled. No one laughed. Forran and Coopbird, however, wore expressions of amusement.

"Gentlemen, let's get to work." The Death Merchant pushed back his chair and stood up.

Chapter Twelve

With Captain Boris Ruzorkaski walking rapidly beside him, Colonel Anatole Bersenko hurried from the radio room on the first bridge deck to the briefing room on the second deck of the forward superstructure. When Bersenko and Ruzorkaski entered the room, the four men at the table became silent and watched the two men take their places at the table.

"The American ships have stopped dead in the water," Bersenko said. He pulled his chair closer to the table and reached for the half-empty bottle of fruit juice. "I talked with Captain Rozichev. The *Cesarevitch* has moved to within five miles southeast of the Americans. Rozichev reported that the Americans are apparently having trouble with either the rudder or the propeller of their destroyer. Divers with cutting torches and other equipment have gone below the waterline. Rozichev doesn't dare send diver scouts to ascertain the validity of the Americans' difficulty. Evaluations, gentlemen?" He finished pouring a small amount of juice into the glass of warm tea, and recorked the bottle.

"None of this is logical," Lieutenant General Vladilen Zudin said, frowning deeply. "The Americans slaughtered the Cubans we sent against them and all of our own divers, except one who had the good sense to turn his vehicle around and come home. It was a catastrophe! Antipin, Chovensky, Likaro, Bogachiev—all of them dead! Why should the Americans run? Somewhere along the line we are missing something."

"Right after our defeat, they should have attacked," Major Feliks Turkin said. A slim but powerful man, with sunken eyes and a soft voice. His coal black hair that always looked uncombed made him resemble a bomb-throwing Bolshevik of the early 1900s. He was second-in-command of fifty sea commandos, or *Ziaistvo Yennaya*.[1] Lieutenant General Vladilen Zudin was his superior.

Captain Sergei Soidra, the skipper of the *Mikhail Tukhachevsky*, looked steadily at Colonel Bersenko. "Did Rozichev mention the American submarine?" In his fifties, Soidra was an ugly man of medium height, with a large nose, steel-rimmed glasses, and a mass of thick brown hair decorated with long streaks of gray.

"There isn't any sign of the American submarine," Bersenko said slowly. "Frankly, I'd be less concerned if our boat had the enemy sub in sight. Rozichev said they'd been using long-range radar scan constantly. Nothing. The American sub has vanished."

"Exactly like our three divers," said Albert Didov, who was the first officer of the *Mikhail Tukhachevsky*. "Remember how it was? Their deep-dive vehicle was on sonar when it disappeared."

Captain Soidra made mocking sounds with his thick lips. "Come, come, Albert. Don't tell us that you believe in Dr. Trovtsev and his 'Other Intelligences'?"

"We are very close to the Bermuda Triangle," pursued Didov. Toying with his glass of tea, he kept his eyes downcast. "All the strange happenings have been documented; they're not just rumor." He looked up, his eyes sweeping the other men. "We can't deny that 'something' grabbed three of our divers. We can't pretend they're not missing."

"The disappearance of the American nuclear vessel is something to think about." Captain Boris Ruzorkaski glanced at Didov, who was broad-shouldered with a long scar on his right cheek. He usually wore a pair of dark sunglasses and always chain-smoked. "Suppose whatever it is in the Bermuda Triangle did kidnap the American sub and its crew? That could well be the reason why the American force has left the area."

"There could be some truth in that," Feliks Turkin said. "The *Kingfisher* was their best weapon, their best deterrent against us. It was there only for show. They no more intended to use nuclear weapons than we did." Turkin's eyes went from face to face, looking for agreement.

"Comrade, even if you are only half-right, none of that explains why all our missiles missed during yesterday's attack," said Lieutenant General Zudin, grim-visaged. "I can under-

[1] The literal translation means "Fighters of Water."

stand one or two missing, but all of them—hundreds of feet off the mark! Ridiculous."

"We can't be certain they missed that far," Turkin offered. "No one came back to report, with the exception of the single diver. He was under the water and didn't see where the *Lzumruds* hit. But they were far off the mark, according to his report about concussions."

"There's other evidence," Colonel Bersenko said. "The three American ships sustained no damage. If they are having trouble with the destroyer, it wasn't caused by any of our missiles, or they wouldn't have gotten as far as they have. They're roughly a hundred and sixty kilometers west of us."

Albert Didov said firmly, "The misses of our *Lzumruds* don't surprise me, not in this section of the Caribbean."

"Nonsense." Boris Ruzorkaski dismissed Didov's words with a wave of his hand. "You're talking science fiction, comrade." He laughed slightly and crushed his cigarette butt. "I'm not inclined to believe that the 'Other Intelligences' made our missiles fall off target. That's too much."

"This Bermuda Triangle business is nothing more than a clever bit of American propaganda." Lieutenant General Zudin was wearily ironical. "There isn't any mystery. The Americans have either been ordered to pull out or else their submarine developed some kind of trouble. It left the area and was somehow missed by the sonar on our own U-boat. Who cares what might have happened? The Americans are gone, and we can continue with the project."

"It's a damned shame that the *Cesarevitch* can't finish off the Americans." Feliks Turkin was bitter. "It would be so easy with rocket torpedos, and we owe those capitalist swine for what they did to us yesterday."

"That's quite enough of that war-mongering talk," snapped Colonel Bersenko, his tone a clear warning. "Our orders from Moscow, in spite of yesterday's disaster, are implicit. We are not to pursue or take any further action against the three American ships. We don't want history accusing us of starting a world war."

Lieutenant General Zudin opened his mouth to speak, but Bersenko raised a restraining hand. While Zudin outranked him, Bersenko was not only the real boss of the Soviet force, he was KGB. Anyhow, Zudin was in the Soviet Army. He and the others maintained a respectful silence and waited for Bersenko to speak.

"I recall reading some years ago of an experiment that United States Navy made in October of 1943. They conducted a series of tests in an attempt to make a destroyer disappear. As I remember, the U.S. Navy made use of an artificially induced magnetic field in the experiment, which, reportedly, was a success, except for the deleterious effect on the crew. Some of the crew never reappeared. Others died after reappearing. Many who did return were stark raving mad. Gentlemen, that happened almost forty years ago. Who knows what progress the Americans have made since then, assuming the original experiment really took place?" He paused to take a sip of fruit juice.

For several moments there was silence. Captain Ruzorkaski lit a cigarette. Feliks Turkin avoided Albert Didov's gaze, afraid that the always suspicious Bersenko would think that he and Didov were sharing thoughts not complimentary to what Turkin suspected was coming next.

Captain Sergei Soidra was the first to speak. "Comrade Colonel, is it your belief that the American submarine is still out there—close to the American ships—but *invisible?*"

"Such a possibility exists." Bersenko put down the glass and dabbed at the corners of his mouth, all the while looking at Lieutenant General Zudin, who had an intelligent, raffish face, and was an immense man, weighing 325 pounds.

"I presume you disagree with me, Comrade Zudin?"

"I think your theory is ridiculous!" Zudin said without hesitation. "If the Americans had an 'invisible' submarine, why did they turn west? They're almost a hundred miles away and the *Cesarevitch* is watching them constantly. Those ships can't move an inch without our knowing it."

Colonel Bersenko did not reply. He leaned back, locked his fingers behind his head, and stared up at the ceiling, thinking: *If a submarine could be made invisible, could it be detected by sonar?*

138

Chapter Thirteen

Closing in on the Soviet submarine had been astonishingly simple, but only because the Gf-Mechanism made it impossible for the sonar on the *Cesarevitch* to detect the presence of the American, 4,270-ton, hunter-killer U-boat. To the Soviet captain and his officers and crew, the *Kingfisher* did not exist.

Other than the three sonar technicians wearing headphones, the firing officer, and his two computer experts, there were four other men in the fire-control compartment, or attack center. The Death Merchant, Captain McConachie, Josh Forran, and Cullen Torway were all four clustered around the operator of the target position indicator.

There in the infrared viewer of the T.P.I. was the dark silhouette of the *Cesarevitch*, a killer-attack sub similar to *Kingfisher*.

They stared at *Cesarevitch*, and for the moment there was silence, except for the low-pitched humming coming from the equipment in the crowded compartment.

While still staring at the Soviet submarine resting motionless on the sea floor, Captain McConachie said, "Give me the plot check."

"She's at two hundred fifty fathoms, sir," replied Lieutenant Ellsworth, the firing officer. "Her range from our surface vessels is five point two miles southeast. Her position from us is two thousand yards southwest, sir."

"All we have to do is let her have it," Forran half-whispered, glancing at Camellion who shook his head and put a finger to his lips. One does not distract a commander of a nuclear submarine.

"Exact range on the torpedo date computer?" said McConachie. "I want it in feet."

"Six thousand one hundred and ten feet to her stern, sir." Ellsworth replied promptly.

"The arc intersects?" inquired McConachie.

"Two point six, sir. Thirty-four seconds maximum to firing before we have to take a new bearing."

Captain McConachie stared intently at the Cesarevitch. He was the captain of the Kingfisher, and the sole responsibility for success was his alone.

"Fire all four fish in a salvo," McConachie said, his voice the tip of a whip.

Lieutenant Ellsworth's fingers pressed orange buttons on the console in front of him. "Salvo fired, sir."

At one-second intervals, four slight jolts shook Kingfisher as four Mark-48 torpedoes left the bow tubes and streaked toward the doomed Soviet submarine. Instead of the Mark-48, McConachie could have used the HARPOON, a submarine-launched guided missile that was much faster and more powerful than the Mark-48, and could be used against either underwater craft or surface ships. McConachie had chosen the Mark-48 because it was less costly and could do the job equally as well against the Cesarevitch, which was a stationary target—a sitting duck!

The four streaks of the Mark-48s could clearly be seen in the viewer screen, the four torpedoes, not diverging an inch, speeding straight toward the target.

"Those poor bastards in that tin can will never know what hit them," Cullen Torway exclaimed, his voice cracking from tension.

"Their sonar will pick them up about ten seconds before impact," Captain McConachie said. "They'll have time for only a 'God help us.' "

"The joke's on them," said Forran mockingly. "They're all atheists."

The four acoustic homing torpedoes closed in on the Soviet sub. Utilizing a liquid monopropellant fuel, each Mark-48 had a diameter of 21 inches and weighed 3,600 pounds, 1,800 pounds being a warhead of TNT.

Anticipating the explosions, the sonar technicians removed their headphones. Suddenly the round screen of the target position indicator revealed a boiling tornado of water, a mixture of water, mud, and ripped-apart steel. Even through the triple hull of Kingfisher, Camellion and the others heard the detonations, tremendous hollow booms, and braced themselves for the shock wave. It came seconds later, the pressure rocking the boat, the floor underneath their feet swaying and shivering slightly. As suddenly as the concussion had come, it was gone, and conditions were back to normal.

There was no sign of *Cesarevitch* in the view plate. All that the men could see were several large pieces of wreckage sinking rapidly to the sand. The Mark-48s had pulverized the Soviet submarine.

"That is that," muttered Josh Forran. Perspiration streamed down his heavily tanned face. "If the rest of the plan goes according to schedule, we might even get back to the good old U.S. of A."

The Death Merchant, his expression one of satisfaction, swung to Captain McConachie, a small part of his mind going over Forran's comment. The rest of the plan, while uncomplicated, demanded some luck and extremely careful timing. The explosions of the four torpedoes had served as a double signal. To the American force on the surface, they indicated that the Soviet underwater craft had been destroyed and that it was time for the three American ships to move west again, very slowly, under the protection of "Emma." To the Soviet force, a hundred miles to the east, the explosions, picked up on their transponders and other sensing devices, would indicate either the destruction of *Kingsfisher* or *Cesarevitch*. The Soviets would have no way of ascertaining which until they tried to contact the *Cesarevitch* and did not receive a reply. They should then be positive within fifteen minutes.

"Captain, I'll be in the briefing room with Norris and his boys," Camellion said diplomatically. "Please let me know when we're within fifty miles of the Soviet dome. That will give us more than enough time to get suited up. I know this boat isn't the *Concorde*, but I'd appreciate full speed ahead."

"You'll get it," McConachie said crossly. He didn't like "civilians" on his boat, particularly intelligence "spooks," and he made no secret of his feelings. "We can get sixty-two knots. You'll have more than an hour. I'm basing the time on the prediction that the Soviets don't saturate the area with Shaddocks[1] and blow us to kingdom come."

The half-smile vanished from Camellion's mouth, and his pleasant manner changed to the charm of a cobra. "I don't like playing games, McConachie. The pig farmers ahead aren't going to waste their ASW missiles on a hundred square miles of open water, certainly not on a sub they can't detect. I know it and you know it. As I said, call me."

---

[1] Similar to the American SUBROC system, but less accurate and less efficient.

Camellion turned and stalked out of the fire-control center. Forran and Torway, who avoided looking at a stunned McConachie, walked through the door and soon caught up with the Death Merchant.

Hurrying down the passage with Camellion and Forran, Torway said, "I think it will take an act of Congress to get those choppers there on time. Thank God they have ten minutes leeway."

The CIA case officer glanced nervously around him, as the shrill whine of the turbines began to drown out the pumps. *Kingfisher* had increased speed, and a small amount of vibration had begun to creep into the tough steel structure of the submarine. The floor tilted forward. As had been agreed on at the final meeting aboard *Mohawk,* the *Kingfisher* would travel submerged as deeply as possible to increase propeller efficiency. The deeper the boat, the more effective the propellers, all of which made a big difference when running at high speeds.

The submarine inclined downward until she was at 2,000 feet; then the automatic depth-keeper leveled off the boat. Again the floor was level and the vibration stopped. But *Kingfisher* would travel at this depth for only 46 miles. She would then rise steadily as she approached the Soviet underwater base and the Soviet ships on the surface.

Camellion hurried along the passage, confident that the submarine was charging through the dark depths at full speed. "I admire the crews of those three helicopters," he said and stepped through a bulkhead into a short midsection gangway. "Flying just above the water will protect them from Soviet radar, but only up to a point. It's still an enormous risk they're taking."

"Sure, I give them credit," Torway said sincerely. "I'm giving us credit, too. We're not going to a church social."

Forran, quickening his pace to keep up, sounded pessimistic. "I only hope that McConachie and his experts can place that torpedo with pinpoint accuracy."

"It's that puny two hundred and six pounds of TNT that bothers me," grumbled Torway. "That small amount doesn't seem enough to blow a big enough hole in the side of the *Mikhail Tukhachevsky.* She's the biggest and the best vessel in oceanography the Soviets have—triple-hulled and with outside plates two inches thick."

Torway was surprised and slightly angered when Camellion laughed.

"Don't worry about it. By the time we swim over to her,

you'll see a fair-sized opening and the inside compartment will be filled with water. Just hope—and pray if you're so inclined—that the choppers and their chain-guns are doing their job upstairs when we swim in."

"I still say that we would have a better chance if we went inside the *Tukhachevsky* through one of her bottom observation ports," insisted Torway. "She's supposed to have two. Why a hand grenade would shatter the glass easily."

"No dice. Remember what we got out of Major Bogachiev? Colonel Bersenko and Lieutenant General Zudin are not fools. If they suspect an underwater attack by SEALs, the observation chambers will be the first places they think of. Those chambers will be locked and armored and pig farmer commandos waiting."

Camellion stepped through another bulkhead and entered the long briefing room next to the stern diver-lockout chamber, where Red Norris and sixty of his men were checking their deep-dive suits and stuffing Ingrams, bags of ammo, and various kinds of grenades into 4-foot-long, 18-inch diameter, plastic cylinders.

Camellion walked up to Norris, who was strapping two Seecamp Bobcat .45 auto-loaders around his waist. SEALs were permitted to carry sidearms of their own choosing—a psychological measure that made for greater efficiency in fighting. Any man can kill better with weapons he is comfortable with.

Some of the SEALs wore Diamondback revolvers; others wore Star PDs, AMT Hardballers, Mossbergs, and Llamas of various calibers. One man even sported a pair of chromed nine-millimeter Brownings.

"Red, have you figured out the underwear problem yet?" Camellion picked up the two Auto Mags from a table and began strapping them around his waist. "We'll be wearing sidearms and need more room in the suits. My only solution is to leave off the cotton underwear and the nylon-pile insulating. With coveralls, we'll still have a tight fit, but I know we'll be able to manage. I've used that arrangement before on other jobs."

"Yeah, I figure the same way you do," Norris said. "We could try and eliminate the electrically heated woolen suit, but it's too risky even in these comparatively warm waters. A chill sets in and a man's had it." He chuckled and moved his long fingers through his closely cropped red hair. "We sure as hell don't have to worry about swimming back. We'll board the sub directly from the surface—those of us alive. There's still the danger of sharks unless the *Mikhail Tukhachevsky* stays

143

afloat long enough for McConachie to surface and send over rafts." Norris looked down at Camellion, who was seated on a bench pulling off his black Wellington boots. Forran had already slipped on thick rubber-soled moccasions that could be laced to the ankle and over the instep to prevent slippage.

Norris, who felt that, when it came to Communists, Camellion's right wing feelings were not too far removed from Hitler's, persisted in his opinion of the strike on the *Mikhail Tukhachevsky*.

"Don't think I've changed my mind. We're only wearing out our shoes and our souls in attacking that goddamn boat. And don't tell me that the odds of our grabbing any of the Russian bigshots are with us. They aren't and you know it."

"It's a ship. This sub is a boat," Camellion said. He fastened the lace around his left ankle, then started to tie the lace of the other moccasin.

"Let's not get technical," growled Norris. "You know what I'm talking about."

Cullen Torway stood up, moved his feet within the moccasins, and said resignedly, "I suppose you're still convinced that the Soviet Command in Cuba won't send fighter-bombers? If they do, we can kiss ourselves and maybe this sub goodbye forever. And if they hit us, they'll hit the three ships."

"They won't," Camellion said, standing. "They won't because they don't want the Last Big War. The Soviets are just as afraid of us as we are of them." He sighed loudly. "As for the KGB and scientists, we must try. I don't cotton to doing half a job. The bottom line is that we have more to gain than to lose."

Torway looked mournfully at Red Norris, whose face was devoid of emotion. Nonetheless, Torway knew what Norris was thinking, what all the men must be asking themselves: how do you argue with a man who viewed dying and death as insignificant and irrelevant?

You don't. . . .

Richard Camellion and Captain Claude McConachie stared at the Soviet titanium dome in the viewer tube of the target position indicator. At a distance of 9,120.30 feet—a mile and a half—the silvery gray structure, with the nine Quonset-hut-shaped modules arranged around it, looked like something from a science fiction motion picture set, the iodine-vapor floodlights adding an eerie glow and making the picture, centered in the screen, seem even more ghostly.

McConachie said, "The bearings have been set by the computer and the inputs fixed in the HARPOONs?"

"Yes, sir," replied Lieutenant Ellsworth, his tone mechanical, "including the special missile for the large Soviet vessel."

"Sequence firing plot?"

"First three missiles for target dead ahead fired as a salvo, sir. One each for the platform and the two surface vessels, at two-second intervals. A fourteen-second pause for the special HARPOON to be fired at the remaining Soviet ship."

The Death Merchant spoke, "You're positive of the coordinates on the *Mikhail Tukhachevsky*?"

"Sir, I tripled-checked the torpedo data computer," Ellsworth replied stiffly. "The *Mikhail Tukhachevsky* is at anchor. The computer in the guidance system of the missile will carry the HARPOON to the bow of the ship. Forty feet from the prow and just slightly below the waterline. I might add, sir, that I know my job."

"Thank you. I'm sure that you do, Lieutenant."

Captain McConachie gave the order. "Fire the first three, then according to sequence."

Ellsworth's finger pressed three orange buttons. A locking of the circuits and a faint *whoosh* as the three rocket-powered wire guided missiles left the stern tubes. Unlike torpedoes, which required a straight course to smack the target, the HARPOON missile was radio-controlled by preset coordinates and could travel in any direction.

The three HARPOONs shot a hundred feet from the aft tubes, performed graceful loops, and, as a trio, streaked through the dark water at almost 120 knots—straight for the dome. The three missiles left no wake and traveled too fast to be seen on the viewer scope. During those tense moments, Ellsworth fired the next three missiles.

The Death Merchant, Captain McConachie, and the operator of the T.P.I. saw the explosions. For a slice of a second the water, a mile and a half forward, churned with unbelievable violence. The iodine-vapor lights vanished. The dome disappeared. The explosions thundered against the hull of the boat, the shock rocking the submarine.

Seven hundred and ten feet above and slightly more than a mile and a half to the southeast, three more explosions announced the the destruction of the Soviet work platform, the *Suarez Gayol*, the Cuban ship, and *Vitiaz*, the Soviet supply vessel.

The water cleared as Lieutenant Ellsworth was pressing the

final orange button. The submarine shuddered slightly and the most important HARPOON of all was on its way.

Where the dome had been was emptiness, except for an enormous rounded rim of metal, the top jagged, bent, and twisted. What was left of the dome could be compared to a derby hat, three-fourths of which someone had cut off very crookedly, several inches above the brim.

The operator of the T.P.I. said in an odd voice, "It must have been like Boulder Dam breaking through on a colony of ants. God!"

Most of the nine modules were gone, crushed by the wave of concussion from the three HARPOONs. The modules that had not been caved in had been blown from their foundations, some even lying upside-down or on their sides.

They all heard the final explosion, the low distant *berruuummm* of the HARPOON that had found the hull of the *Mikhail Tukhachevsky*.

"Time for me to go," Camellion announced. He was surprised when Captain McConachie stuck out his right hand and intoned solemnly, "Good luck, Camellion. Watch yourself."

The Death Merchant pumped McConachie's hand. "Thanks. We'll all need it."

He turned on his heel and hurried from the attack center, a slight smile on his face. Human beings were such odd creatures. They came naked into the world, existed for only a whisper, yet acted as if they could never die, as if they were eternal!

The Death Merchant and the 64 other men swam in the cold, pressing darkness. Each man was connected to his neighbor by a 20-foot length of line that contained a telephone cable, and each was pulling his plastic, watertight container filled with kill-instruments. Camellion and Lieutenant Commander Norris were connected to each other by an umbilical 30 feet long. A hundred-foot line connected them to Sergeant John Day. In turn, Day was attached to the other SEALs. Included in the 60 SEALs were Forran, Coopbird, and Torway, the last of whom was going along to get first-hand information.

The Death Merchant and Red Norris carried underwater, infrared, binocular-type viewers, which utilized a 25mm 3-stage intensifiers with automatic brightness control and high speed objective lenses. Each Kron-D nightsight device intensified particles of received light—too little to be detected by the

146

human eye—100,000 times. To Camellion and Norris, this was the equivalent of swimming in early twilight. Without effort, they could see where the dome had been and the wreckage of *Vitiaz* and the *Suarez Gayol*. Each vessel had been blown in half by the missiles and had sunk within seconds, going straight down to the bottom.

Now, five hundred yards ahead, they could see the long gray hull of the *Mikhail Tukhachevsky*. There wasn't anything they could do should the Soviets decide to start lobbing depth charges into the water. Should that happen, they would die instantly, crushed like walnuts beneath hammers.

"There's the big bastard." Norris's voice floated over the wire and through the tiny speaker in Camellion's helmet.

"Affirmative. In a short while we'll know whether the TNT did its job in the right spot."

They swam steadily; yet the push forward was very slow and especially a strain on Camellion and Norris. Not only did they have to pull their cylinders of weapons by straps slung over their shoulders, but every now and then they had to pause to look through the infrared devices.

Desperately hoping that he had not made a miscalculation, Camellion thought of the *Mikhail Tukhachevsky*. Enormous for a vessel engaged in research in oceanography, the ship was 490 feet long, displaced 5,670 tons, and carried a complement of 310 men.

Gradually, Camellion and Norris closed in on the port side of the vessel and, hearts pounding, began to swim upward. As they drew closer and moved upward, they could hear a faint racket from the surface, a strung-together staccato volume of noise, discordant sound irritating to one's ears.

The helicopters had arrived and their chain-guns were in action.

Camellion and Norris soon found where the Harpoon missile had struck. Forty feet from the prow there a was a jagged 15-foot hole in the hull, three-fourths of it below the waterline.

"That's what I call accuracy," Camellion said, his own breath coming back at him within the helmet.

"Yeah, I see it," said Norris. "Happy days are here again. . . ."

Chapter Fourteen

Souls of the damned approaching the redhot gates of hell could not have been more apprehensive than Colonel Anatole Bersenko and his men on board the *Mikhail Tukhachevsky*, a vessel that was not a conventional type of ship. Instead of a single midsection superstructure, the *Mikhail Tukhachevsky* had a forward superstructure and a smaller one toward the stern. The main control bridge, navigation, engineering, the radio room, and other vital functions were in the forward structure. The officers and the crew's quarters, the galley, and the mess for the officers and for the crew, were all located in the superstructure toward the stern. On top of the aft superstructure was the radar dome used for tracking satellites.

Between the two superstructures, the deck was filled with equipment essential to the complex study of oceanography— four decompression chambers, divers' dressing stations, swing-out booms for lowering small 4-man subs, air compressors for oxygen makeup systems, gas cylinder storage, a helicopter on its pad, the heavy crane and various workshops. Midways were missile launchers. On each side had been added depth bomb "shooters."

Long-range radar had locked in on the three American vessels, and Bersenko had ordered that the enemy ships be saturated with 30 "Emerald" missiles. But had the "Something" again engineered a miss?

Bersenko had then had his navigators calculate the time it would take the American submarine—if there was a sub—to cover a distance of 95 miles.

"It's a mistake," insisted Lieutenant General Vladilen Zudin. "The *Amerikanskis* do not have to come to us to attack. If it is a sub, it could use SUBROCS to do the job."

149

"Of course they can!" Bersenko declared angrily. He stared dismally out of one of the stern windows on the main bridge. The blue water was as calm as a sleeping baby. "We should pull up anchor and leave this area with all possible speed. We can't and you know why. Moscow has ordered us to stay put."

"*Da*, I know, I know," Zudin conceded reluctantly. Standing next to Bersenko, he shifted his walrus-like bulk from one foot to the other. "Moscow underestimated the *Amerikanski*s and—"

"I said so in my last radio message to the Center," Bersenko said sourly, then lit a cigarette.

"And we are to be sacrificed to save face." Zudin thought of his wife, two sons, three daughters, and five grandchildren in the mother country and somehow knew that he would never see them again. A deep believer in the occult, a belief he concealed from his associates, he felt that his feeling of doom was more than pessimism. It was a presentiment. "Moscow knows that the Americans wouldn't sink one of our submarines unless they also intended to attack our surface vessels. All we can do is saturate the area with *Lzumruds* and hope that one of them gets the American submarine."

Bersenko turned and gave Zudin a look of disgust. "We have ten *Lzumruds* and how many hundreds of square miles between the Americans and us. Where would you suggest we target them?"

"At least we have depth charges," Zudin said quickly. "But that isn't much protection. We're practically on top of the dome and sitting still. Why not move away from the area?"

"It wouldn't be worth the effort," Bersenko said dismally. "A sub could fire torpedoes or missiles from miles away. Comrade, we can do nothing but sit here and wait."

HSR radar detected the three Hughes XM230 helicopters. The three choppers were 7.4 miles southeast of the stern.

"They're just hanging there directly above the water," radar reported. "We can't be sure, but they can't be more than ten feet above the surface."

Bersenko was about to give the order that would send Nighthawk missiles at the three American helicopters when a monstrous rumbling boiled up from the depths several hundred yards southeast of the ship. Bersenko and everyone else on the bridge knew at once that the dome had been destroyed.

"My God!" cried Pavel Kazikovchek. "There were several hundred of our people down there!"

Came the shock wave. The water swelled momentarily and

then broke into ten-foot waves that smashed against the port side of the *Mikhail Tukhachevsky*, rocking the vessel from side to side, forcing the bow to tug against the anchor chain.

They all saw the work platform disappear in a huge flash of red-orange flame. Men and machinery became mixed in a squeezed-together mess of flesh and metal, the wreckage shooting skyward, part of an A-frame winch tumbling over and over in the air.

The wreckage had not yet had time to fall back into the water when a tremendous explosion came from the *Vitiaz*, a quarter of a mile starboard. An instant of fire and smoke, and the supply ship was dead. Several moments later, while *Vitiaz* was sinking in two sections, both her stern and bow upended, the *Suarez Gayol* disintegrated in an expanding ball of fire. By the time the last chunk of metal from the work platform fell from the sky and splashed into the water, the *Vitiaz* was gone and only 20 feet of the bow of the Cuban ship was sticking out of the water.

"Rocket underwater missiles!" a stunned Boris Ruzorkaski croaked. "It's a submarine and it used rocket missiles!"

"Impossible!" First Officer Albert Didov's voice was almost a shriek. "There has been absolutely nothing on sonar. Submarines can't be invisible."

"We're next!" Feliks Turkin said hoarsely. "The Americans—"

An explosion chopped off his words, a thunderblast to port below the superstructure. As if an earthquake had struck, the floor shook violently, the vessel shuddering from rudder to fore peak.

Yet every man on the bridge was still alive.

The ship was not breaking up.

Whatever it was that had hit the ship, it had not been an American HARPOON missile!

Captain Sorgei Soidra raced to the right side of the bridge, almost running past a terrified helmsman and several ordinary seamen. Next to the echo-sounder read-out, the digital depth indicator, and the forward-scan sonar read-outs was the pressure board. A red light was blinking on and off below a label marked L-14. As Soidra stared at the blinking red light, two smaller green lights began glowing.

"It's the core analysis laboratory on the third deck," yelled Soidra. "The bulkheads have already closed automatically and sealed off the compartment. The explosion couldn't have been a torpedo or we'd be listing heavily to port."

"Divers!" The word exploded from Colonel Bersenko's

mouth. "American divers intend to board us, or the Americans would have sent us to the bottom." Full of blind hatred, he stared at Captain Soidra. "Use depth charges from both sides. We'll crush them like ants. The pressure will—"

"American helicopters!" screamed the radar operator. "Coming right at us port and stern!"

If the radar operator's attention had not been diverted by the explosion, he would have seen the three choppers a few minutes earlier. Now it was too late. Captain Soidra didn't have time to pick up the phone and contact the men stationed at the depth charge tubes. No sooner had the radar operator shouted the warning than the three Hughes XM230s began firing their chain-guns.[1] Each Hughes had two chain-guns protruding from the port and the starboard sides of the fuselage, a .50-caliber machine gun and a 20-millimeter cannon on each side.

Within seconds, six .50-caliber machine guns and six 20 mm cannons were raking the deck of the ship with a rain of projectiles that were devastating in their destruction, the roaring of the three choppers and the firing of the twelve chain-guns sounding like the heart of a tornado.

The glass of the bridge windows—fore and aft—shattered, then showered the Russians who were diving to the floor. One of the seamen uttered a choked, "*Uhhhhh!*" and slumped over, a big, bloody hole in his chest.

A full minute had not passed before 26 Russian sailors lay butchered on the deck. The cylinders of gas were riddled, the hiss of escaping helium lost in the roaring of the three helicopters and their twelve chain-guns.

Scores of .50-caliber and 20mm projectiles wrecked the four decompression chambers and the divers' dressing stations. Five technicians in the workshop died when projectiles poked hundreds of holes in the building and hacked their bodies into numerous pieces.

[1] Designed in 1973. As its name suggests, the gun mechanism is driven by an electrically powered bicycle-type chain, but instead of a multibarrel configuration, as used on many contemporary aircraft guns, the Hughes weapon has a single barrel fed by a revolving chamber. The chain-gun is operated via an extremely sophisticated fire-control system, incorporating a gyro-stabilized telescopic sight mounted below the fuselage, with laser range-finding/target designation equipment and infrared for night operations. For sheer firepower the Hughes chain-gun is one of the most terrifying weapons in the world.

A blast of 20mm missiles chopped into one side of the radio mast—at the bottom where it was bolted to the roof of the main bridge—and it sagged to starboard, ripping the hi-gain antenna from the mast on the aft superstructure.

Strangely enough, not one projectile hit any of the depth-charge tubes on the port and the starboard sides of the vessels. The gunners knew that should any of the depth charges explode, a chain-reaction might occur. All the depth charges could explode and plunge the vessel to the bottom of the Caribbean.

On the bridge, Colonel Anatole Bersenko belly-crawled toward the elevator, yelling to make himself heard above the racket. "We've got to get out of here before we're all killed!"

The Death Merchant was the first to swim awkwardly into the interior of the ship, going in through the center of the hole and speaking into the mike fastened to his neck. "Men, stay next to the hull. I'll keep you informed of what I see inside."

Norris chimed in, "I'm going inside with him. Sergeant Day will wait outside the hole."

With the weapons' cylinders dragging through the water behind them, Camellion and Norris moved into the flooded compartment, peering through the Kron-D night vision devices. In the deep twilight, made possible by the Kron-Ds, they saw that they were in an area where rock core samples, bored from the ocean floor, were analyzed, then stored in bins. The blast had demolished much of the equipment and had turned over some of the bins. Rock cores, some six feet long lay scattered. Many were broken.

Camellion and Norris saw that a bulkhead at each end of the area was closed. To blast either door would have been useless, would have been an exercise in sheer futility. Water would flood the compartment, then the next area after its bulkhead was exploded, and so on through the length of that level, of that deck.

For that reason, Camellion had chosen a deck whose ceiling was above the waterline, but whose floor was below the waterline. Water always seeks its own level, and now, as Norris and Camellion swam upward, the Death Merchant knew that he would soon know if he had made the right decision. His head popped out of the water and he saw that he had. There was a two-foot space between the top of the water and the ceiling, that is, the bottom of the next deck above. Should there have been an opening in the ceiling, he wouldn't have had any difficulty in pulling himself up and through.

153

"A half a pound of stuff should do nicely," Camellion said happily to Norris. "I'll place it in the center of the ceiling."

Norris didn't sound enthused. "I just hope the concussion doesn't travel too far, or we'll be hearing *ding-ding-ding* for a week!"

"The force of the blast will travel upward," Camellion said. "As a SEAL, you should know that. Most of the concussion will be absorbed by the ceiling and the empty space."

He looked around again through the night-sight device, swam ten feet to the left, and let the Kron-D drop around his neck and rest on the cord. He opened one of the watertight pockets on the legs of his Neoruperine suit, took out a small flat package of RDX, pulled the length of wire at one end of the block, kicked to give himself momentum, and placed the magnetic mine against the metal ceiling.

"Let's go," he said. "Twenty feet to stern. We have three minutes."

He raised the Kron-D night viewer, turned in the water, swam downward, and headed for the gaping hole in the side of the Soviet ship, feeling the Plastoperene line tighten as Norris swam ahead of him.

Quickly they moved through the gaping cavity, turned, swam a short distance to stern, and waited. They didn't have to wait more than ten seconds. There was the sound of a muffled explosion from inside the ship. Water churned in a frenzy around the hole and the hull vibrated.

"Let's go have a look-see," the Death Merchant said easily. "Sergeant Day, you and the men get ready."

Calling on extra reserves of strength, Camellion swam back into the hole. He swam with such speed that he quickly outdistanced the younger Norris—in spite of the strap of the weapons' cylinder pulling against his left shoulder. Halfway in, the life-line grew tight, and he was almost jerked to a halt by Norris, who was trying to catch up with him.

Camellion chided Norris. "You should get more exercise. You're out of shape."

Lieutenant Commander Harris, smarting from the way Camellion had taken over, did not reply.

Camellion did not have to use Kron-D to find the damage done by the RDX. Light from the deck above filtered down through the hole into the water that rippled with a faint yellow glow. Still under the water, he swam to one side of the hole, popped up his head into the open space between water and ceiling, and saw that the RDX had ripped out a ten-foot section of the above-deck floor. All around the edge steel plates were curled upward, the wooden decking splintered.

Kicking to stay afloat, he moved closer to the opening, his sweat-dotted face a mask of tension. This was the crucial moment, the twilight between success and failure. What lay above? The worst of all possibilities was that the enemy was waiting above and would start lobbing grenades into the water. If that happened—*Goodbye life, hello death!*

He opened the waterproof pocket on the other leg of the suit, unclipped an M26 fragmentation grenade, and, kicking furiously to stay afloat, raised the grenade out of the water, pulled the pin with the fingers of his left hand, released the safety lever, counted "one thousand and one" to insure airburst, and threw the grenade out of the hole, heaving it with all his might to the left. He was pulling the pin from the second grenade when the first one exploded and sent shrapnel flying across the room. Glass shattered; other kinds of equipment was wrecked. *Yet there aren't any shouts!* he thought. *Any screams of pain! Not a single damned cry of agony. How about that?*

He threw the second grenade to the right and heard it explode and shower whatever was above with hundreds of pieces of shrapnel.

Suddenly, Red Norris's helmeted head popped out of the water, and his nervous voice came over the wire to Camellion. "We're going to have to hurry it up. Those chain-guns upstairs don't have an inexhaustible supply of ammunition."

"So what else is new, damn it!" Camellion growled, thinking that there comes a time when all planning ends and one must take a chance and depend on pure luck. Now was such a time.

He kicked with both legs, moving his body upward, grabbed the rough edge of the opening with both hands, pulled himself through the blasted hole, and looked quickly around. He guessed, judging from some of the equipment still intact, that the place was a lab for distilling fresh water. Tubes, bottles, and other delicate equipment lay scattered on the floor.

Not a single Russian was in sight!

"Attention men. Come in and come in fast," Camellion said, his voice coated with tension. "Watch the edges of the hole outside in the hull. The rim is damned sharp in places."

"Let's go up," he said to Norris. With effort, he lifted himself out of the water and crawled over the jagged steel edge onto the wooden floor. Glancing at Norris hoisting himself out

155

of the hole, Camellion pulled the plastic cylinder from the water, but instead of opening it, he pulled a sealed-in-plastic-wrap Ingram submachine gun and two magazines from the right outside pocket of the deep-dive suit. While Norris opened his own plastic container, the Death Merchant tore the wrapping from the sub-gun and the two magazines, shoved one of the magazines into the Ingram, and pulled back the cocking lever. All the while he kept glancing at the doors at each end of the room and at the stairway leading upward, at the stern end of the lab. From the two pockets of the suit, he took four more M26 grenades and another half-pound block of RDX.

By this time, Norris had unscrewed the top from his cylinder, had stripped off his air tanks, and was getting out of the Neoruperine suit.

Sergeant John Day started pulling himself out of the hole.

It was then that the aft bulkhead door opened and several Russian sailors, Stechkin machine pistols in their hands, walked straight into Camellion's line of Varner .25-caliber bullets, which exploded on impact and turned the front of the pig farmers into a bloody mess of ripped flesh and shredded uniforms.

Free of his diving suit, Norris jerked two IMP machine pistols from the cylinder, jammed in magazines, cocked the weapons and, half a minute later, fired off a short burst of 5.6mm Fireball slugs at the half-closed door, just to let other Russians know what they could expect.

Desperately, the Death Merchant and Sergeant Day unbuckled their air tanks and weight belts and crawled out of the suits, as other SEALs began crawling from the opening onto the deck. Day and Camellion pulled canvas shoulder bags from the plastic containers, slipped the straps over their shoulders, and soon were ready for action.

"Do we go up or toward the stern?" inquired Norris, who secretly felt that everyone was entitled to Camellion's opinion.
"If we take the stairs we'll need a diversion."

Josh Forran, who had just gotten out of his D-D suit, shoved a magazine into an Ingram. "The bigshots should be in the bow superstructure. Who knows where the scientists might be?"

A burst of IMP machine pistol fire from Sergeant Day knifed into the conversation. Day was positioned where he could see the bulkhead at the top of the stairs toward the stern. The door had opened slightly, and Day had wisely raked the edge of the crack. Some of the Fireball slugs lodged in the thick rubber of the rim; several others ricocheted from metal with loud, screaming whines.

By now, several dozen fighters had stripped off their swim suits, opened their cylinders, slung bags of ammo and grenades over their shoulders, and were ready to kill—or be killed. All the while, more SEALs were coming up through the hole in the deck.

The Death Merchant looked around the crowded area filled with men and discarded deep-dive suits. *Damned ironic,* he thought. *We, the willing, led by the unknowing, are attempting the impossible for the ungrateful!*

"We'll go upward," he said. "We don't have time to skip up and down the lengths of the decks."

"The rest of the men should be ready in a few minutes," Norris said in a low undertone. "Then we can start with the THI [Thermite]. Do you have a better suggestion?"

There was more IMP firing at the bulkheads at each end of the area and at the third one at the top of the steel steps. The instant one of the doors started to crack open, SEALers opened fire. The men were massed in the area and, should the Russians succeed in opening one of the bulkheads and tossing in grenades, the explosions would turn the wrecked lab into a slaughterhouse.

"Have you noticed," said Forran, "the helicopters are gone. We're on our own, and McConachie won't surface until he sees our signal flare."

Camellion finished adjusting the Menten gas mask over his face, his voice muffled. "We've come this far. We've done so much with so little we are now almost qualified to do anything with almost nothing."

"The last three men just came up," Norris said and pulled his gas mask from one of the shoulder bags. "We'll be rocking and rolling in a few more minutes."

Colonel Bersenko and the other officers had successfully reached the second deck and were receiving a report from several of the ship's junior officers. Lieutenant General Zudin and Captain Feliks Turkin were off to one side talking in hushed tones to one of the sea commandoes.

Finally, Zudin and Turkin hurried over to the other group, Zudin waddling as he walked, his fat face a cloud of menace.

"The Americans blasted a hole in the hull on the third deck," started Captain Soidra. "They then—"

"We know," snapped Zudin impatiently. "Our *Ziaistvo Yennaya* have them bottled up at the bulkheads at each end of the laboratory, as well as the bulkhead at the top of the stairs. I've ordered an all-out assault. We'll kill them where they stand."

"Is there any chance we can capture some of them?" Bersenko's brown eyes narrowed and he made no effort to wipe the sweat from his ruddy face.

"Or force them to surrender?" asked Boris Ruzorkaski anxiously.

"Surrender? *Nyet*. It's possible we might get some of them alive, but don't count on it." Zudin made a motion of total helplessness. "What difference does it make. I rather suspect that the Americans have arranged to send some kind of signal to their submarine, to—"

"We can't be positive that there is a submarine," interjected Captain Soidra, panic poking holes in his voice.

"You nitwit! Where do you think the divers came from?" hissed Zudin. "The American submarine has some kind of device that makes it impossible for sonar to detect it. That sub is no doubt zeroed in on us right now, all set to fire if the American commandos lose."

"In that case we could use missiles to sink the bastard," suggested Boris Ruzorkaski. "At least we'd be safe until help arrived from Cuba."

"Didn't you hear what I said?" growled Zudin. "The instant the commander of the American sub saw us lifting the missiles, he'd fire. He'd blow us out of the water."

Colonel Bersenko spoke quietly, "How have you deployed your men, Comrade Zudin?"

"Fifteen at each end of the lab's bulkheads. The others are waiting above the steps on the third deck. Armed sailors will act as backups, although I don't think they will be needed."

A deep explosion rumbled from below.

Captain Felix Turkin inhaled loudly. "Those aren't our boys. They haven't had time yet to put together armor plate to use as shields."

Four grenades exploded from below.

"Apparently our commandos are better than we thought." A smile slid across Zudin's washtub of a face. "It's the beginning of the end for the Americans."

Realist that he was, Colonel Anatole Bersenko was not so sure.

Chapter Fifteen

When the Death Merchant had said, "Upward," Red Norris and the others had assumed he had meant that they would use the stairs to reach the next deck above. He hadn't.

"We're going to get out of here by way of the bulkhead at the stern end," he said, once all the men had been assembled into six squads. "The pig farmers know we're going to head for topside and they'll be thickest at the top of the steps on the third deck."

"They'll be at each bulkhead, too," Norris declared thickly. He suddenly had the idea he was in the center of a graveyard. "Either way, we still need some kind of diversionary tactic."

"We'll have it." Camellion reached into one of his shoulder bags, pulled out a half-pound block of RDX, handed the explosive to Norris, and quickly explained his plan. Sergeant Day passed on Camellion's scheme to the squad leaders, who in turn told the men in whispered tones.

While Norris tied the packet of RDX around a grenade and other men pointed dozens of automatics at the bulkhead toward the bow, and at the bulkhead at the top of the stairs. The Death Merchant and six SEALs ran to the bulkhead at the stern end of the room. Under the watchful barrels of five IMP machine pistols and one Bushmaster, Camellion took out four flat packets of THI with magnetic bases and carefully placed them against the bulkhead—two on the left side, in the vicinity of the huge hinges on the other side of the door, two to the left, one at the top, the other a foot from the floor.

With a great caution, he turned the knob of each detonating timer attached to each package, allowing a four-second margin between the turn of each knob. The time on the first knob was 50 seconds; 38 seconds on the fourth knob.

The Death Merchant and the men with him were scurrying back from the bulkhead when Red Norris pulled the pin on the grenade, and dropped it and the package of RDX into the water two feet below the level of the hole in the floor. Norris and Day, Forran, Coopbird, and Torway then moved away from the hole and rushed toward the bow end of the room. Giving the hole a wide berth, the Death Merchant and the SEALs with him ran in the same direction.

The grenade and the RDX, falling through the water to the floor of the fifth deck, exploded with a subdued roar that shook the Soviet vessel, splashed up half a ton of water through the hole, and ruptured the plates between the inner hull, the large tear permitting fuel oil, stored throughout the length of the vessel in the inner bottom, to flow into the water of the core compartment.

Twenty seconds more and the four packets of thermite went off with a giant *whoosh*. Dazzling blue-white fire enveloped the entire side of the bulkhead, a solid wall of loud sizzling fire burning at a temperature of 4,000 degrees. At such an incredible temperature, it was only a matter of seconds before the hinges and most of the three-inch steel door had been reduced to molten metal, which flowed like miniature rivers of white lava, the terrific heat burning through the wooden deck and filling the air with the pungent smell of burning wood. The Death Merchant and twenty of the men moved closer to the burned-out bulkhead.

The *Mikhail Tukhachevsky* was tilted slightly toward the bow because of the water filling the rock core analyzing lab. What remained of the door—a shapeless blob of metal—fell inward with a loud crash.

The door had not had time to settle when four SEALs raked the opening with four streams of submachine-gun fire. At the same time, the Death Merchant, Norris, and Sergeant Day tossed MK3 offensive grenades through the red-hot opening, and Forran, Coopbird, and Torway tossed cannisters of DC gas.

On the other side of the burned-out bulkhead, fifteen Russian commandos and a dozen ordinary seamen had been pushing shields of metal—steel plates fastened by bolts to wooden frames—toward the door, the first line of commandos only six feet from the door when the thermite went off. They had moved back and waited, hunched down behind the shields as streams of machine gun projectiles screamed off the steel plates, their confidence rapidly going down the drain.

Came the grenades. They exploded ten feet beyond the doorway and killed nine of the Soviet commandos outright. Some were crushed by the very shields that were supposed to protect them; others were sent to a commie paradise by shrapnel that sliced them to ribbons. A few screamed. Others didn't have time; they died as fast as a light bulb is turned off, all to the tune of metal shields clanging loudly against walls, and bits and pieces of flesh and clothing slapping against ceiling and floor of the storage room.

The six remaining *Ziaistvo Yennaya* and the horrified seamen might have lived if they had retreated. It was the DC[1] as that prevented them from doing so.

Hit by the DC gas, the six commandos and dozen sailors might as well have been struck by invisible lightning. Vomiting at one end, defecating at the other—both uncontrollably—and deprived of all strength by waves of violent nausea, the eighteen men were as helpless as babies.

An Ingram in each hand, the Death Merchant and his force stormed across the area, every man jumping in a crazy pattern to avoid the burning wooden floor and puddles of rapidly cooling metal.

Camellion leaped through the red-hot opening, the Ingrams in his hands crackling out streams of .25-caliber slugs, which, exploding on impact, quickly put an end to most of the racking noise of vomiting. Red Norris and Billy Coopbird finished off the last three sailors, stitching them with 5.6mm Fireball slugs.

The storage area was filled with boxes of canned goods, but Camellion didn't stop to read the labels. He raced toward the end of the storage area, his destination the open bulkhead and the gangway beyond, the rest of the men right behind him. Most of the SEALs were fleeing down the length of the storage room when the Soviet *Ziaistvo Yennaya* attacked from the bow bulkhead and from the one at the top of the stairs.

[1] Diphenylcyanoarsine—DC for short—is a colorless, odorless as that causes the victim to vomit instantly on inhalation, but it not a normal form of vomiting. It is the result of a muscle contraction and is referred to as "projective vomiting," i.e. the ejection of the contents of the stomach over several feet. As well as vomiting, there is intense nausea and instant diarrhea. There is no protection against this gas, except two methods—running like hell and wearing a special Menten gas mask. The Menten mask named for Casper J. Menten, its inventor, a biochemist who worked for Turner Dynamics Corporation in Syracuse, New York.

The Russians first tossed in grenades, which exploded harmlessly, then raked the entire area with PPS and AK-47 fire some of the solid-based, boat-tailed projectiles streaking through the opening of the hot, stern bulkhead and hitting the last two SEALs, killing them within several seconds of each other.

Four other SEALs reacted like well-oiled robots. They raced the short distance to the smoking bulkhead and flattened themselves against boxes close to the entrance. Two stood guard, IMP machine pistols pointed at the open bulkhead. The other two reached into their bags and pulled out TH3 incendiary grenades, each of which contained 26.5 ounces of thermate.[2]

Altogether, the two men tossed seven grenades through the bulkhead, the first two landing in the center of the Soviet commandos, who had raced down the stairs and attacked through the bulkhead toward the bow.

During the next 35 seconds the seven TH3 incendiary grenades turned the wrecked laboratory into a roaring hell filled with Soviet sea commandos, most of whom had been turned into shrieking torches, blazing from combat boots to metal helmets. Everything was consumed by the molten thermate— uniforms, metal buttons, leather holsters and straps. And when the thermate had eaten through these materials, and bullets in ammo packs were still exploding, the TH3 burned through flesh and bone, leaving only "half-eaten" corpses.

The four SEALs checked to make sure the two men who had been shot were dead, then hurried after the rest of the force, one man remarking, "Camellion sure knows his business."

"Yeah," agreed another man. "So did Jack the Ripper."

"Exactly what we need," said a third SEAL.

"Hell, he acts as if all this is no more annoying than a mild attack of athlete's foot," said the fourth commando.

The Death Merchant skidded to a halt to the left of the open bulkhead and motioned for the others to get down. Something was rocking his dreamboat, and that something was time. According to his own private calculations, the force was ten minutes behind schedule; and there was a definite limit on how long Nervous Nellie McConachie, worried about the precious Gf-Mechanism, would wait.

[2] A mixture of thermite, barium nitrate, and sulfur in an oil binder. It burns for about 18 seconds at 4,500 degrees.

Were more Russians beyond the door? Let's find out.

Camellion got down on one knee, shoved fresh magazines into the Ingrams, and placed the two small machine guns on the floor.

"Get the lead out," Norris said, his voice flat and muted through the Menten G-mask. "We're a hell of a long way from the main control bridge."

"We don't even know that the Russians are still on the bridge," Josh Forran said harshly.

Camellion tossed one canister of DC gas through the doorway. He tossed the second canister to the right. Loud hissings. But no sounds of confusion, no sounds of vomiting.

He stuck his head around the left side of the opening and studied the T-shaped hallway. The length of the T was a 20-foot-long gangway. At its end was an ordinary door—closed. The cross-section of the T was the gangway in front of him. It lay in a port to starboard, left to right, position. At both ends were closed oval-shaped bulkheads. Ten feet in front of the right bulkhead was a stairway that moved up to the third deck. At the top of the steps, the door was closed—a steel door, apparently, since Camellion could see the rivet heads.

"To coin a metaphor, 'the coast is clear.'" Camellion said as Red Norris, Forran, and John Day looked up and down the T-shaped passageway.

"This tub is certainly compartmented," Day said. "I've never seen so many damned bulkheads in so short a space."

A muscular young man with a broad chest, narrow hips, and an enormous mustache, he made it a ritual to use an electric razor on his skull every morning. Now, he clipped the IMP machine pistol to his belt, pulled two stainless steel .45 Vega auto-pistols from hip holsters, pulled out the clips, and placed them into one of the leg pockets of his combat fatigues. From one of the shoulder bags, he took two Taylor Mark-1 drums, checked to make sure each clip was secure to the drums, then shoved the 30-round drums into the Vegas.

"Cover me," ordered Camellion. "I'm going to blow the steel door."

"It could be unlocked," Forran suggested hopefully.

"I'm not going to try to find out," Camellion said, clipping one of the Ingrams to his wide leather utility belt. "I could throw open the door and get my head blown off. The hinges are on the other side. The door will blow inward. If the pig farmers are waiting, the explosion will give us an edge. We have to move fast. Our schedule is tighter right now than the tail feathers on the rump of a prairie chicken."

"Don't tell me your troubles," growled Norris. "Get going. Sometime between now and eternity we have to get to the bridge."

Under the protective barrels of a dozen automatic weapons and with an Ingram in his right hand, Camellion dashed out, raced up the steps, and planted a half-pound magnetic pack of RDX against the left edge of the steel door. The timer was already set in the pack. He turned the knob of the timer to 30 seconds, ran back down the steps, raced through the doorway, and got down.

Within the confined space, the blast sounded like a baby H-bomb. The loud clang of the door being slammed against the floor sounded almost like a gong—a terrific banging accompanying Camellion and Forran, who dashed to the foot of the steps. The Death Merchant tossed up an offensive grenade that sailed through the square opening. Forran let fly a canister of DC gas. Both men then raced back to the safety of the doorway.

The grenade exploded and the canister began to hiss out its vomit gas. Shrapnel *zing-zing-zinged* against the walls and ceiling.

"Let's saddle up," Camellion said. He dashed out and began to race up the steel steps, firing short bursts at the smoking square opening. Norris, Day, and the rest of the men ten feet behind him.

Camellion darted in low through the doorway, to the left, almost tripping over the lower edge of the blasted door lying on the floor. He had not heard any uncontrollable retching, so he was surprised when AK-47 and PPS slugs began zipping all around him. One bullet almost kissed his left cheek. Another 7.62mm hard-core slug cut through one of the straps of a shoulder bag, tugging at the bag. A third bullet raked across his right leg and tore through the black material of the jump suit while he was falling toward the deck and firing long horizontal bursts. Still firing, he hit the floor on his left shoulder, but saw four sailors in dungarees, blue shirts, and gas masks falling, riddled from his popping .25 projectiles.

Three other sailors were against the wall to the Death Merchant's right. Another was down on one knee in the middle of the passage. Two more were against the left wall.

The sailor in the center of the passage tried to swing his AKM down on Camellion, who fired by instinct, not only at at the single sailor but at the other two against the left wall. Slugs exploded all over the four doomed men and sent parts of uniform, and pieces of lungs, hearts, and ribs flying against the walls, floor, and ceiling.

An Ingram and several IMP machine pistols chattered to the right and slightly behind the Death Merchant. The other three against the right wall jerked, spun, and went down, their lives terminated by Norris, Forran, and Coopbird, all three having fired over the top step. But two of the sailors had triggered off final bursts while going down, and some of the slugs had come dangerously close. One 7.62mm had torn through the top of Coopbird's helmet, narrowly missing the top of his skull. Another had scratched Forran's right cheek, clipping his right ear lobe. Another bullet had glanced off the steel door, and had cut a not too deep gash in Norris's right wrist. By the time the firing was over, blood was moving along Norris's hand and dripping onto the forward pistol grip of the Individual Multipurpose Weapon.

"I thought you said only Menten masks were effective against DC gas?" grumbled Forran, coming up to the Death Merchant, who was getting to his feet.

"The last I heard the Menten masks were." Camellion reached for a full Ingram magazine and stepped back slightly to make room for SEALs racing by to secure the other end of the gangway.

"Maybe the canister didn't go off?" suggested Cullen Torway, who was uncomfortable in his gas mask. He glanced from Camellion to Sergeant Day, who was wrapping a bandage around Norris's wrist, then at Coopbird who was examining the bullet hole in his helmet.

Camellion reached into one of his pockets, took out a book of matches, and struck one. The match burned with a pale green flame. Proof positive. The air was alive with DC gas.

Philip Ayer, one of the squad leaders who had gone down the passage, came back, ran up to Norris, and let Camellion have a quick look.

"We've found another set of stairs," Ayer reported, his voice muffled through the Menten mask. "There's another gangway at the end of this passage, as you can see. The steps are in the right side passage. Do we take it or what?"

"Hear that, Camellion?" Norris sounded jubilant. "We have a way to the second deck." He jerked a thumb toward the direction in back of them. Not only was the air thick with fumes from explosive and thermite, but with another kind of smoke, smoke that was on the verge of being tar-black. "You know what that means. We have to hustle."

Cullen Torway touched Camellion on the elbow. "What does he mean?"

"The fuel oil's burning," Camellion said. "Probably ignited in the water by one of the thermate grenades our guys tossed in."

"Could we sink?" Coopbird asked. "Or could the oil explode and blow out the bottom?"

"A blast is unlikely, but"—Camellion and the other men felt the deck jerk and tilt to the bow—"as the fire spreads, it could pop other bulkheads on the fifth deck and even on the fourth. The ship would fill with water and gradually go down. We don't have to worry."

"By then, we'll either be back on *Kingfisher* or dead," added Lieutenant Commander Norris. "That's the bottom line."

"Let's go take those steps to the second deck," Camellion said. "By the way, Norris. How many of your boys have crossbows?"

"Four."

Into each life some rain must fall, but a cloudburst was inundating Colonel Anatole Bersenko and the other Russians, all of whom listened in shock and rage as the five sea commandos, who had survived the massacre, reported how the Americans had incinerated most of the *Ziaistvo Yennaya*. All of them were crowded into the lecture hall on the second deck. Included in the group were Dr. Paul Trovtsev, Dr. Igor M. Servadda, one of the Soviet Union's best marine biologists, and Dr. Raya Selnikova, a structural engineer.

Sergeant Ilich Darensky said nervously, "We were fortunate enough to have been coming down the steps when the incendiaries went off, or we too would have been reduced to ashes."

Inserted Thomas Kvashin, looking at a furious-faced Lieutenant General Vladilen Zudin, "It would have been suicide for only five of us to have attacked the entire American force. We decided it was best to report to you, Comrade General Zudin."

"And the oil is burning in the inner hull," Lieutenant Vasili Malyshev said, clearing his throat and shifting his PPS machine gun to his other shoulder.

"My God!" cried Captain Soidra. "The ship will sink within an hour. All we can do is take to the lifeboats."

Colonel Bersenko gave Soidra a savage look. "Such talk borders on treason, Captain. I have no intention of permitting the American swine to capture us. News of what is happening

166

here will leak to the world. We can't, under any circumstances, appear as cowards."

"We can't stay in our present position," Boris Ruzorkaski said bitterly to his boss. *We can't win either*, he thought, *not against gifted killers.* But he didn't say so.

Surprised at the anger in his subordinate's tone, Bersenko ignored Ruzorkaski, and glared at Lieutenant General Zudin and Captain Feliks Turkin with icy disdain.

"Don't suggest the superstructure," spit out Bersenko. "We'd be too exposed to fire on all sides."

Zudin, visibly shaken at the loss of all but five *Ziaistvo Yennaya*, felt the muscles in his fat face twitching. "The small submarine storage midships offers the best defensive position," he said, his voice sounding strange even to himself. "There isn't any other place that is safe. Even there . . . who knows?"

First Officer Didov said hastily, "The bulkheads there are double strength. Another plus is that we'll have the protection of the two deep-dive craft stored there. Their hulls are titanium."

"We outnumber the Americans," Feliks Turkin commented hopefully. "Counting the sailors not fighting the fire below and guarding the stern superstructure, we'll have a three-to-one edge." He indicated the ashen-faced scientists with a jerk of his head. "Even they can fire a machine gun."

Colonel Bersenko shrugged contemptuously and slowly looked over the group. He saw only lack of will and deep fear. "Comrade Turkin, we don't have enough weapons for all the sailors." His voice was just as contemptuous. "And the gas masks are not effective against the devil gas the Americans are using."

"It's some kind of riot control gas," Lieutenant General Zudin said pensively.

"Who gives a goddamn what it is!" stormed Bersenko, throwing both hands out and upward. "What matters is that after fifteen minutes or so the gas is able to penetrate the filters of our mask."

Once more his sinister gaze raked over the group. Corpses! He was looking at dead people and he knew it. Without a word, he turned and stalked out of the lecture hall. Captain Boris Ruzorkaski walked slowly after him, motioning for the others to follow.

Like the rest of the Russians, Ruzorkaski knew they were doomed. Bersenko did have a point though. It was better to die fighting like wolves than to surrender like sheep. Why they'd all receive the Order of Lenin posthumously—for all the good it would do them!

Ruzorkaski jumped, along with the others, at the sound of the explosion. The floor shook violently. The blast had been on the second deck, about 125 feet ahead, toward the starboard bow. The damned *Amerikanskis* had reached the second deck.

Bersenko, Ruzorkaski, and the rest of the Soviet force began to run toward the submarine storage area.

The Death Merchant and his group blew the bulkhead with a pound of RDX, and then received a pleasant surprise when they found the passage devoid of Russians. With great caution, they moved down the smoky gangway, turned left, crept down another port-to-starboard passage, and stopped when they came to a much wider hallway on the second deck, this one in a bow to stern direction. From the mouth of the shorter passage, they could see an open elevator, to the left, in the much wider corridor. Not far from the elevator, to the left, was a stairway that led to the main deck.

The long, wide passage was empty. Lieutenant Commander Norris sent four men to recon the main deck from the steps to the left of the elevator. They zigzagged across the area and soon were moving up the stairs.

"It's a trick," Forran said. "They sent down the elevator to make us think they're not on the bridge."

"I'd like to know where the sailors are," Coopbird said, sounding worried. "I'm always afraid of an enemy I can't see."

"You've got a lot of company." Forran was still fighting the nostalgia he felt over having been forced to leave Kingston, Jamaica. All his Dvorak records were still in Kingston.

During this very brief period, Red Norris and John Day had been pouring over a diagram of the *Mikhail Tukhachevsky*.

"Camellion, come here for a moment," Norris called. "I think we have something."

The Death Merchant was getting down on his knees between Norris and Sergeant Day when there was a long burst of PPS fire from the main deck, about midships. Several IMPs answered with a short, cracking blast.

Norris tapped the diagram. "Unless Intelligence goofed, right here on the second deck is a storage for small, explorative deep-diving submarines, vehicles something like our Cubmarines."

"Yeah, I see."

"Notice the bulkheads at each end of the storage—double-strength!"

The Death Merchant's eyes roamed off the scaled drawing. "You're inferring the pig farmers are holed up in the storage area."

"It's their best bet," Norris said. "The fore and aft superstructures are too exposed. The decks below are too hot. By now the oil firm must have popped three or four bulkheads in the fourth and fifth decks. The bow is tilting more than it was ten minutes ago." He tapped the diagram again. "I say they intend to make a last ditch stand here."

John Day looked up at Camellion. "We sure don't have time to explore the ship. I think they're in there waiting, packed closer than two nudists in an igloo." He glanced up. One of the SEALs, who had been on recon, ran toward them.

"Russian sailors," the SEAL reported, grinning within his gas mask. "They're lowering lifeboats on both port and starboard."

"The bigwigs might be with them," suggested Norris.

"We'll soon know," Camellion said. "Sergeant, get those guys with the crossbows."

Blowing open the bulkhead did not take long, but it took four pounds of RDX to do the job, to tear the door off its massive hinges and send it crashing to the deck, the explosion of such intensity that it wrecked a small section of the main deck above. The last rays of the twilight sun slanted through large cracks, throwing a red-yellow pattern on the floor.

The thick steel door lay six feet from the oval entrance—all very convenient for four SEALs who bellycrawled to the door, two with crossbows. Four other SEALs raced to the smoking sides of the bulkhead opening; two of these four also carried "Tiger-Claw" crossbows made of aluminum.

Eight M14 incendiary grenades had been attached to the shafts, and it was not the least bit difficult to fire the grenades through the opening into the storage section beyond. Once a shaft and its grenade was fixed in the bed, the bow drawn back, and the man sighted in, the SEAL beside the shooter pulled the pin on the grenade, and the shooter pulled the trigger. In a minute and a half, all eight incendiaries had been shot through the bulkhead. The four SEALs at the opening then followed through with eight offensive grenades and four canisters of DC gas. Last of all, they tossed four canisters of M34 standard smoke through the blasted bulkhead.

The Death Merchant and the force then charged through the bulkhead.

They didn't pace themselves. Now, it was either kill or be killed.

Colonel Bersenko and his force, which included a dozen of the *Mikhail Tukhachevsky*'s officers and seventy sailors, had secured for themselves the best protection possible under prevailing conditions. With forklifts, the Russians had used crates and boxes of spare sub parts and other equipment to form half a defensive rectangle in front of the bulkhead. The longest part of the rectangle was 40 feet in front of the open bulkhead, each side of the rectangle almost to the hull of both the port and the starboard sides of the ship. Oddly enough, none of the Russians wanted any part of the two midget submarines resting on their skids. No one wanted to be trapped inside one of the weird-looking contraptions.

Behind crates filled with spare diving suits and boxes containing empty cylinders, Bersenko, Zudin, Turkin, and the other Soviet officers felt fairly safe. The Americans would first have to get past the sailors, a feat that was not likely to happen. Twenty of the seamen had PPS submachine guns; others were armed with AKMs or handguns, mostly Tokarev auto-pistols.

With all that firepower pointed at the open bulkhead, Bersenko and Zudin concluded that not a single American would live long enough to throw a demolition or incendiary grenade.

The Russians assumed they had thought of everything. They hadn't.

They hadn't thought of crossbows and the expertise with which SEALs can use the modern versions of these ancient weapons.

The four SEALs didn't just shoot each incendiary in a haphazard manner. Each shaft with its grenade struck in a different position. The other SEALs were careful to spread out the offensive grenades, the DC canisters, and the smoke.

The Soviets didn't expect what they got, the eight incendiaries taking them completely by surprise. The first burst over the small conning tower of the first midget sub in line, and transformed it into what appeared to be a bright white ball of fire. The other seven incendiaries blossomed one after another. One exploded on top of some crates of the long defensive line in front of the bulkhead, and splattered thirteen sailors with droplets of molten thermate. Two more exploded behind the crates of the long line, splashing liquid fire over more Russian seamen, who screamed like lost souls, and jerked and danced in a futile effort to stop the man-made lava that had ignited their clothes and was eating through flesh and bone. The fifth and sixth incendiaries landed far to the left, on machinery used to keep the midget submarines in tip-top shape. Several drill presses and a lathe were reduced to rubble, the fire igniting oily rags, which burned with a lot of black smoke, like a smudge-pot. The seventh shaft and its thermate bomb curved through the air and struck the floor 30 feet behind Colonel Bersenko and his group, all of whom were keeping as low a profile as possible, First Officer Didov and Second Officer Pavel Kaznikova even lying flat with their arms over their heads. Crates in back prevented some of the thermate from splashing over Bersenko and the others. In the same manner Dr. Paul Trovtsev and the scientists with him were saved from a horrible death. The last thermate grenade went off not far from where they were hiding behind large reels of cable. Some of the dazzling white-hot fire fell on top of the drums and splattered against the thick steel cable wound around the lower drums. However, luck stayed with the Soviet scientists. None of the thermate reached them.

In 115 seconds the organized group of Russians had been transformed into a disorganized mass of terrified men. Twenty-six had been turned into human torches, which still smoked and gave off the strong odor of a barbecue at a family get-together.

The eight offensive grenades went off with crashing roars, each explosion creating more panic, and wounding and killing more Russians. The DC gas and the thick white smoke were icing on the cake that the Death Merchant and his men intended to chop into crumbs.

Camellion, in a low crouch, darted to the right. In each hand he carried an Ingram submachine gun, which he was using the way one would use an auto-pistol. To conserve ammunition, he had set the firing time of each Model 11-I to 3-second bursts.

Zigzagging behind Camellion came Norris, Day, and the rest of the force. The round opening of the bulkhead continued to vomit gas-masked SEALs, who zigzagged either right or left, their eyes darting around like ball bearings.

Instantaneously the battle turned into a kill or be killed free-for-all. The SEALs had the edge; they had been bloodied and tested in Vietnam and other operations, many of which the world's public had never heard about. The Russian sailors lacked firefight experience, but they were cornered and driven by fright, a half-insane fear that gave them extra strength and made them forget all caution. They had no choice but to fight, including Colonel Bersenko and his group. Automatic weapons in hands, they came out shooting, motivated more by blind hate than a desire to live.

The Death Merchant dodged to the left to avoid a stream of slugs from a wild-eyed seaman and, as he ducked into drifting smoke, triggered both Ingrams, moving them longitudinally. The train of PPS slugs missed him, but punched a dozen holes in a SEAL close to Forran, several of the 7.62mm projectiles raking across Forran's back, ripping through his fatigues and slashing deep cuts through the skin. Josh cried out in pain and anger; yet he realized from the lengths of the burning cuts across his back that the wounds were not serious. With Billy Coopbird beside him, he dropped to one knee, thinking again of his complete set of Dvorak records he had left in Kingston. Calmly, the "Odd Couple" began to pick off pig farmers with four .45 Combat Mossbergs.

The Russians would have had a much better chance if they had remained calm and stayed behind the crates. But, terrified of the thermate, they had rushed out to attack the Americans, impelled by the false logic that the sooner they came to grips with the SEALs, the safer they would be. An enemy can't throw an incendiary while he's standing directly in front of you. But he can blow your head off! Or turn you into a cold cut with a knife. Two facts not considered by the Russians.

On the whole, the SEALs fought in circular positions, seven men to a circle, a formation that made it impossible for the pig farmers to sneak in from behind. Yet because of the smallness of the area and the proximity of Russian to American, the two sides soon clashed and were fighting eyeball-to-eyeball—an even worse mistake by the Soviet dumbbells, who had as much chance against the battle-hardened SEALs as a blind man has of climbing Mount Everest.

Not having time to reload their IMPs and Ingrams, the SEALs pulled sidearms. Some had pistols in both hands. Others had a pistol in one hand and a knife in the other.

Lieutenant Commander Norris shot one man in the face at pointblank range, the Russian piece of trash so close that flying flesh and bone splattered all over the front of him as he slammed a second pig farmer against the head with the other Seecamp Bobcat, then shot a third red cabbage eater in the chest with the Bobcat in his right hand, the big flat-nosed .45 bullet knocking the dying man back into three other "comrades" about to attack Sergeant John Day, who, snuggled behind the corpses of two Russians—one having fallen across the other—was killing Russians with all the precision of a man in a shooting gallery, using his two Vega .45s to which were attached the Taylor Mark-1 drums. Two of the Russians took .45 slugs in the chest; the third got one in the stomach. A fourth and a fifth crashed to the deck when Day slammed .45 projectiles into them.

Almost as quickly, Day died at the hands of Captain Feliks Turkin. The Russian commando, only 20 feet away, stitched him in the right side with a dozen PPS machine gun slugs. Day jerked violently. Blood flowed from his mouth and he lay still, face down.

Norris had seen Turkin kill Day, but so had Josh Forran, who snapped off a shot at the Russian commando officer. A moment before Forran pulled the trigger, Turkin turned to fire on a SEAL who had just ripped open the belly of a pig farmer with a bone-handled Schrade Scrimshaw knife. Turkin's movement saved his life. Forran's bullet, instead of hitting him in back of the head and scrambling his brain, cut across his scalp, a graze deep enough to slam him unconscious to to floor.

By now, there were so many bodies in the area that the sub storage space resembled a coffinless morgue struck by an earthquake. Cullen Torway was the next man to be added to the dead, only a few moments after he had put three nine-millimeter Hi-Power Browning projectiles into the right side of Captain Sergei Soidra. First Officer Albert Didov fired half a magazine of 9MM Stechkin projectiles that stabbed into Torway's chest and stomach. The CIA officer had time for only one lightning quick thought—*This is ridiculous!*—then he died.

Didov didn't have time to congratulate himself. Red Norris fired both Bobcats and the two bullets smashed into him, one mushrooming in his upper right chest, the second expanding in his groin. The double grand-slam pitched him against a crate, and he slid slowly to the deck, his mouth fixed and open in shock, his eyes snapping shut in death.

Camellion, bleeding from half a dozen near hits, had lost count of the pig farmers he had butchered. For a minute he had been using his twin International Auto Mags, yet was careful to save ammo when he could. One damn fool of a Russian tried to push a Tokarev in his side. Camellion pushed the pistol away and crushed the man's skull with the long barrel of the AMP in his right hand. Almost at the same time, he kicked another man in front of him squarely in the testicles, and, as the man doubled over, caved in the back of the man's head with the barrel of the left Auto Mag. Just as swiftly, he shot Thomas Kvashin in the chest with the right AMP.

Kvashin was pitched toward Lieutenant General Zudin, who was aiming a short-barrelled Draskanov machine pistol at Josh Forran. Zudin fired a moment before the dead Kvashin knocked him off balance. The stream of 7.65mm Draskanov peppered Forran's back, tearing off tiny pieces of fatigue cloth before they tore through his heart and lungs and took their exit through his chest. Dead within the blink of an eye, Josh Forran pitched forward and fell on his face.

"You're dead, 'Fat-Boy'!" muttered Camellion. He snap-aimed and pulled the trigger of the left Auto Mag. The big weapon boomed and the balloon-body of Lieutenant General Zudin jerked from the impact of the dynamite-fisted .357 Jurras bullet that tore a tunnel through his belly and took part of his intestines out the larger hole it made in the small of his back.

Camellion had more trouble. Coming at him were two other Russians—KGB officers from the way they acted. One was a cold-eyed fish with ruddy skin, a Stechkin M.P. in his right hand. The other was a broad-shouldered goof. Neither man wore a gas mask, a sure sign that the DC gas had been dissipated.

Lieutenant Commander Red Norris was having even greater difficulty. Sergeant Ilich Darensky had twisted the .45 Bobcat from his right hand and was trying to twist his arm into an armlock, while Yuri Kipov attempted to cave in his head with the butt of an empty AK-47 automatic rifle.

Norris ducked the butt of the AKM and snapped six of Kipov's ribs with a left-legged heel-drive kick. Yet the SEAL commander would have still died if Billy Coopbird had not arrived in time to prevent Nikolai Lazarev from stitching Norris with a train of 7.65 slugs. Lazarev, 8 feet in front of Norris, was in the process of aiming down on Norris, wanting to make sure he did not hit Darensky. At the moment, the barrel of the machine pistol was pointed upward; in another moment Lazarev would level the weapon and pull the trigger. He didn't because he couldn't! It was then that Billy Coopbird chopped off Lazarev's right hand with a 21-inch machete, the broad blade swishing through the air. Lazarev screamed. Blood spurted from the stump of his arm and he started to pass out from shock.

Sergeant Darensky was even more terrified, so much so that he let go of Norris's arm, and, with a gurgling kind of sound, tried to pull a knife from his belt. The doomed *Ziaistvo Yennaya* might as well have tried to put out the sun with a mouthful of spit. Coopbird's machete swished again through the air. The head of Darensky, a gas mask over the face, jumped six inches from the neck, then fell to the floor, looking silly and out of place on the deck.

"I'll be damned!" mumbled Norris in surprise. Forran had told him that Coopbird was a past master with a machete. Jamaicans who cut sugar cane usually are. Well, Forran had not exaggerated. Coopbird could use a machete the way Camellion could kill—expertly and without emotion.

A river of blood gushed from Sergeant Darensky's neck. Spurting blood, the corpse wilted to the floor.

Coopbird wiped his bloody blade on the pants of the dying Nikolai Lazarev as Norris picked up the .45 Bobcat and put a bullet into the head of Yuri Kipov, who was down on his knees hugging his ribs.

The series of muffled explosions below decks shook and shuddered the entire ship. The deck tilted sharply forward, the motion so unexpected that Norris and Coopbird and most of the other SEALs were thrown off their feet. Camellion also went down, as did Colonel Anatole Bersenko and Captain Boris Ruzorkaski.

The Death Merchant was much too fast for the two men. He fired both Auto Mags at the two KGB officers who were getting up off the floor. One bullet hit Colonel Bersenko in the left hip, bored all the way through the lower part of his body, broke the right ilium, or hip bone, and went bye-bye through the skin. Another .357 Magnum projectile punched Boris Ruzorkaski in the midsection, doubled him over, and pitched him back to fall on top of another corpse. Both men continued to jerk, so Camellion put another slug in Ruzorkaski. He then exploded the head of the dying Bersenko with another .357 AMP projectile.

Cautiously, the Death Merchant looked all around him. *Yeah, it's been a real barn-burner!* he thought. Norris and Coopbird stared at him. All three then looked at the SEALs still alive, and at the piles of dead bodies filling the area. Slowly, men pulled off gas masks.

Camellion came up to Norris, whose fatigues were as dirty and as bloody as his own.

"Torway and Forran bought it," Norris said resignedly. "So did Sergeant Day." Abruptly his manner changed and he became the mechanical professional. "I'm going upstairs with several men and get a signal flare off to Captain McConachie.

175

We've got to get the hell off this tub. You take charge down here."

"Yeah, I'll clean up down here," Camellion said. He shoved a fresh clip into one of the AMPs and cocked the big shiny weapon.

Norris was about to call out to three of his men, but stopped and turned in the direction of a man who had moaned and rolled over on his back. It was the same man who had killed Sergeant Day. Norris recognized him from his mop of black hair, and the white sports shirt with horizontal blue stripes.

Camellion started to drop the barrel of the Auto Mag toward the man, but Norris held up a hand. "No. He's mine. He's the son-of-a-bitch who gave the business to Day."

Feliks Turkin opened his eyes. His head throbbed and his mouth was full of hot, dry sand. The first thing he saw was Norris and the .45 in Norris's hand. He tried to speak. He couldn't. He raised his right hand as if somehow the motion could prevent the .45 from exploding. It couldn't. Norris pulled the trigger, the bullet going through Turkin's half-open mouth and blowing out the back of his neck. Twice more Norris pulled the trigger, tasting the sweetness of revenge at the sound of each shot.

Richard Camellion and the others stood on the slanting deck and watched the dozen inflatable rubber boats, powered by outboard motors, speeding from *Kingfisher* toward the dying *Mikhail Tukhachevsky*. Waves were already lapping at the boat deck of her forward superstructure.

A half-mile to port was the tall conning tower and the rounded top of *Kingfisher*'s hull, the killer submarine resembling a sinister sea monster in the soft, mellow moonlight.

Other than Camellion, Norris, and Coopbird, there were thirty-six SEALs—seven wounded and half-unconscious. And seven Soviet prisoners: five scientists who had been found hiding behind drums of steel cable, and two other pig farmers. One was the second officer of the ship, Pavel Kaznikova. He had been shot in the leg and the shoulder, and was unconscious. The other prisoner was Lieutenant Vasili Malyshev. He had been knocked in the head by a SEAL and had a fractured skull.

Holding onto the rail to keep from sliding on the deck, Camellion and the others watched the rubber boats draw closer. In several minutes they'd be at port side and shooting up rope ladders and stretcher slide ropes.

Lieutenant Commander Norris had contacted *Kingfisher* by PRC radio and had received a report concerning the three American ships to the west. In spite of protective "Emma," some of the Soviet "Emerald" missiles had done considerable damage. One missile had detonated close to the starboard stern of *Mohawk*. Pressure had smashed in the plates—almost with the force of a torpedo—and forty-six men had drowned. Bulkheads had been quickly sealed, but *Mohawk* was limping along at greatly reduced speed. The *South Dakota* had not been scratched. Two missiles had exploded close to *Atlantis II*. She was leaking from stem to stern, her pumps working furiously to keep her afloat.

Red Norris held onto the railing to brace himself on the slanting deck. "What counts is that we succeeded. The Soviets now realize they don't have a chance in the Caribbean. Thank God it's over."

It hasn't even begun. This era is about to end, Camellion thought, but only said, "Me, too. I hate violence."

Billy Coopbird, keenly feeling the loss of Josh Forran, gave Camellion an odd look. He didn't know whether to envy Camellion, hate his guts, or feel sorry for him. Whoever or whatever Richard Camellion was, he didn't need anyone. Nor did he seem to feel anything. And one always had the impression that there was something alien about him . . . another kind of presence staring out through his eyes.

Coopbird sniffed the air. Different parts of the sea have different smells at different times. Here there were no odors of the sea. There was only the stink of smoke and of things burning.

The stench of destruction.

The smell of death. . . .

177

The Number 1 hit man loose in the Mafia jungle . . .
nothing and nobody can stop him from wiping out the
Mob!

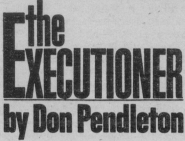

the EXECUTIONER
by Don Pendleton

The Executioner *is without question the best-selling action/
adventure series being published today. American readers
have bought more than twenty million copies of the more
than thirty volumes published to date. Readers in England,
France, Germany, Japan, and a dozen other countries have
also become fans of Don Pendleton's peerless hero. Mack
Bolan's relentless one-man war against the Mafia, and Pendleton's unique way of mixing authenticity, the psychology of
the mission, and a bloody good story, crosses all language bar-
riers and social levels. Law enforcement officers, business ex-
ecutives, college students, housewives, anyone searching for a
fast-moving adventure tale, all love Bolan. It isn't just the real-
ism and violence, it certainly isn't blatant sex; it is our guess
that there is a "mystique"—if you will—that captures these
readers, an indefinable something that builds an identification
with the hero and a loyalty to the author. It must be good, it
must be better than the others to have lasted since 1969, when
War Against the Mafia, the first Executioner volume, was
published as the very first book to be printed by a newly born
company called Pinnacle Books. More than just lasting, however—as erstwhile competitors, imitators, and ripoffs died or
disappeared—The Executioner has continued to grow into an
international publishing phenomenon. The following are some
insights into the author and his hero . . . but do dare to read
any one of* The Executioner *stories, for, more than anything
else, Mack Bolan himself will convince you of his pertinence
and popularity.*

The familiar Don Pendleton byline on millions of copies of Mack Bolan's hard-hitting adventures isn't a pen name for a team of writers or some ghostly hack. Pendleton's for real . . . and then some.

He had written about thirty books before he wrote the first book in *The Executioner* series. That was the start of what has now become America's hottest action series since the heyday of James Bond. With thirty-four volumes complete published in the series and four more on the drawing board, Don has little time for writing anything but *Executioner* books, answering fan mail, and autographing royalty checks.

Don completes each book in about six weeks. At the same time, he is gathering and directing the research for his next books. In addition to being a helluva storyteller, and military tactics expert, Don can just as easily speak or write about metaphysics and man's relationship to the universe.

A much-decorated veteran of World War II, Don saw action in the North Atlantic U-boat wars, the invasion of North Africa, and the assaults on Iwo Jima and Okinawa. He later led a team of naval scouts who landed in Tokyo preparatory to the Japanese surrender. As if that weren't enough, he went back for more in Korea, too!

Before turning to full-time duty at the typewriter, Don held positions as a railroad telegrapher, air traffic controller, aeronautical systems engineer, and even had a hand in the early ICBM and Moonshot programs.

He's the father of six and now makes his home in a small town in Indiana. He does his writing amidst a unique collection of weapons, photos, and books.

Most days it's just Don, his typewriter, and his dog (a German Shepherd/St. Bernard who hates strangers) sharing long hours with Mack Bolan and his relentless battle against the Mafia.

Despite little notice by literary critics, the Executioner has quietly taken his position as one of the better known, best understood, and most provocative heroes of contemporary literature—primarily through word-of-mouth advertising on the part of pleased readers.

According to Pendleton, "His saga has become identified in the minds of millions of readers as evidence (or, at least, as hope) that life is something more than some silly progression of charades through which we all drift, willy-nilly—but is a meaningful and exhilarating adventure that we all share, and to which every man and woman, regardless of situation, may contribute some meaningful dimension. Bolan is therefore considerably more than 'a light read' or momentary diversion. To the millions who expectantly 'watch' him through adventure after adventure, he has become a symbol of the revolt of institutionalized man. He is a guy *doing something*—responding to the call of his own conscience—making his presence felt in a positive sense—realizing the full potential of his own vast humanity and excellence. We are all Mack Bolan, male and female, young and old, black and white and all the shades between; down in our secret heart of hearts, where we really live, we dig the guy because *we are* the guy!

The extensive research into locale and Mafia operations that make *The Executioner* novels so lifelike and believable is always completed before the actual writing begins.

"I absorb everything I can about a particular locality, and the story sort of flows out of that. Once it starts flowing, the research phase, which may be from a couple of days to a couple of weeks, is over. I don't force the flow. Once it starts, it's all I can do to hang on."

How much of the Bolan philosophy is Don Pendleton's?

"His philosophy *is* my own," the writer insists. "Mack Bolan's struggle is a personification of the struggle of collective mankind from the dawn of time. More than that, even Bolan is a statement of the life principle—*all* life. His killing, and the motives and methods involved, is actually a consecration of the life principle. He is proclaiming, in effect, that life is meaningful, that the world is important, that it does matter what happens here, that universal goals are being shaped on this cosmic cinder called earth. That's a heroic idea. Bolan is championing the idea. That's what a hero is. Can you imagine a guy like Bolan standing calmly on the sidelines, watching without interest while a young woman is mugged and raped? The guy cares. He is reacting to a destructive principle inherent in the human situation; he's fighting it. The whole world is Bolan's family. He cares about it, and he feels that what happens to it is tremendously important. The goons have rushed in waving guns, intent on raping, looting, pillaging, destroying. And he is blowing their damned heads off, period, end of philosophy. I believe that most of *The Executioner* fans recognize and understand this rationale."

With every title in the series constantly in print and no end in sight, it seems obvious that the rapport between Don Pendleton and his legion of readers is better than ever and that the author, like his hero, has no intention of slowing down or of compromising the artistic or philosophical code of integrity that has seen him through so much.

"I don't go along with the arty, snobbish ideas about literature," he says. "I believe that the mark of good writing can be measured realistically only in terms of public response. Hemingway wrote Hemingway because he was Hemingway. Well, Pendleton writes Pendleton. I don't know any other way."

Right on, Don. Stay hard, guy. And keep those *Executioners* coming!

* * *

[Editors note: for a fascinating and incisive look into *The Executioner* and Don Pendleton, read Pinnacle's *The Executioner's War Book,* available wherever paperbacks are sold.]

The Destroyer by Warren Murphy

Remo Williams is the perfect weapon—a cold, calculating death machine developed by CURE, the world's most secret crime-fighting organization. Together with his mentor, Chiun, the oriental martial arts wizard, The Destroyer makes the impossible missions possible.

Over 13 million copies sold!